THE DRYAD

THE DRYAD

THE DRYAD

JUSTIN H. McCARTHY

WILDSIDE PRESS

Originally published in 1905.
Published by Wildside Press LLC.
wildsidepress.com

ΕΙΣ ΤΗΝ ΦΙΛΗΝ ΚΑΛΛΙΣΤΗΝ

Most dear, most fair, these pages go
To you, who watched this story grow
Through days of sun and days of snow,
A legend of the Long Ago.
Where Wonder-Wood is all aglow
With godlike forms, and far below
The bland Athenian breezes blow,
The faint Athenian fountains flow.
Take up and read, and reading know
How much to you these pages owe
Since first we bandied to and fro
Sweet fancies, swift to come and go.

—J. H. McC.

1

IN THE WONDER-WOOD

Simon of Rouen—Simon, the soldier of fortune—trampled the grass of the Eleusinian wood with a heart as light as his wallet. His garments were wrecks of former splendor, degraded now by the tramping of high-road by day and the sleeping beneath hedge by night; but Simon carried himself as if he bobbed on the high tide of prosperity. A great sword clung to his thigh; his right hand brandished a massive oaken cudgel; a rusty iron lantern hung from his girdle, incongruous enough. He whistled as he went a tripping tune, and now and then he shouted some words to it:

> *"When I was no more than a span,*
> *Honey and gingerbread pleased me highly."*

That was the beginning of it, and, for much of the journey, was the middle of it and the end of it as well, for it was Simon's own song, and Simon's first adventure in the lyrical, and Simon was but a child at rhyming. He had a grudge against the world, and he wanted to sing his grievance the better to blow it abroad, but he would have given any man his fist in the face who dared to call him poetical.

It was naught to him that the ground he covered was sown with splendid memories. Truly he knew nothing about them, but he would have cared as little for the condition of his journey had he been wiser. To the mind fanciful those memories might seem as many as the leaves that year by year had greened and withered and fattened the forest soil through long generations of men. Greek gods, Greek kings, Greek heroes, beautiful Greek women, had been the children of that magic land. But Simon, the soldier of fortune, whistling as he fared, cared no jot for his lack of knowledge. Though he had left behind him the land of Agamemnon, and was setting his face steadily towards the city of Theseus, for him Peloponnesus was the place where the French noble dwelt who called himself Duke of Corinth, against whom he nursed his grudge; for him the capital of Attica was the city where the French noble reigned who called himself Duke of Athens, from whom he hoped to gain favor. For Simon, the soldier of fortune, flourished in the dusk of the thirteenth and the dawn of the fourteenth centuries of the world's age since the birth of the world's Saviour; and Simon, the soldier of fortune, took it for granted contentedly that from all time titled French adventurers had held by the hard hand the pleasant land of Greece.

The time of the year was May-time; the time of the day was hard on to sunset. Simon had tramped sturdily since morning and had not broken his fast since noon—his stomach was crying cupboard. There were onions in his wallet, there was nothing in his gourd; he must hope for a spring in the forest to moisten his provender—little cheer. This was why he looked about him so closely as he followed the dubious way between the trees, for his thoughts paid no reverence to the evening glories of the ancient wood.

The young knight whom he had passed on the road an hour or two before saw the forest with other eyes, being a poet and a reader of poets. When Simon, tramping the white highway, had come up with him he was reclining beside his tethered horse in the shade of the trees on the edge of the little wood, reading in a little book. Simon first questioned the young knight if there might be a short cut for him if he quitted the highway and went through the wood. The young knight, laying down his book, answered him that there very well might be such a short cut. But he added that he could not tell him for sure, as he was himself but newly come to Greece. Simon thanked him and decided to try for the short cut. But he saw that the book which the knight held had little painted pictures in it. Simon, ever curious, asked him what he read. The youth answered him civilly that he read what a rhymer had written of a dreamer who became a lover because of his great love for the mystic rose. Whereat Simon grunted his disgust that anyone should be fool enough to waste his life in reading of other folk's love-affairs when he might be making love for himself briskly.

"'Tis all one," he averred, "with thinking of tables spread with dainties while the hunger-belt nips your middle."

He had spoken feelingly, for he fasted, and, fasting, fretted. But the young knight carried no provant to temper Simon's edge of appetite, and the young knight smiled at Simon's view of life, and returned to his reading of *Good-Greeting and Sweet-Looking* and the kiss given to the mystic rose-bud. Whereat Simon rattled angrily the lantern that hung at his girdle and took to his journey again, climbing up the slope into the fringe of the forest, and telling himself as he did so that no man deserved to be called honest who squandered his manhood over love-tales. And so, hot with his scorn, Simon strode into the coolness and the twilight of the wood. If Simon had been travelling from Athens instead of travelling towards Athens he might not have chosen to journey through the wood, at least when night was near. The Athenians believed the wood to be haunted. They knew not why they believed this; they had the tale from their mothers, who had it from their mothers before them; and so the Athenians skirted the forest by day and shunned it by night. The French masters of Attica, taking everything they could take from their Athenian subjects, took their superstitions as well and gave the wood a wide berth. Simon did not know that the forest was haunted; he did think that it made a short cut to go through its avenues instead of following the main road that wound in a great loop below. Others before him that day, ignorant as he, had done as he did—gentles of an ancient guild, devotees of St. Nicholas. If Simon had known of his predecessors it would not have changed his purpose; he still would have chosen to travel by the woodland way.

If Simon had been a poet, like his disdained acquaintance of the roadside, he would have been delighted with the May-day graces of the place—with the new-green livery of the ancient trees; with the deep glades and dim aisles, down which the dying sunlight lingered; with the fantastic shapes that bole and bough put on under the enchantment of the waning day; with all the mystery and piety of the wood. But to Simon a wood, in the main, was a place where enemies love to lurk in ambush, and though Greece was for the hour at peace, custom made Simon look about him as warily as if he walked in time of war. Custom, to his surprise though no whit to his alarm, was justified of her pains. Something glittered in that clump of bushes; something stirred behind that mighty tree. Simon swung his staff to his right hand, and those who waited, guessing themselves detected, came leaping from concealment, left and right, and faced him—two men with drawn swords, ruffians of the kind that follow camps, soldiers in name, robbers in fact and act, never fighters unless the odds were hot on their party. Simon knew the kind well enough and despised them highly, not because they were plunderers, but because they were skulkers, shufflers, fluffers, mean moths in a rich coat. The jack-rascals were clad in habits fitted to their forest play of trap and catch—dull greens and sullen tawnies, good for lurking in, easily commingled, for the unwary, with the green and tawny of a wood. The rogues would have rushed Simon, but he stood so steady and made so mighty a mill-wheel with his monstrous cudgel that they were daunted, and bayed at him.

"Stand and deliver," cried one. "Deliver and stand," the other varied.

Simon eyed them composedly, plainly unperturbed. He felt that he was master of the match, and made merry in the sense of his strength.

"Good-evening, crimps." Thus he greeted them cheerfully. "Why should I stand and what should I deliver?"

"The contents of thy wallet, fat rascal," made answer the man who seemed to hold a kind of chieftainship in the little league of two.

Simon grounded his cudgel.

"Fellow," he said, "I am not a rascal, neither am I fat. What you call fat is brawn, solid brawn. For the other matter, I am as poor as the ancient patriarch."

"We will not take thy word for that," the second robber grumbled, and the brace of knaves moved a little ways nearer to their quarry. Simon guessed that their game was to get at him, one on each side, and to counter their purpose the hunted became the hunter. He moved up on them whirling his baton, so valiant a piece of anger that the robbers yielded ground and their hearts were as water. He thundered at them as he moved:

"Also, I am a little less strong than Samson, the gate-snatcher, and will tackle twenty such as you."

One faintheart called to the other faintheart:

"I like not the looks of this Christopher," and the other faintheart, at one with his comrade, lowered his blade and cried at Simon, to placate him:

"If you be indeed penniless, there is no use in molesting you."

Simon's staff lay at ease again, balanced in his big fist. He was good-humored with the rogues, being tickled at the thought of their possible plunder—the brace of onions in his bag.

"Well reasoned, lads," he laughed. "No logical doctor in Byzantium could have come to a better conclusion. Are you very hot to pick pockets?"

He who seemed the leader of the pair seemed surprised at the simplicity of the question.

"Every honest man is anxious to push his trade," he affirmed, sagaciously.

Simon grinned.

"Is this forest your playground?" he pursued.

The robber shook his head.

"No, no," he said; "we come from Corinth, where we have plied our craft blithely this many a day. Among the light-fingered of that bright city I am Captain Fox, at your service," and the lean, leather-faced rascal made Simon a bow; "and this my comrade goes as Captain Gander," and he pointed to the fat rogue, his companion, who had seated himself on a tree-trunk to await the result of the negotiations.

Simon nodded, and queried:

"Where are you going, good Captain Fox and good Captain Gander?"

"We make for Athens," Captain Fox replied. "There are great doings in Athens—jousts, feasts, dances, banquets, pageants. We should do famously in Athens."

The other ruffian took up the tale.

"Every knight's purse will leak gold pieces, and the lovely ladies will rain pearls from their petticoats. 'Twill be but stooping to pick them up."

Simon leered at the pair maliciously, and his misanthropy hatched a plan.

"Though you take no toll of me, yet the devil is your friend tonight, for yonder on the highway at my heels comes, by-and-by, a young gentleman riding all alone, and one that is sure to carry gold in poke."

Captain Gander rubbed his plump hands.

"St. Nicholas be praised for sending us game," he chuckled.

Simon, in malice, dashed the rascals' hopes with a grin.

"It may be," he suggested, "that it will prove too proud a quarry for two such gibbet-kites as you to pike at. The featherhead in the fine clothes may be a fool, but I do not think such a brace of barn-filchers would show very fearsome even in a fool's eyes."

He that called himself Captain Fox snarled with lips that were as leathern and teeth that were as yellow as his jerkin.

"Do not vex your liver for that," he answered. "We have comrades otherwhere in the wood that we will call to our comfort: Captain Rat and Captain Badger, Captain Bat and Captain Chanticleer, no less—valiant captains all."

Simon laughed heartily as the fantastic catalogue swelled.

"Here is an army out of Noah's ark," he applauded, "with as many generals to it as ever followed Alexander. Ye lack only the leader and the led. Well, go your ways. I give you Golden Jacket for a guerdon."

Again Captain Gander chuckled, but Captain Fox looked at Simon with some show of suspicion.

"Why do you tell us this?" he asked.

Simon answered him in the honesty of his malevolence.

"To help you to the gallows and him to his hurt, for he is a book-reading noodle. Go your ways, I am tired of you," and he pointed with his staff in the direction in which he knew the highway ran, though he could see no sign of it through the clustering trees. "You cannot miss him, for I have seen no other rider this eve, and he shines like a star, for his coat is of cloth of gold and he has jewels in his cap."

The rogues licked their lips. Captain Fox saw himself already in the coat of cloth of gold. Captain Gander, in imagination, pocketed some of those jewels.

"We thank you," Fox cried; and—

"Good-night," cried his fellow. And the pair made off at a pace between a walk and a trot in the direction indicated. Simon looked after them till they disappeared in the deepening dusk.

"I misdoubt me much," he meditated, "if reading of romances of roses will help that lad to tackle these grab-alls." Then he dismissed the matter from his mind and resumed his journey.

A little way farther he came upon a quiet glade which seemed very reposeful in the dying light, and here, in default of water, he decided to rest and munch his onions dryly. He sprawled at his ease on the soft grass and bit thoughtfully at his vegetable, pricking his wits for verses. This ballad was to be his biography, but so far it had not travelled beyond the nursery. The sharpness of his root stimulated fancy:

> *When I was no more than a span,*
> *Honey and gingerbread pleased me highly;*
> *When I came to the height of a man,*
> *Women and vintages used me vilely.*

This quick flow of inspiration fascinated him. The rhymes were as true as they were beautiful. He must needs try again while the fit was on him:

> *When I went to lovemonger school,*
> *Poppets and fopperies killed my credit;*
> *All my sweethearts thought me a fool*
> *While I had pence; but when poor they said it.*

He was hugely amused at this fruition. A man might read verses and yet prove no fool, if the verses were of such stuff as this ballad he fashioned. Here was no nonsense about a rose, but a plain tale of a brave man's life, bravely told, meat for heroes. Thinking it over, he felt that it had gone far enough. It said with a noble simplicity all that he wanted to say; there lay his life by and large. Love of women, love of wine; and for result, your penniless misanthrope yawning in a forest. For Simon was yawning noisily. The unwonted intellectual effort had overmastered his activity; he ought to be up and doing, but sloth pawed at his eyelids and the dusk was all a-humming with lullabies.

"Well, thanks be," he murmured, as he chewed on the last bite of his onion, "there is no woman-thing in this wood to worry me if I choose to slumber."

Even as he spoke he closed his eyes, and, as it seemed to him, had scarcely closed them when he opened them again, suddenly conscious that a woman was standing before him and staring at him.

2

RAINOUART

The studious young knight lay for some little while in the pleasing shadow where Simon had left him, busy with his book. In the enchantment of its pages he had soon forgotten Simon and his lantern and his angry face. In that warm May evening it was very agreeable to lie stretched at his ease there in the green shade and to read the wonderful story of the *Romance of the Rose*. The little volume was very neatly written on vellum in a clear, clerkly hand, and a hand that was more than clerkly had enriched it with many agreeable pictures in which wonderful attenuated youths and slender maidens with yellow hair, all in garments of vivid green and blue and red and yellow, wandered over enamelled fields that were studded with daisies, and in pleasances of fantastic trees. The book was not new to Europe, but it was always new to the youth. He had brought it with him from the court of Philip the Fair, who had given it to the young knight on the occasion of his departure from Greece. Now because Philip the Fair, a shrewd discerner of humanity, knew his man, his gift contained only that early part, which was written by William of Lorris, and which exalted love and ladies, and not that later part, from the hand of John of Meung, which treated ladies with scant ceremony and would have spelled love after another fashion. For the youth who lay in the shadow and read the *Romance of the Rose* was, in the first place, a youth of a high mind and gentle heart, whose spirit swam in the clearest ether of chivalry; and, in the second place, he was son and heir of the reigning Duke of Athens, Duke Baldwin of the Rock.

In all the stormy stories of the conquest of Greece by the Frankish princes, few histories were more stormy or more splendid than those of the Princes of the Rock and of their connection with the city of the Violet Crown. For long enough the Princes of the Rock had ruled in Athens in the direct line, but in the year 1308 the torch was blown out by the death of Guy II., who died childless, and the title swerved off to a cousin of the dead duke, Count Baldwin of the Rock, who at that time was living a brisk, piratical, and filibustering life in the East, much to the discomfort of those with whom his turbulent, truculent nature brought him at loggerheads. Baldwin was a whole-hearted soldier of fortune who loved the bustle of battle, the sacking of cities, the filling of his pockets with other people's money, and the cheering of his occasional solitude with other people's wives. Baldwin had been married himself years before in France to the Lady Isabeau of Hainault. She had loved him much, having been deceived, as sweet women sometimes will be deceived, into the belief that the manners of a savage were truly the manners of a man. He had loved her a little just because her pale graces were new to him, and of her and her pale graces he soon heartily wearied. It was not Count Baldwin's way to trouble himself long about anything that wearied him, and he flung himself headlong into a life of fierce adventure in the scrimmage-ground of the East, leaving his lady, who by that time was not broken-hearted to lose him, in France, with his infant son to take care of.

It was not unnatural that Isabeau of Hainault, having known what it meant to be companion for a season to Duke Baldwin, was honestly and honorably determined to bring up her son to be as unlike his father as, God willing, might be accomplished. Melancholy, heart-sick Isabeau worked out her purpose well. For all her pale grace and fragile person, the Lady Isabeau of Hainault was a strong woman with strong thoughts. She recognized very frankly and very fully from the first how she had been deceived in Count Baldwin, and she made it her whole purpose and endeavor that no other woman should be so deceived by Count Baldwin's son. She had a kind of clear seeing that many such women have, and as she rocked the cradle of the sleeping boy she believed that his days and his ways might prove beautiful. Over the child she prayed one strange prayer morning and night—"I pray that you may never love till you find the loveliest, nor woo till you find the worthiest," and because she knew in her soul that the child would be strong of limb, and because she loved all the old tales of chivalry, she named the child Rainouart, after the noble youth with the giant's strength in the ancient tale of Aliscans.

As the new Rainouart grew from infancy to boyhood, day by day he redeemed his mother's prayers and fulfilled his mother's wishes. He showed from the first an extraordinary strength of body. His physical frame had in it nothing of the bull-bulk of Count Baldwin, but inside his slender form and smooth skin he seemed to be compact with steel. The Lady Isabeau was too brave a lady to forget that a man's first business is to be a man, wherefore the young prince was well trained in arms and skilled in all bodily exercises. As he grew into years and proficiency in martial arts, the contrast between his slender juvenility and his extraordinary vigor and power grew more remarkable. It was curious to find this amazing heritance of the paternal strength so intimately allied with, and subject to, the spirituality of his mother. Rainouart was never quarrelsome, and could scarcely be provoked into a brawl save by some deed of injustice or dishonor; but if ever he were forced to fisticuffs it always went hard with his adversaries, though the odds were heavy against him, as they always were in such cases. Youths of his own age, but youths of greater breadth of body and show of muscle, taken unawares by his appearance, would often challenge him to feats of strength, confident of easy victory, only to be amazed and discomfited by the gentle serenity with which he overcame their sturdiest efforts.

The boy's mind was not neglected at the charge of his body. The tastes of the Lady Isabeau were lettered for an age which did not overprize letters, and she saw to it that her son had a breeding more scholarly than would have pleased the mind of Count Baldwin, who lustily despised and damned all clerks and cared for nothing in manhood but big-boned fighting-engines. The boy was early trained to read and write, to taste some tincture of Latinity, and to find his inspiration and his ideal in the chivalrous epics of France and Britain. When he came to young manhood and entered the service of the King of France, he was soon recognized as one of the most promising knights of the king's following, and the friendship of many men was given to him and the friendship of many women offered to him. The friendship of the men he took amiably and modestly, though no man was his superior of all the king's men in strength or skill. The friendship of the women he let go by him, also very modestly but always with decision. There were many that longed to knock at the door of his heart and enter in, and there were some that showed their longing, most notably of all the beautiful Esclaramonde of Bayonne, whom most men worshipped for her dark, imperious loveliness, and whom all the women, her rivals, hated for a witch, and upbraided beneath their breaths for her skill in philtres. But Esclaramonde, who had won many hearts, and was said to have shown herself generous in reward for her victories, gained no greater favor in Rainouart's eyes than any other lady of the many dainty ladies in the court of Philip the Fair. It would seem as if the prayer his mother had prayed over his cradle had acted on his nature like a charm. Consciously or unconsciously, those words were the governance of his life—"Never love till you find the loveliest, nor woo till you find the worthiest." Truly the Lady Isabeau so loved her son that she thought no woman born of woman worthy to be his wife, and truly she was pleased to believe that in this, as in all other thoughts, Rainouart was of her mind. Moreover, the Lady Isabeau was, as became her rank, familiar with the family histories of the great houses of which the fine court ladies were the fairest flowers, and what she chose to tell or suggest to her son had its service in steeling his spirit against temptations. Anyway, Rainouart served all the fine court ladies with the high-bred homage of an equal and even courtesy, but no pretty face out of all those pretty faces had ever blotted the sun from his mind's firmament, and no white hand of all those white hands had ever held his spirit its prisoner. Esclaramonde of Bayonne, in chagrin, it was whispered, married the ancient, doting Lord of Nemours, who had gained a duchy in Greece, where he reigned as Duke of Thebes, and whither he carried his passionate, magical, dangerous lady. Rainouart paid no heed to her passing; he knew only three services in life—his service to God, his service to his king, and his service to his mother. And from two of these services he was, to his sorrow, soon to be set free. A little while before destiny called upon him to quit the service of Philip the Fair destiny denied him the present service of his mother. The Lady Isabeau passed away from a world of which, had it not been for her son, her pale and gracious presence had long been weary. When the time came to leave him, the last words she said to him were:

"It is good to be brave, it is better to be good; strive to be both," and so she passed away and left him very lonely.

The young Rainouart deeply mourned his mother's memory, for she had ever been his ideal of gentle womanhood, and he made it a mighty resolve in all his life so to act as if she were still with him and her approbation still to be won. Losing thus his best friend, he would have been well content to remain in the service of the adventurous French king, but the death of Guy II. changed his fortune. When the Duchy of Athens came to Count Baldwin, and that jovial freebooter hurried hot-foot to Greece and found himself in unquestioned possession of his duchy, he remembered, belated, that he was a family man. His wife was dead, indeed, but his son lived, and a son was an advantageous possession for the holder of a great title and the ruler of a great state. So messengers were sent speeding across seas to the court of King Philip the Fair, summoning the young man by his filial allegiance to Athens and to the father whom he had never seen. It is by no means overlikely that Rainouart would have thriven at the court of Philip the Fair. For though that astute and unscrupulous monarch had a high regard for the strength, the courage, and the scholarship of the young knight, Rainouart had other qualities which Philip disliked exceedingly, chiefly, indeed, the candor of his mind and the frankness of his speech. He would never consent to condone King Philip's savage treatment of Pope Boniface VII., which had ended, as it seemed, in the pontiff's death at the hands of Philip's men. He held his peace about it, as was meet in the servant of a king, but once when Philip plied him for his opinion, and would take no denial, Rainouart said what he thought, simply and straightly, and the king never plied him for his opinion again, deciding that he was better as a king's fighter than as a king's councillor. Yet he liked the lad for his comeliness, and Rainouart liked the king as his lord. So the young man regretfully said farewell to the king, his master, and his master gave him the beautiful painted manuscript of William of Lorris's romance as a farewell gift, and the young man journeyed over-seas to his father's duchy.

Chroniclers of the age do not seek to deny, though they strive to attenuate, the fact that the meeting of father and son was not wholly felicitous. The young soldier who read poetry on all days and even wrote poetry on some days, and who venerated the memory of a fair and unhappy lady, found his inherited delicacy something offended by the boisterous joviality of Baldwin, the huge eater and drinker, the furious fighter, the promiscuous wooer, quarrelsome when sober, quadruply quarrelsome in his cups. Duke Baldwin, for his part, thought his son's native delicacy of taste effeminate, sneered patently at his sobriety, ramped like a madman at his passion for books, and was flagrantly disgusted by the indifference with which a son of his blood viewed the genial and yielding lemans of the paternal court. But if the young man failed to satisfy his father's wishes in all things, if he failed to explain his tastes for reading and luting, at least he proved satisfactory in other matters. His physical strength was an abiding joy. When Duke Baldwin grasped his son's hand in greeting he strove to crush it to pulp between his merciless fingers, but young Rainouart gave him back grip for grip and squeeze for squeeze till the blood came from the finger-nails of both, and Duke Baldwin was glad in two fashions to unclinch that clasp.

Thereafter it something consoled Duke Baldwin to reflect that if the lad from Paris had a womanish weakness for books and music, at least he could ride as straight and wield lance and sword and axe as well as any youthful paladin of Greece. And if the youth disdained the snares spread for him by the amorous damsels of Athens, he soon made himself friends with the gallantest of the young swaggerers, who learned to love him more for his sinews of steel than for his heirship to the duchy. Duke Baldwin was as volubly proud of his son's skill in arms as he was bitterly ashamed of his skill in arts, and he would have been willing enough in his rough-and-tumble way to let his pride of the one blot out his contempt of the other. But the son would have found it hard in any case to forget Duke Baldwin's neglect of his mother, and he saw nothing to his credit to commend in the man whom he knew to be his father. So it came about that the duke and his son did not see very much of each other, and that while the duke was holding prolonged revels with rollicking swashbucklers and frolicsome, complaisant ladies, the young prince mostly chose to ride abroad, a solitary explorer of the lovely Attic land, dreaming his dreams. He knew little more than honest Simon or than any other French adventurer, gentle or simple, then in Greece, of the ancient days and the ancient fame. When his horse carried him abroad to Colonos or Marathon, or, as it had carried him this day, to the farthermost edge of the Eleusinian wood, his memory was neither pleased nor troubled by thoughts of Œdipus or Miltiades or the rites of Demeter. All he asked when he took the road was to pass through pleasant champaigns and presently to dismount and lie at ease in shady places and read unceasing in the *Romance of the Rose*, and wonder unceasing if ever Good-Greeting would take him by the hand and lead him through the thicket to the place where the Holy Rose-bud awaited him. For

Rainouart dreamed day and night of the rose that he had never found. He had sailed across the seas to Athens with a whole and lonely heart. Whole and lonely his heart had remained at the court of the Duke of Athens, though there, too, as at the court of Philip the Fair, beautiful women swarmed like butterflies, spreading out their colored wings in the ceaseless sunlight, and ever ready to smile their brightest when the young prince came a-nigh. But Rainouart paid them no heed. He was courteous to them because they were women; he disliked them because they were light women; he dreamed of a star. Not yet had he loved the loveliest or wooed the worthiest.

3

ARGATHONA

Simon sat up and rubbed his eyes while he stared back at the damsel. At first he thought that he must unawares have slipped into sleep and that he was still dreaming. Primarily he had heard no sound of footsteps through the wood; further, the girl who faced him was radiantly unlike any woman he had ever seen—and Simon in his time had seen many women. To begin with, she was taller than is the wont of womanhood, seeming tall even to him, who carried four inches over six feet. This was the first thought in Simon's drowsy mind, surprise at the stranger's height; the next, as his brain escaped from the nets and snares of sleep, was conviction that the stranger's face was fairer than any woman's face he had ever seen awake or dreaming. It was beautiful with an unfamiliar type of beauty, though he remembered dimly some ancient statues once seen and little heeded in the garden of a house of pleasure in Byzantium whose features were like the features of this woman. Her head was nobly set upon her neck; her yellow hair was gathered into a knot above the nape; her eyes shone with the most wonderful, changeful blue—they were like the sea, they were like the sky, they were like the waters of forest fountains, the floods of mountain streams. Her comely, upright body was clothed in a kind of smock of white stuff girdled about her middle with a golden girdle of ancient handicraft; her arms were bare from the shoulder; her legs were bare from the knees; her feet were shod with sandals of leather. From the smoothness of her cheeks, from the soft color of her lips, from the slimness of her limbs, from the firm swell of her breasts beneath the fine garment, Simon would have guessed her age to be eighteen or thereabouts. Yet she seemed at once child, girl, and woman, with something boyish, too, in the firmness of her forms, in her balanced carriage, supple as an athlete's, in her air of alert repose. Never had he seen anything so vividly young; the very spirit of youth and joyousness seemed to shine in her glance, to hover on her lips, to quiver about her body as summer air quivers with the heat. Her naked arms, her naked legs were neither tanned by the sun nor stained with forest-travel; on the strong fingers of her fine hands the nails were clear-pink as sea-shells; through the candor of her skin he could see the blue veins wander. She held a bough of myrtle in her right hand, and played with it as she gazed at the man on the grass, and a childlike mirth danced in her kind, wise eyes. Her sweet mouth smiled at his awakening senses, and then she spoke—and here was a marvel! He knew what she said as well as if she were his countrywoman, and yet—it was odd—and yet she did not seem to speak as folk spoke any French that he had ever heard from salt Normandy to the Spanish hills.

"Good-evening, traveller," the girl said, and at the sound of her salutation Simon knew that he was not dreaming but wide awake, and he scrambled clumsily to his feet.

"Saints and angels!" he said, crossing himself.

The girl laughed, and her laughter was as pleasant as the tinkling of sheep-bells in a meadow.

"Do not be fearful, friend," she said, in that same flowing, unfamiliar, appreciable speech; "I will do you no harm."

Hearing this astonishing promise, Simon was quite himself again. That a lass should pledge her word not to hurt him was hugely amusing.

"No, I should guess not, prettykin," he guffawed. "But what does a fair maid in this forest?"

The girl's forehead wrinkled a little in displeasure as the bray of his laughter jarred the serenity of the cloistered trees.

"I live in the forest," she answered.

Simon stared anew at her white arms, her white legs, her unscorched face and unstained raiment.

"I live here all alone, too, save for the birds and the beasts and the trees and the flowers. The foolish Athenians are so fearful of the forest that they never come near its kindly shelter. You are not an Athenian?"

Simon shook his head stoutly.

"No, I thank Heaven," he said; "I am a Frenchman from Rouen." He spoke with a proper pride.

"I thought you could not be," the girl said, gravely, "when I saw you lying so at your ease on the grass and heard you snoring. No Athenian would do that."

Simon reddened a little. Frenchman of Rouen though he was, he had this in common with lesser men: he resented the imputation of snoring.

"Do no Athenians snore?" he questioned, grumpily. The girl laughed again.

"Nay," she said, demurely, "I meant that no Athenian would lie here in the twilight. I have seen no one sleeping in these shades for ages, though I have lived in the forest all my life."

"No great slice of time, I take it," Simon suggested, gallantly. His slow mind was much puzzled by the maid, but his quick flesh was enamoured and he was much the body-servant. The girl looked at him thoughtfully.

"Longer than you think. I cannot tell how often I have seen spring swell into summer, mellow into autumn, and descend into winter, for the years in their seasons are alike to me; but, I suppose, more than a thousand times."

Simon stared agape.

"More than a thousand times? Pray, how old may you be, young woman?"

"I cannot tell," the girl answered, thoughtfully. "I do not think of time. Why should I, being come to my full growth? Time will change me no more. I shall be as I am for always."

Simon frowned in dubiety.

"What is your name, young woman, and where do you belong?"

"My name is Argathona. I belong to the forest. I am a dryad."

Simon's education had been something neglected, and he had no idea what a dryad might be. But he was always superstitious, and now suddenly suspicious.

"Are you a fairy?" he gasped, fearfully.

Argathona shook her head, and waved the myrtle-bough as if to dissipate his fears.

"I have naught to do with the fairies, nor they with me. I am the daughter of a dryad, but my father was a mortal man."

"Like me," Simon suggested. Simon plumed himself on his good looks, but the dryad disagreed.

"I do not think he can have been like you, for my mother said he was beautiful."

Simplicity's frank arrow quivered in vanity's ample target. Simon swallowed an oath.

"Oh, oh," he thought, "this is some rustic minx who is making game of me. Well, I'll humor her whimsy; perhaps we may end with a kiss." He went on aloud, "When were you born, bonnie lassie?"

"Long ago," the girl answered, gravely, "when the old gods still dwelt in Hellas."

Simon's bulk was as full of stifled laughter as a pillow is full of feathers.

"Perhaps you remember the old gods," he hinted, with a grin. The girl's calm eyes widened with wonder at his folly.

"Assuredly I do. How could I forget my earliest friends? They loved me so dearly that though I was the child of a mortal they gave me the gift of immortal youth."

Simon gave a long whistle.

"So you are immortal?"

"My mother was a true dryad," Argathona answered, "born in a tree, living the tree's life, and dying when the tree died. But she loved an Athenian and bore me, and as there was no tree in all the woodland that I could call my own, Zeus gave me this gift to live forever so long as a tree should grow in Greece."

"And your parents?" Simon inquired, politely. He was so taken with the girl that he would not quarrel with her crazy tale.

"My father died long ages ago," Argathona said, "when I was a baby. He died in fight upon the plain of Troy, died by the hand of Paris, the lover of Helena. Hermes brought the news to my mother here in the wood, and my mother wept sorely and sighed in vain to die. This was long ago, long before the time came for the gods to go."

She sighed as she spoke, as one who lingers with tender, pathetic memories. Simon continued his humoring, though the girl was flagrantly insane.

"When was that, pray you?"

"I cannot truly tell you. I was but a child, and had seen no more than some few hundred summers. They were banished, all the beautiful gods, into the twilight, into the Hollow Land. They came to say us farewell, the great gods, the Cloud-Compeller and his queen, and the Lord of the Sun and the Lady of the Moon and sea-born Aphrodite and Virgin Athena and all the Olympians with them. They rode away in a noble company, and I stood with my mother under the shade of my mother's oak and watched them as they went."

This was more than Simon could patiently stomach, and he let some laughter slip.

"Of course you expect me to believe all this?" he chuckled, irreverently. The dryad answered him tranquilly.

"Why should I deceive you, mortal? My mother could not leave her oak, so the gods would have taken me to dwell in the Twilight Land, but I would not leave my mother, and we lost the adorable gods and lingered here in the greenwood. Here my mother taught me all the woodland arts, woodcraft, and glamour, and the speech of the beasts and the meaning of what the birds sing and the trees whisper, and the properties of the plants for heal and for hurt, and how to weave and spin and be familiar with the stars—and all the things that it is needful for a dryad to know. But soon my mother vanished as a mist of the morning, for the oak grew old and withered, and its time had come and hers. I have lived here all alone ever since."

"All alone!" Simon echoed, sceptically, and "All alone!" the white child repeated simply. There was no sound of sadness in her voice, no shadow of sadness in her eyes. She spoke of strange things as naturally as Simon would have talked of his breakfast or his boots or any other workaday matter. Cunning leered in Simon's eyes, cunning lurked in Simon's voice as he chuckled his next question:

"No mortal lover?"

Argathona answered him with a grave simplicity that took the sting out of his sneer.

"I have never left this greenwood; I have never longed to leave it. What use were it for me to make friends with your race who die in a day?"

"Excuse me," Simon interpolated; for Simon was thirty years old, and hoped to live to ninety, but the dryad took no heed of his interruption.

"For many generations few mortals have come to this forest; none, I think, since Alexander died."

"That was not the day before yesterday, neither," Simon commented. He was wondering if the maid were truly mad or merely a piece of mystification. Anyway, she was very fair, the grass was soft, the night air kindly, a rising moon smiled through the trees, and Simon was always ripe for love-making.

"Sweeting," he began, jovially, "if you have never loved mortal man it is high time that you quarrel with this continence, and though I do not greatly credit your tale, I am ready to woo you merrily."

It is always disconcerting to a swain, be he sentimentalist or sensualist, to find that his proposals of passion are entertained with hilarity. So it was with Simon when the girl greeted him with a peal of the cheerfulest laughter that ever had rattled about his ears, while she swayed on her shapely legs like a bell-flower to a breeze. So children laugh at their play; so gods laugh at the muddles of mortals, bright, sweet, whole-hearted laughter, brilliant as the songs of birds.

"You foolish Bœotian," she said, when a pause in her laughter left her breath to speak, "you do not think I would welcome your wooing?" And once again the musical gusts of merriment shook her, and her eyes danced and her whole body trembled with delight.

Simon glowered at her, very red-faced, very sulky, very hot on his purpose. He had overcrowed coy reluctance ere this.

"Welcome or no welcome," he cried, "I mean to clip you in my arms. The forest is silent, you are my prize, you shall follow your mother's example."

He made a step towards the girl as he spoke, with his face as red as a peony, and stretched out his big, brown hands to seize her white body. To his surprise she made no effort to evade him, and for one wild moment it was pleasure to clasp her soft body close to his; but before he had time to turn his clasp into an embrace he found himself, to his bewilderment, plucked from the ground as if he had been caught in the clutch of a whirlwind, and then in another astonishing instant he realized that the maiden had flung him from her as if his mighty mass of manhood had been no bulkier than a cradled doll, and that he was travelling rapidly through the air towards his mother earth. Then he countered the ground with a prodigious thump that seemed to squelch the breath out of his lungs and to shake every bone and strain every sinew of his body. Sick and dizzy and all of an ache he lay on his back on the grass, rigid as a man in a catalepsy, and staring in unfamiliar terror at the maiden, whose beautiful face was suddenly fierce with anger.

"You fool," she cried, "learn that I rule in this forest. I have dealt thus gently with you for this once"—Simon groaned inwardly as she said this, and wondered if he had a whole bone left in his body—"but if you vex me again I shall be tempted to do you some hurt."

Simon made an effort to move, and the effort hurt him sorely, and he marvelled at the girl's ideas of gentleness and hurting. The Olympian sternness of Argathona's brow softened a little at the sight of that supine image of misery.

"Will you promise to offend no more?" she asked, and Simon cried back at her, speaking from the very core of his heart:

"I promise."

The dryad's frown faded, her serene calm rekindled.

"You will do well to keep your word," she said, merrily, "for my sinews are knit with the vigor of the Age of Gold, and I have no need to fear the children of men."

"As to that," Simon protested, as stoutly as he could under the somewhat undignified conditions, "I have my failings, it may be, but I am an honest soldier, and I never broke my word in my life."

"Then get on your feet again," said Argathona, gently, and she reached out her hands to his, extended, and lifted him up standing as easily as if he had been a baby; and at the touch of her fingers Simon felt instantly that his blood was running anew and that the chill which gripped at his heart dissolved before the flame of life revived. He made to stretch his stiff arms, and found to his joy that he succeeded. He moved his legs this way and that with a painful relish in their obedience. It was good to find himself still all of a piece.

"Ah," he sighed, "how stiff I be! It is tedious to feel like a tree."

Argathona's brows knitted slightly, and Simon saw that he had bungled, and tried to gloss his blunder. He had no doubt now as to his companion's powers if he still questioned her narrative, and he thought it well to show respect to her alleged sylvan kinship.

"Of course, there are trees and trees—" he began to stammer, but the dryad with a whisk of her myrtle twig warned him to keep his peace, and he shut his mouth tightly. She sat comfortably down upon the turf, crossing her legs under her as a lad might, and motioned to him to take his ease. Simon gingerly lowered himself to the ground with his chin in his hand. He was not a little afraid of the amazing maid, for which he was scarcely to be blamed; but he was also heartily her admirer, for which he was wholly to be commended. She stared at him and smiled, and Simon stared at her and rubbed his head wistfully.

"Here is a wonder out of a wood," he said. "May the devil fly away with me if I know what to make of you."

"There is nothing to wonder at," Argathona answered, gravely. "I belong to the old, strong race, the kin of the gods, and the strength of the gods runs in my body though my sire was a mortal man. Also I know something of the secrets of the ancient wood. Otherwise I am like yourself, thinking the same thoughts, living the same life, sharing the same pleasures of hunger and thirst, sleep and waking, and the change of the seasons. The only difference is that there will come a time when none of these things can live for you, and that time will never come for me. I shall go on with the dawn and the sunset and the wheeling stars and the changing seasons and the perpetual years."

"The difference is a pretty big one," Simon grunted; "but let that pass."

He looked at the girl curiously; he was now quite prepared to be devoted to her, though he was also quite prepared to believe her a witch. There were witches and witches, and this seemed an honest one. But her claim to endless existence bewildered him. He admitted to himself that it would sound very pleasant if applied to his own case. It must be agreeable, he thought, to go on cheerfully eating and drinking and making love, and fighting and sleeping and gaming and riding a-horseback and experiencing all the other enjoyable processes appertaining to a strong man's life, day in and day out, year in and year out through the centuries, with never any fear of finding wine and love and pastime uninteresting or condemned to end. At least, the maid was not making game of him; she was fixed in her strange story; and, anyway, he was pledged her friend.

"There is one thing that puzzles me," he said, bluntly—"how does it happen that you, who have lived in this wood since your old friends the gods decamped from paradise, and who talk, as I should think, the jargon of ancient days, can converse with me, who remember no more than thirty summers and was born over-seas in France?"

Argathona smiled amiably at his quandary.

"It is given to us," she said, "who are kindred with the gods, to say in our speech the thoughts of all men, and to understand with our ears the thoughts of all men. When you speak I hear your meaning in the words of the woodland, and when I speak to you my meaning takes possession of you and you shape it for yourself into the usage of your familiar speech, and so it will be for me always, wherever I go."

Simon nodded. If this were so he could understand that something in her utterance which seemed alien and quaint to him. Here truly was a gift scarcely less enviable than the grace of perdurable life. Argathona interrupted his meditations.

"You have asked me many questions," she said, looking straightly at him from under level brows; "now answer some for me. Is it the manner of mortal man to make love in your fashion?"

Simon looked awkward and fumbled with his beard.

"There are many ways of making love," he confessed. "Some are more formal," he admitted, after a moment's pause.

The nymph looked thoughtful.

"Such would please me better," she said. She eyed Simon circumspectly, then questioned, suddenly, "Why do you carry that lantern?"

Simon unhooked it from his girdle and held it at arm's-length, a formidable piece of furniture for a traveller.

"There was some fellow of old time did the like for my reason—looking for an honest man or an honest woman."

The dryad smiled at memories.

"I have heard of that; it was a mad Athenian called Diogenes."

"I care not what his name was," said Simon, "but I like his humor and I follow his quest. Not that the lantern is of much use to me in the daytime, but it shows my good faith."

"Have you found no honest folk?" Argathona asked, sympathetically. Simon shook his red head.

"Never since I came to these regions of Greece," Simon protested. "There were honest folk in Rouen, or, at least, I used to think so. Alain, the armorer, he was an honest man. He made this blade," and Simon patted the stout sword at his side. "I never met with a better. But since I came to Corinth to serve the duke I have found no honest soul or body."

Argathona gave a little shiver.

"I am glad that I dwell here in the greenwood, and not with your clan."

Simon rambled on with his narrative.

"When I came to these parts I still had the bulk of a pretty little patrimony. Where is it now? Every light o' love in Corinth has filched her bit of it; every cozener with the dice has picked his share. While I was rich my friends fawned on me; when I fell poor they turned their backs, lads and lassies. I have written some rhymes on my misfortune."

He paused, hoping that the maid might ask to hear them, but as she did no such thing he resumed, plaintively:

"So now I trample this planet seeking an honest human."

"Do you hope to find such in Athens?" Argathona asked.

She was quite interested in this strange, russet-colored man, with his wild words and his wild wits—as interested as she would be if she came upon some new kind of fawn or unfamiliar moth in the forest. Simon grunted uncertainly.

"I have my doubts," he said, "though every great lord and every little lord in Attica will be there. But I do not go to Athens solely to that end. I hope to find service with the Duke of Athens, who loves, so they tell me, such stout fellows as I be."

He stretched his great arms apart as he spoke, in pride at their mighty muscles. Then, remembering how little their strength had availed him against the witchery of the nymph, he grinned a thought sheepishly. But Argathona was honestly admiring his force, and only pitying him for not being comely. They sat for a moment looking at each other, thinking their own thoughts. About them all was very still in the moonlight, silence only troubled by the wheeling of bats and the droning of insects. Suddenly from the distance came loud shouts, furious cries, and then the angry clash of steel on steel and the clattering of a horse's hoofs in furious flight.

4

THE MYSTIC ROSE

The young prince lay in the shadow while his horse cropped at the fresh grass, and he read the *Romance of the Rose*, and as he read it seemed as if he, too, lay there dreaming with the dreamer, and that all the amazing pageant of the tale moved before him as the figures on the woven arras of a great room move, stirred by the wind. For he, like the teller of the tale, seemed to wake from sleep on a May morning and to stray into the meadows to hearken to the matins of the birds. Like the dreamer, he wandered over flower-starred fields beside a river broader and shallower than the Seine till he came to the garden and the castle whose walls were adorned in gold and colors with the hideous images of Hate, Felony, Villany, Covetousness, Avarice, Envy, Sorrow, Eld, Hypocrisy, and Poverty; and it seemed to him that after he had sated his awed fancy with the study of those strange devices, he, too, sought if by any means he might get into the garden. Then in this waking sleep he found at last a small wicket, and he smote thereon, and the gate was opened to him by a damsel who told him that her name was Idleness, and that she was the friend of the master of the castle and garden, whose name was Mirth, and she gleefully bade him enter, and he obeyed and found himself straightway in so fair a garden that he deemed himself to have arrived at the earthly paradise. His dream spirit, following fast on the dainty heels of Idleness, came to where apple-faced Mirth and his jolly company, fair men and fair women, entertained themselves with song and dance.

But while he was with that genial congress and sharing in their sports, the God of Love came over the grass with Sweet-Looking by his side, and Sweet-Looking carried two bows, one crooked and knotty, the other even and comely, and two quivers, each holding five arrows, and the arrows in the quiver in the right hand were Beauty, Simplesse, Franchise, Company, and Fair-Semblance, and those in the left hand were the arrows of Pride, Villany, Shame, Wanhope, and New-Thought. Then the dreamer fled away from these presences, and as he went the God of Love dogged his footsteps with the fair bow and the fair arrow in his hand, and the dreamer came to that clear fountain where Narcissus drowned himself for self-love. In the waters of this fountain the dreamer beheld the reflection of a rose-bush all on fire with roses, and the desire of that rose-bush filled his heart so hotly that he would not have parted with one bud thereof, might he hope to gain so much, for the city of Paris or the city of Pavia. And while he hungered for the rose, the God of Love came up with him and pierced him with the five arrows of Beauty and Simplesse and Franchise and Company and Fair-Semblance, and with each wound he became more and more Love's servant and vassal, and then Love locked his heart with a golden key and left him with but one desire in that shut heart, the desire to obtain the noble rose.

And so in his dream the youth pursued his adventure till he came to where the rose-bush flourished and found it guarded by all manner of evil passions, who grinned defiance at him and knotted their gnarled hands to make a barrier to hold him from the lovely, lonely rose. And even as he despaired of success Queen Venus came to his aid—Venus with roses in her hair and roses at her feet, a beautiful, alluring presence, and cheered him with sweet smiles and urged him with sweet words to complete the achievement of the rose. Line by line and page by page the story of the wonderful book seemed to tell itself over in living pictures to his dreaming eyes, and the gracious women with the gracious names courtesied to him and kissed their pink fingertips, and the evil faces mowed at him, and behind and beyond the fair faces and the foul he could see the glorious flower that he longed for. And he thought that Venus led him by the hand till he was close to the flower, and gave him leave to kiss it, and he stooped and kissed the rose, and his blood ran fire and his spirit was sanctified.

Then, with a shiver, Rainouart woke, and realized that he was lying alone by the highway to Athens, and that the day had darkened and the shadows were falling, and that his horse was fretting impatiently at his tether, and that the book had fallen from his relaxed fingers, and that he was very much alone on the earth. And he wished with all his unblemished soul that he could slip from the world he lived in, from the world where he loved no woman, into that kingdom of dreams, and achieve through all impediments and obstacles the love of his unknown lady. Wishing thus with a deep sigh, and realizing the vanity of the wish with a deeper, he thrust the book back into his bosom, and unfastened his horse and mounted him and turned his head towards Athens, letting him go at his own gait. Muffled in his melancholy musings, he suffered the bridle to drop on his horse's neck and rode with folded arms, meditating upon the power of poesy, and wondering if it were truly well for him that it had pleased Heaven to make his spirit so unhappily different from the spirits of the light-hearted knights of his father's court, who loved and were content, or who loved and were discontent, but who were always blithe of spirit and seemed to ask nothing better of fortune.

As he thus jogged and mused, trusting to his horse to find its way to the city, suddenly from the shadow of the trees that bordered the white highway came leaping from either side menacing figures, and the dusk was troubled with the gleam of naked steel. And then, before the prince could realize what had happened, his horse gave a great scream of pain, for one of the skulkers had wounded the animal in the side, aiming to hamstring it, and missing his mark in the dusk and flurry. The horse reared, and the prince, taken unawares, lost his stirrups. But Rainouart was too skilful a rider to be thrown, for instinctively he gripped the sides of his horse with his thighs and caught at the crupper, and if he had chosen could have escaped from his assailants easily enough astride of the galloping steed. But it was not in him to avoid danger thus or to fly from any odds; so, leaning forward, he caught on the bridle and brought the frightened animal to a moment's stand-still, and then deftly swinging himself from the saddle alighted on his feet on the highway. In another moment his sword was out to meet the swords of his antagonists, who rushed on him, a hurly-burly of shouts and swords, and the quiet of the night was broken by the fierce clash of steel on steel and the thundering of the frightened horse's hoofs as he sped along the highway towards Athens.

5

THE SONG OF THE FOREST

When the noise of the clash of steel and the clatter of flying hoofs echoed through the greenwood, Argathona leaped to her feet and the warm color fled from her face. Simon, flatling on the grass, indifferent to a noise the cause whereof was shrewdly guessed by him, thought the girl more than ever akin in her pallor to those old stone statues he had lightly noticed in that garden of pleasure in Byzantium. At that time he decided easily that the living women who served his squandering humor in that garden were much more fair than those ladies of old time whom the unknown sculptor had hoped to commemorate. Now rolling the problem over carefully through somewhat sluggish processes of thought, he began to hold it little less than reasonable to change his mind.

"What is the matter?" the dryad cried, pressing her hands against her breasts and widening her eyes, catlike, as she peered through the moony gloom of the wood. Her attitude in her companion's eyes was that of a wild creature troubled, and alert to pounce.

Simon rolled lazily on the grass and gave a self-satisfied snigger.

"I met a loon by the highway at the edge of the forest poring on a foolish book, and his folly vexed me. Then I 'countered a covey of thieves in the thick of the trees and told them of my blockhead coming. From what we hear I take it that he has fallen into their fingers. Belike they are cutting his throat at this present."

He chuckled at the ugly thought. Argathona turned upon him a pale, set face and blazing eyes of rage.

"You will not suffer this!" she cried, indignant; "you are a strong man."

Simon laughed again, a fat laugh, and aired his cynical philosophy.

"Marry, will I!" he answered. "Every man oaf that kills another man oaf rids me the world of one pestilent fellow, and gives an honest man more elbow-room."

Simon had angered the dryad much before, but now he angered her more. Probably he had never heard of Medusa or he might have believed that he beheld her. Argathona's adorable face was terrible to behold in its wrath, and her tresses in the moonlight gleamed like golden serpents. The scorn in her eyes might well have scared his bulk to stone.

"Oh, you are hateful, you humans," she protested, with hands uplifted to heaven; and then she shrilled in a voice there was no resisting, "Run to his help."

Very reluctantly, for his tumble still irked him, Simon found himself obediently scrambling to his feet. The moment he stood erect Argathona clutched hold of his right hand with her left, and in another instant she had started to run in the direction from which the clangor came. Simon would have liked to resist, but he might have liked equally well to be proclaimed emperor of the East for any self-satisfactory result his wishes were likely to have. His strong right hand was a helpless prisoner in the grip of the girl's white fingers, and his limbs seemed only to obey the volition communicated to them by her swift pulses. Whether he liked it or whether he did not—and indeed he knew very well that he did not—he was scampering at the top of his speed beside the smoothly running maiden. Oh, the appalling rapidity of that race through the forest! Simon, for all his bulk, had ever been counted swift of foot among his fellows, but he had never known till that moment what it truly meant to move swiftly. His hand captured in the irresistible grasp of Argathona, the big man bounded along through the alleys and over the glades of the forest trying to keep pace shoulder to shoulder with the flying maid. It was like being tied to the tail of a comet and careering through space; or, rather, it reminded Simon's homely fancy of a dog he had once seen tied to a farmer's wagon when the farmer's horse had bolted, covering ground in reluctant hurry with trailing paws and tail. It seemed to him as if his legs no longer touched the firm earth, but floated behind him foolishly, swimming in the air, while his companion swept quicker than the wind through the interminable avenues of the wood. That frenzied flight was like the worst part of an ill dream, but it was an ill reality, and Simon's bulk suffered wofully. His heart was strained like a swollen wine-skin, the sweat rained from his aching body, there was not so much breath left in his lungs as would blow a single hair from the beard of a seeding dandelion; it was death in life to travel at that pace. After what seemed to Simon an eternity of breakneck journeying, they swept into a clearing of the forest fringed at the foot by the white highway. In that clearing, as in a theatre, Simon saw a youth with his back to a tree engaged gallantly in steel-play against a group of dusky figures that came at him by rushes and fell off again before the steady sweep of his long sword. Simon's breath and senses came back to him like a trick. He saw that the man so vehemently attacked and so shamefully outnumbered was defending himself valiantly, and he thought better of bookworms from that instant. As he watched the craft of single man against many, the assailants gave ground, and one of their number fell to the earth like a log and lay there loggish. The man attacked had a breathing span, and waited watchful with his weapon poised.

"Go to his aid," the wood-nymph whispered in Simon's ear, pointing to the man who was fighting for his life.

Simon shook his head doggedly, thinking of the rules of his misanthropic game. He had made up his mind to dislike mankind and womankind, and it seemed a declination from principle to help anyone in peril of a paltry life.

"He would not thank me," he grumbled; "he is holding his own well enough."

Even as he spoke, however, the conditions of the struggle were suddenly altered. Again the robbers had made to rush the youth, again they had retreated, and this time the youth, quitting the bastion of his tree-trunk, charged his retreating foes, who fled swiftly before him hither and thither. In making this attack he left at his rear, unheeding, the man who had fallen, and this one, suddenly quickening from his seeming lethargy, rose to his feet directly behind the advancing knight, and struck at close quarters a murderous blow at his head with what seemed to be a short club or mace. The youth gave a groan and reeled as he turned and tried to face this unexpected onslaught, and instantly all his enemies came swarming at him again.

"Will you not help him?" Argathona cried, in fine scorn. "Then I will."

A fallen tree-trunk lay in their way; the dryad leaped upon it just as the harassed youth, stumbling under a second treacherous blow, tripped and fell, and the robbers came swooping from all quarters upon their quarry to despatch him. Argathona flung up her arms.

"Help me, help, ye forest powers," she cried, in a great voice that seemed to Simon to fill the four corners of the world.

At the awful sound the startled robbers turned from their victim and stared in terror at the white figure perched upon the stricken tree. Simon to that moment had noted no signs of rising storm, though it was no news to his experience that storms rise and fall swiftly in the land of Greece. But on that instant it seemed to him and to the confounded robbers that a fierce wind came roaring through the forest while a black cloud like a dragon swallowed the moon at one bite, drowning the wood with intolerable darkness, ripped at swift intervals with zigzags of lightning, blindingly bright. Furious volleys of thunder rolled through the blended terror of light and darkness, and the clamor of heaven was horribly mimicked on earth by a bellowing as of innumerable wild beasts, fierce citizens of the forest, disturbed in their slumbers by the sudden hubbub. Simon, frankly frightened, fell on his knees and tried to stammer a prayer, while the robbers, utterly discomfited, shrieked their fears, and turning from that figure standing preternaturally white against the blackness, fled for their rascal lives. It appeared to Simon as he knelt that the dryad high above him chanted a wild imprecation upon the fugitives which rang thus:

> *Chase them, wolves, but do not slay;*
> *Scare them, snakes, but do not sting;*
> *Glow-worms, guide the rogues astray;*
> *Hedgehogs, trip them as they spring*
> *Helter-skelter through the night,*
> *Dumb and deaf and blind with fright.*

Though Simon deemed it an age-long time before the last sound of flying feet died away and the last words of the wood-nymph's imprecation faded into silence, yet the storm died with a suddenness only equalled by its birth. The thunder ceased to rumble, the lightning ceased to fly, the great, black dragon of cloud fell asunder dissipated into a myriad vanishing fragments, and in a quiet sky the sweet moon shone supreme again, filling the glade with brilliance. Simon staggered to his feet and made an end of his paternosters.

"That was a very pretty piece of work," he stammered, wiping the beads of sweat from his wet forehead as he turned to address the wood-nymph. The remark was intended to be a compliment, but it proved a soliloquy, for he found that he stood and spoke alone. Argathona had already quitted the tree-trunk and skimmed across the intervening grass to the field of battle. She was now bending over the wounded man. Simon followed her as quickly as he could, fearful of his own black shadow as it trailed raggedly in the moonlight. When he reached her side Simon, bending by her, peered into the rigid face of the fallen fighter. The man was, indeed, his book-reading knight of the afternoon, who lay now very still and pale in the moonlight with his eyes shut, and there was blood upon his bright hair and blood upon his colored coat. The dryad looked up imploringly at Simon with clasped hands and face strained with sorrow.

"The beautiful boy!" she sighed. "What have they done to him? I hope he is not dead. Tell me, you who are human and should understand your kind."

Simon stooped closer over the body and examined it dexterously enough. In the rough-and-tumble of his life he had had plenty of experience of wounds, and knew what to do. The heart was beating satisfactorily, and Simon nodded approval.

"Have you never seen death before?" he asked of his companion, while his big paws began to search more gently than seemed natural to them for the man's wounds.

Argathona wrung her hands.

"Never of human creature," she wailed; "but I still weep for the forest creatures, the beasts and the birds and the insects who seem so happy in their little lives."

By this time Simon had plucked open the knight's coat, and his fingers travelled dexterously over flesh that seemed womanly white and smooth in the moonlight.

"You are mighty compassionate," he grunted.

Argathona gave him a glance of pathetic reproval.

"I should be, being immortal," she answered, with a girlish dignity which was quaint in such a case.

Simon nodded silently. He had forgotten the girl's claim to immortality, but he was now very sure that she was a witch and her words did not worry him. Patiently he finished his examination of the body. A stroke aimed at the side had slipped on a buckle, causing only a gash where a hole had been hoped for. The loss of blood was not enough to account for the knight's helpless condition. Simon lifted him carefully to one side and then saw the cause of unconsciousness. The murderous blow that had been struck at the back of the knight's head had been struck at close quarters, and struck to kill. It had come pretty near to carry out its purpose, if the striking arm had been stronger.

Simon turned an encouraging countenance to the girl's grave face.

"Your knightling is not dead nor in great danger of death, though he has a nasty nick in the side that had better be bunged."

As he spoke he tore away a great piece of the youth's shirt and laid bare his side while he twisted the linen to shape a bandage.

"The worst of his business is that crack at the back of the head which has knocked him silly. It were well if we had some water."

"Let me do that," Argathona ordered, pointing to his employment. "I know how to stanch wounds. I saved the life of a stag lately that Alcibiades had wounded. Run you to the spring in the forest and bring me water."

When Argathona commanded in Argathona's woodland, Simon felt that it was for him to obey without question.

"Where is the spring?" he asked, as he rose to his feet.

Argathona drew from her girdle the myrtle-bough that she had thrust there when they began their wild race through the forest.

"Hold this so in your hand," she showed him, "and go straightly moonward, pressing it lightly between your palms. When it begins to quiver and twirl in your fingers you will know that you are near the spring. It is but a little way from here."

Simon had heard ere this of such ways of finding water, though in his country folk did the business rather with witch-hazel than myrtle; yet he had little doubt but that Argathona knew her woodland ways, and he took the bough from her hands and made at the top of his speed for the forest.

6

LIKE UNTO ADONIS

Argathona, bending on one knee over the wounded man, lifted his shoulders with firm, supple fingers upon the other knee, and, tenderly supporting the bruised head with one hand, breathed quickly and repeatedly upon his parted lips. The breath of those who are deathless can fan the dying flame of the lamp of life till it burns again serenely. As she worked thus, tending a mortal man for the first time, touching the curling young head and the smooth young skin, unwonted tremors stirred her and unwonted fancies fumed. "If it were not for the red blood," she thought, "surely this youth might be of kin with the immortal gods. Adonis must have looked so when he lay with his life-blood dabbling the brake and reddening the petals of the roses, and widowed Aphrodite wept."

There were tears in Argathona's eyes as she thought thus, and they fell warm upon the cold face and kindled color in it, for the tears of those that are deathless quicken the flesh as the rains from heaven quicken the earth. After a little the youth opened his eyes and looked up in wonder at the beautiful, sad face that compassionated him, the beautiful body that neighbored him.

"Who are you?" he asked, faintly, wondering where he was, for his wits were still wool-gathering, and wondering why his voice sounded so weak and foolish to him, as voices sometimes sound in dreams.

"I am—" Argathona began, and faltered. She thought that she would not again tell a stranger the truth about herself and be doubted, as Simon had doubted her, so she changed her purpose a little and went on:

"I am a woman, and I live in this wood."

Rainouart struggled somewhat to get up, for it vexed his strength exceedingly to feel helpless and it fretted his courtesy to trouble a woman with such care of him. But Argathona gently laid a hand upon his breast, and for all his strength he could not resist that pressure, and she kept him pillowed on her knee. He put a hand that seemed unusually clumsy to his aching head, and then stared in amazement at his naked chest and weakly strove to claw his coat together. Argathona whispered to him very softly, and he understood her without marvelling, being unable for the moment to marvel at anything.

"Robbers set on you—wounded you."

Again Rainouart struggled to rise.

"Now I remember," he said, fiercely; and looking about him, though it hurt him much to move his head, he saw how his sword lay on the grass a-nigh him, and he made a grab for the weapon. But Argathona put her beautiful, strong arms about him, and held him thus while she whispered motherly to him, as children have whispered to their dolls since the first child played with the first mandrake:

"You must keep still; you are sorely hurt, but I have stanched the blood."

Rainouart's wits were none too muddled to forget reverence. He stooped his head and kissed the girl's hands where they met about his breast. The touch of his lips upon her seemed to sting her virgin flesh through to the pure heart, and she unclasped her hands with a little moan. Rainouart looked up at her.

"Why do you cry out? Why do you withdraw your hands? My gratitude would never offend you."

"You do not offend me," Argathona whispered, very softly, so softly that he could scarcely hear her. But he did hear her, and so hearing he now wondered, as Simon before him had wondered, how it happened that his own dear French speech should sound at all strange to him. As the girl's hands no longer restrained him, he struggled a little and sat erect, and stared into her eyes as she kneeled beside him. His troubled thoughts seemed to lapse again into a trance; surely he had strayed in the guarded garden, surely he lay in the mystical pleasance, surely he had touched with his lips the petals of the noble rose.

"What is your name?" he whispered, and she told him, and he repeated it softly, "Argathona," and found it very sweet to say and hear.

"When I kissed your hands, Argathona," he murmured, "all the pain of my wounds seemed to leave me, and I drew new life, new vigor, from the kiss. But when you withdraw your touch from me the smart returns and my head aches wearily. If you will let me kiss your hands once more I think that would surely banish pain."

He pleaded not because he dreaded to bear pain, but because he longed with all his heart to kiss her hands again, and he hoped to win her to yield through pity. He asked no more in his speech than to kiss her hands, and he asked no more in his heart. For this, though he knew it not, was his first acquaintance with the meaning of love, and his white chivalry would have died blithely for less grace than this from the loved one.

"You must not suffer pain," the girl said, looking with troubled doubt into his bright, mortal eyes. For this, though she knew it not, was her first acquaintance with the meaning of love. Then she yielded her hands to him sweetly as one who, being great, grants a favor, and granting it is glad to be humble in the granting. The young French knight took her white fingers in his and kissed them very tenderly, very courteously, and as he kissed them he looked up into her pitying eyes and longed to weep for the very keenness of the joy that filled his being. It seemed to him on the instant that he had waited through all the love-loneliness of his spring for the touch of those hands, for the regard of those eyes. Surely Lord Love had locked his heart with a golden key, to keep it as a shrine vacant till this hour and dedicated to this image.

"You have the most wonderful hands in all the world," he stammered, tremulous with a sense of intimate revelation. "Their touch yields life. But you have the most wonderful face in the world, the most wonderful eyes."

He had clean forgotten how he came there, he had clean forgotten Athens, forgotten everything except the glorious certainty that he had found the rose of the world. Argathona neared her face to his till she almost touched his cheek with her lips. She knew with the wisdom of the wood that he spoke the truth of his heart. She would have known even, if she had been wise in the wisdom of the world, from the loyalty of his voice, and she gave back the truth of her heart with the frankness of the dawn of time.

"Your hands are strong and shapely, like the hands of the gods; your eyes are bright, like the eyes of the gods; you are good to behold."

Rainouart colored, a little bashful as a gallant lad should be at the high praise of a fair girl, and tried, manlike, to put it by in spite of his wild pleasure at its sound and sense.

"So long as a man be brave, it matters little how he be formed and featured, at least so all men say, but I have heard that some ladies think otherwise." And he smiled shyly at her, hotly glad that she should think well of him, spirit and substance together glad to madness with happiness.

The dryad looked at him gravely. "Are there many mortals like this," she pondered—"so modest, so brave, so fair?" Her heart assured her that this must be the pride and idol of the time.

"Comeliness is a mark of the favor of the gods," she asserted.

Rainouart pressed her hands closely, his spirit rekindling at the exquisite contact, his soul desiring nothing better than this bright hour. Yet he wondered at her words.

"Why do you speak like a pagan?" he asked. "The gods have gone long ago."

The dryad sighed as she thought of the splendid figures riding to the twilight land. Was it yesterday?

"Ay," she sighed, "the gods have gone long ago," and she stared across the moonlit space into the blackness of the wood, and wondered what had happened to her which had changed so strangely the ancient way.

There was a little silence; mortal and immortal troubled with new thoughts. Then Rainouart made to rise. It was strangely sweet to lie there supported by this woman's arms; but Rainouart was a man and a knight, and must not presume on a fair lady's patience. So he got to his knees, and she helped him to his feet with her strength, which could have aided a greater than he; and they stood face to face in the moonlight, mortal boy and immortal girl, and to both alike the moment of mortal immortality had come. The night wind was very quiet, the wood seemed still with a kind of sacred stillness; it was as if the world were asleep and only they awake in all the world. The hearts of youth beat with the mutual pulses of a great passion.

7

LOVE IS ENOUGH

The maid gazed at the man wistfully, a-quiver with mysterious hopes and fears.

"What god do you serve?" she faltered, her memory all alive with the divine faces and the shining forms and that calm, tragic procession to the shadowland.

Rainouart bowed his head, meekly devotional as his devout mother, and crossed himself slowly while he prayed a prayer.

"Messire Christ Jesus, who died for all men and for me, a sinner, thirteen hundred years ago. What other Lord may a knight serve? Do you take me for a follower of Mohammed?"

To Argathona neither name had any meaning. The beautiful gods her babehood knew had journeyed to the sunless land, and her mother had told her how a great voice, louder than all the winds that fill the sky, had cried abroad that great Pan was dead. She had always heard of a power mightier than the gods. That power had triumphed; she knew no more, she asked no more.

"I take you for a brave man," she said, looking him full in the face, and she looked many things that she could not say. In the conquering spell of that night of springtime his glorious youth seemed as abiding as hers, and she forgot to pity his dower of frailty or her dower of endurance, surrendering to a greater force than pity. To the man it seemed as if he, standing there holding this unknown woman's hands and drowning in this unknown woman's eyes, had learned in one noble moment the sacred secret of life, the reason why it is worth while to exist and to endure, live hardily a man's hard life, die firmly a man's inevitable death. All his spirit was at his lips as he spoke, his hands clinging to the clasp of her hands. For he knew that he had come to the crown of his life, that he had caught the clew that he was seeking, that he had found the noble rose.

"Pray God you take me for your loyal lover. My soul has lived alone for this moment, my little life has been spared for this grace." So he began, and then for the first time in all her age-long life the dryad heard the splendid, the terrible words that govern the reeling world.

"I love you," the man cried from the heart of his heart, and again, "I love you," and yet again, "I love you"—the mystical three words repeated mystically three times, as is meet in the litany of love. He would have caught her in his arms, but she held his hands fast, and for all his strength he could not pluck them away from her grasp. Joy and sorrow struggled for the supremacy of her being.

"Do you really love me, you mortal man, me whom you have never seen before this night?" she asked, with a tender pity, with a tender irony. The pity was for him, the about-to-die loving the undying; the irony was for her, that she spoke with the speech of doubt knowing with all her heart that he loved her, knowing with all her heart that she loved him.

"I am a mortal man," Rainouart answered, passionately, "as you are a mortal woman; but love is immortal, and true knights who are true lovers only think so of love. They ride and they ride and they see fair faces in lattice or orchard, and they vow the world is a pleasant place; but they pay no heed to the fair faces, and they ride on in the quest of the rose. Then at a thoughtless turn of the road they see one face and the world is heaven or hell—heaven if they win and wear the rose, hell if they may not attain to its petals. No, not so," he corrected himself, quickly, "for to love the loveliest is well whether she smile or frown, and so, come what may, it is my glory to love you, but I wish you could love me a little."

She answered in racking anguish to the rapture of the man:

"I think I could love you very dearly, but I do not think it would be wise."

"Do not mistrust me," he pleaded. "I could be nothing but loyal to my lover, loyal to the death."

As the words rang from his lips Argathona gave a great cry, and loosing her hold of him covered her face with her hands like a frightened child, and her body shook with sobs.

"Alas, to the death!" she wailed, shuddering at the gulf between them and the doom laid upon immortals to see their mortal lovers die.

Rainouart trembled; liberated from her fingers, his life seemed to ebb again furiously, the very strength her touch had given him made him the weaker at the withdrawal of that contact. His wound ran red anew, and the hurt in his head burned horridly. But he cried vehemently, catching at his breath:

"We must all die, young or old, gentle or simple; but we die in the hope of salvation, and today we two live, today I love you, today I pray God that you may love me."

She was stirred by his passionate enthusiasm, by the vehemence of his speech, by the earnest meaning in his eyes. Loving him, she was eager to be loved according to the simple creed of the woodland, and she tried like him to forget the unavoidable.

"Give me your love," he cried to her again. "Give me your love. Come with me into the wide world. I am Rainouart of the Rock, son of the Duke of Athens. You shall live like a queen in the sweet city."

A sudden pain tugged at the dryad's heart, and she shook her head sadly. This was not what she understood by love, to go and dwell among mortals and watch them die as summer flies die in a day.

"If I gave you my love," she said, "I could not go with you into the wide world. My life is here in the ancient wood."

Resolve ruled Rainouart's forehead with strong lines. He was so sure that this was the love of his life, and that to love like this was truly to live, that he was ready to pay his price for paradise.

"Then I will dwell with you in the ancient wood," he answered. "The world is a fine place, full of color and music and honorable strife, but true love is better than all things, and if you love me I will dwell with you in the ancient wood."

The dryad sighed. She longed with all her heart to say yes, longed and dared not. She knew now how her mother felt when the Greek youth wooed her in the days before the heroes sailed to Troy.

"It may not be," she said, but she said it half-heartedly, petitioning secretly if, after all, it might not be. Perhaps she might keep his spirit alive within him with her immortal lips, perhaps she might hold death off with her immortal arms as the demi-god Herakles did when he brought back Alkestis.

The impetuous Rainouart, lip-deep in love, made light of her denial. Heaven had been very gracious to him and he would not lose the rose. What was there to weep for in his father's court? Could its drunken chief and dissolute women and debauched princes restrain him from the religious quiet of the wood? What was there in all Athens to be set against a moment of Argathona's love?

"It must be," he persisted; "we are troth-plighted, you and I. We have exchanged loves and hearts and cannot deny it."

He drew a ring from his finger as he spoke, a heavy gold ring cunningly carved with the image of our Lord upon the tree, and set about with little studs of gold wherewith to say the rosary.

"This is my Master and thine," he whispered. "Wear it and be mine."

She put the ring and his hand away from her, troubled by his words and by the unknown image on the ring. Rainouart misunderstood her gesture.

"Dear," he protested, "I mean all honor and honesty with you. With this ring I will wed you. Hear, my dear lady. A little way beyond the wood between here and Athens there lives apart a holy man; let us go to him hand-in-hand that he may make us man and wife."

The dryad tried painfully and vainly to understand his meaning. What had their loves to do with the little hermitage at the foot of the hill and the lonely man who lived there? To wed meant to her to give herself hand and heart and all to the lover whom she loved, and if ever she dreamed on summer days and nights of what love could be it was as of something that might come to pass when the gods returned, as they surely would one day return from the twilight land. Now she knew that she loved this mortal wholly, now she knew that this mortal loved her wholly, and now, looking at her mortal lover, she knew that he was in peril of the melancholy disease, the ceasing, which mortals call death. For since she had unclasped her hands from his hands his face had grown pale again which had warmed at her touch, and his energies had ebbed with the warmth of his wooing, and his senses sickened with the dizziness in his head. She clasped him again, but her touch could no longer quicken his vitality as keenly as before, for her powers were weaker through love of a mortal. He slipped from her arms upon the grass and his face was grown suddenly gray.

"What has happened," he moaned, "that a scratch can so unman me?"

Argathona bent over him, consoling, comforting, loving.

"I must find the herb of healing," she said. "It hides in the heart of the wood. Sleep here for a little till I return."

She breathed softly upon his forehead willing him to sleep, and the youth's drawn face softened, his limbs relaxed, and he lay motionless upon the turf. A stranger would have guessed that he was dead, but Argathona knew better; she knew that the youth lay drowned in a dreamless, soothing slumber.

"Sleep," she murmured—"sleep till I return with the herb of healing."

Tears flooded her eyes making the moonlight dim, and she beat at her breasts.

"Alas! I cannot deny to love him. My mother's fate is mine, for I love a mortal, and my lover will die in a day and I shall live unhappy till the gods ride back from the twilight land."

She turned from her sleeping lover and ran swifter than a stag across the moonlit space and dived into the darkness of the wood.

8

SIMON SPIES

When the wonderful lovers were speaking together, unstained youth and stainless maid, neither of them dreamed that hMarylanduman eyes were watching them from the thicket; but it was so. Simon, twisting and twiddling the myrtle-bough between his big fingers, had picked his way through the forest till the twig began to spin of itself, and then he found the clear fountain and filled his gourd, after satisfying that private thirst of his own which an unmoistened supper of onions had done much to stimulate. He was in no great heat of enthusiasm about the book-reading youth whom the dryad had rescued. He admitted him a brave fellow, but that was nothing; it was no more than a man's business to be brave, and if the wood-girl must like a brave fellow, why could not Simon serve her turn? He grumbled to himself as he went and returned that he believed the minx had sent him to the waterpool on purpose that she might be left alone with the lad; and he reflected cynically, with a cynicism worthy of such a lickerish lantern-bearer, that a woman is a woman though she be a thousand years old and is pleased to call herself immortal.

Such an aggrieved, sour humor is apt to grow with much dandling and patting, and Simon was in a simmering bad temper with destiny and the sisters three when he reached the fringe of the glade and saw the youth and the maiden standing together. He paused, unseen, unheeded, on the farther side of darkness, rubbing his bristling chin. They looked to be of very good accord together, and his blood boiled at their amity. "It were a shame to spoil sport," he said to himself, apologetically, for what he was about to do, as he drew back a little deeper into the wood, still unseen and unheard. Then, "it were a shame to lose sport," he added, more truthfully to his itching curiosity, and dropping noiselessly on his hands and knees he proceeded to crawl very quietly towards a part of the wood nearer to the pair from which he might certainly oversee their deeds better, and also possibly overhear their words.

He moved quite stealthily and swiftly for his volume of body, for he had learned the primals of forest strategy when he served his apprenticeship to war under Philip the Fair, and his celerity of passage was accompanied by little rustling. At another time, though he did not know this, he could not have hoped to scramble so through the brushwood unperceived by the woodland sense of Argathona, but contact with a mortal sometimes dulls the immortal wit, and Argathona was absorbed by other than woodland thoughts. Indeed, if some faint sound of his patient progress had troubled the night, it would have fallen unheeded on the ears of those two who were wading straight from the shallows into the deeps of love.

At last Simon found his profitable lair and lay hunched up in the darkness with his chin propped on his fists, watching the boy and girl. He interpreted their gestures with a raging heart, hearing now and then something of the words they spoke, for the night was very still. His torpid sense of honor was untroubled by this playing of the spy, for he felt now a very personal sense of enmity to the stranger knight who, as he was inclined to phrase it, had taken his wood-girl away from him. It was Simon's simple creed that if he cast his eyes upon a girl in favor, that girl was his by right; wherefore he watched the mutual wooing with hot eyes of wrath, and there were wild moments when he longed to leap out upon the pair, slay the man, and seize the girl—and perhaps he would have done so had he not been mortally afraid of the maid. But when he saw the youth reclining upon the grass and Argathona bending so tenderly over him, pity began to pull at his heartstrings sorely against his will—pity for the maid, naturally, not pity for the man.

When the dryad, after breathing sleep on the face of her lover, disappeared into the forest Simon groped cautiously from his cover and moved stealthily over the moonlit space to the side of the sleeping man. He looked down upon the young, still face of Rainouart, rubbing his russet chin thoughtfully as he shrugged his shoulders in astonishment.

"What does she see," he asked himself, "in that smooth, unmeaning face that she prefers him to me—to me who know what love means, and war, and how to love women, and carry my liquor, and who never wasted time over a silly, painted book?"

That same painted book was still in the pouch of the young man's girdle, where he had thrust it when he had come from his reverie. There was a corner sticking out and it caught Simon's eye. He stooped and pulled the book from its concealment, a little square of vellum pages, scribed in a fine, clerkly hand, craftily enriched with pictures, and he balanced it curiously on his palm.

"What was there," he asked himself, "in such a lump of ink-stained, pigmented parchment to make a man forget that he was alive?"

Then, after a moment's hesitation, he slipped the volume into his own pouch as a lawful prize, resolving at some future time to see what he could make of its pages. The glimpse of the little, painted book fiercely rekindled his old resentment, which had withered a little at the sight of his enemy lying helpless on the grass. His fingers slipped to the horn handle of the knife that nestled in his girdle, and he moved it up and down from its sheath, enjoying grimly the slipperiness of the steel in the leather. Presently he plucked the blade bare and contemplated its brightness.

"It is but jamming this to the hilt," he thought, "in that quiet, white flesh, and the Duchy of Athens were sadly lacking an heir, and my white witch were sadly in want of a lover."

It was an alluring thought for a very unscrupulous fellow, but he pushed it aside at last, ramming the knife home with an oath, although he made a wry face at his abnegation. "The pretty witch would weep and her tears would grieve me," he thought; "and, besides, the fool is asleep and at my advantage, and belike he has not the blood left to fight with if I kicked him into waking and challenged him to fair battle."

As he thus reluctantly refused murder, he noticed that something glittered on the grass by the side of the sleeping man. Simon stooped and picked it up, and examined it carefully in the moonlight. It was a big, gold ring admirably wrought with the image of the Saviour of the world upon the tree, and set with little studs about the circle for the saying of the rosary.

"By the mass!" said Simon to the surrounding silence, "this is the ring he offered her." But even as he spoke thus, and as he weighed the ring in his palm, he was made aware that he might speak to silence no longer.

9

THE DUCHESS OF THEBES

Through the regal quiet of the night Simon could hear, no great way off, the muffled sound of the tramping of many feet. Turning his watchful face to the white roadway, after a little while he beheld a number of gleaming specks scarcely bigger than so many glow-worms. Then came what seemed like a dark, rolling cloud starred with points of fire, and this presently resolved itself into a mass of armed men, some of them on horseback, some of them bearing torches whose light flowed ruddy over shields and helms and spears. With the help of these earthly lights and of the light of the moon in heaven he saw that the torch-bearers and the armed men formed two bodies, one preceding and one following a number of litters of which the most sumptuous was drawn by four small black horses.

As this procession moved beneath his wondering gaze along the highway, those who led the van suddenly halted and seemed to look in Simon's direction and hold conference together. Instantly Simon remembered that he stood conspicuous enough against the moonlight in the open, and that his presence in that lonely place had naturally attracted the attention of the travellers. But he did not know the meaning of fear, and, though he was ever of a prudent disposition, he felt no need for flight, easy though flight would have been into the concealment of the wood. For he was conscious that he was doing no harm, and he entertained no expectation of harm from a company so numerous, so well armed, and travelling with so many lights by night in a time of peace. In no such fashion did marauders go abroad, so Simon resolved with little self-discussion to stand where he would and see out the adventure.

The new-comers were such a little way off, and so plainly to be observed in the quavering pool of torch-light spilled on the white path, that he could see how first the leaders of van and rear left their ranks and consulted together, and how next the curtains of the leading litter were plucked aside and a woman's head thrust forth, while a woman's imperious voice said something in question which he could not catch. Then the curtains of the other litters were pulled aside and other women thrust their heads into the night, squealing out many questions with sleepy voices. Then he heard the same imperious voice speak again, and the speaker railed at the others, rating them roundly for silly fools, and telling them to hold their peace, at which the pages about the litters tittered, and the women's heads were swiftly withdrawn and their voices silent. Then she who spoke so haughtily gave a command, and immediately the pages who led the four black horses turned them from the roadway and guided them carefully across the grass in his direction. A few of the escort remained on the highway with the other litters, but most of the knights a-horseback, and the men-at-arms and the torch-bearers, accompanied the litter and formed a great circle of steel and flame around Simon, where he stood placidly guarding the sleeping body of the young Lord of Athens, and gazing into the set faces of the strangers, and wondering what was going to happen next.

What did happen was that the four black horses halted a few yards from him, that the silken curtains of the litter were sharply pulled apart, and that a very beautiful face revealed itself to him in the mingled moonlight and torch-light. It was a splendid, sensual face, of the kind that appealed to Simon's directness, skin the color of fine ivory, hair the color of smooth ebony, eyes that seemed to change with every change of light, with every mood of mind, with every phase of desire, like a cat's, and a mouth as ripely red as the berries of the rowan-tree. Such a face might Semiramis have shown nightly to her nightly changing lovers ere they glided into Tigris; such a face might Clytemnestra have shown to her impatient paramour when she had newly butchered the king of men. Simon's simple, straightforward thought was that he wished the lady were for instant sale, and that he possessed the opulence which might purchase her. Simon's reflections in such matters were always direct.

The woman's eyes were fixed on Simon's stalwart body with a cold commendation of its proportions, but she spoke not to Simon but to a page in cloth of gold who stood obedient by her litter side.

"What is the matter, Bohemond?" she asked, in a voice that was wont to govern those who heard it with the sensuous charm of strange music chanted at sunset. Her eyes were still fixed on Simon, and Simon, nothing daunted, gave her back her gaze as boldly as if she had been a staring kitchen-wench, while the knights and men-at-arms stood about as fixed and rigid as armored effigies in audience halls.

"Grace," the golden page answered, "here lies a man dead or sleeping on the grass, and here stands a sturdy fellow with a club that keeps watch over him."

The lady whom the page hailed as "Grace" pushed aside the curtains of her litter impatiently and stepped into the moonlight. She was no more than common tall, but she carried her head high and commandingly, and Simon, still eying her steadfastly, thought that she walked like some old-time empress. Swiftly she stepped to where Rainouart lay, bent over him, and recognized him as the gallant youth whose face and form had stirred her facile pulses when he rode victorious down the lists in Paris, and who denied her as decidedly as he denied all the ladies at the court of Philip the Fair. She swung on Simon like a cat about to scratch.

"This is the young Lord Rainouart of Athens," she cried. "How comes he here and in this case? Have you injured him, villain?"

"I have neither hurt him nor helped him," Simon answered, composedly, "nor, for the matter of that, am I a villain, nor other than an honest soldier; but I can tell you all there is to tell when I know to whom I speak."

The little gilded page stepped a pace forward and addressed Simon sharply.

"It is the Duchess Esclaramonde of Thebes, fellow, who honors you with her speech."

Simon shrugged his shoulders; the woman was a fine piece of flesh were she duchess or no duchess, and his gaze was blatant admiration. The duchess, appraising his bulk, did not resent his possessive gaze.

"Who are you, sir?" she asked, in a voice more amiable, while she motioned to her attendant to rein his zeal.

Simon made her a leg.

"Lady, I am a soldier of fortune voyaging to Athens to seek for service under the bully duke, but your concern is not with me but with his countship yonder."

The Duchess of Thebes looked down again upon the fair sleeping body on the sward.

"How did Sir Rainouart come here?" she demanded, and Simon answered:

"Being foolish enough to overstay sunset near these woods in the reading of silly verses, he was set upon by footpads who thought to kill and strip him, but a girl who lives in these woods scared them away. The rascals took her for a witch, tumbling plump on them from the thicket, and gave leg-bail. It was the devil take the hindermost, I promise you; you would have laughed to see them scamper. The maid tended his wounds, that were little enough save for an ugly clip on the crown, and what should my young gentleman do but fall in love with his sweet nurse and she with him. I think they have plighted their troth, for he has proffered her a ring, and this daughter of the forest bids fair to end her days as Duchess of Athens."

The red blood raged in the woman's face, staining its ivory. "That she shall never be," she said in her heart. "I love this youth, and will not yield him." For, indeed, she had loved him with what Esclaramonde called love, in those painted days in Paris, before in despite she had taken Nemours for her husband, the old Duke of Thebes, who had lately left her an eager widow. What she spoke aloud was:

"A likely tale that Duke Baldwin's son should woo to mate a peasant."

"She is no peasant, I promise you," Simon answered, doggedly. He did not choose to tell what the girl had told him, for he was very far from sure that he believed it himself, and he was very sure, indeed, that no one else would believe it. "She is no peasant, whatever she be. These ears heard him ask her in marriage, and here lies the ring he proffered her."

Simon held out the rosary ring on his brown palm. The duchess's white hand dived at it as a peregrine dives on his prey, and caught it before he could guess or prevent her purpose. He had ever been used to dealing with damsels ready to snatch any trifles they might spy from their chance companions, and, being of a business-like humor in such matters, he made now as if to clutch the ring back again, just as if he were toying with a Corinthian doxy. But the duchess gave a sidelong glance at her escort, and in an instant a dozen swords were naked and aimed at Simon's breast, and Simon, being a sensible man, gave up the idea of further argument or expostulation. The duchess moved nearer to one of the torch-bearers, and in the orange light she looked at the ring covetously, much for its own rich beauty, for she loved all costly toys, and more because it seemed to mean a man's love for another woman, a man's love that should be, might be, hers. For the sanctity of the symbolism of the ring she had no thought at all.

"I will take better care of it," she said, with a strange smile, as she came near again to Simon and the youth at Simon's feet. Her evil wits, shuttles in the loom of deadly sins, were nimbly weaving a web of guile. Rainouart stirred uneasily as she came near, for the sleep that the woodland creatures can give may be molested by the coming of a hostile presence. The duchess looked down into his twitching face.

"See, he begins to wake," she said. "Give place all of you, and keep the tall soldier in ward."

At her command the duchess's people, knights and men-at-arms and torch-bearers, taking Simon, very reluctant, with them, drew away a little distance to the edge of the forest. He could see how, on the high-road eager heads peeped again from between the curtains of the litters of the duchess's women, and he grinned to think how little they could see of the business. But he was heartily wishing himself well out of the whole bother, and was casting about for a means of escape from it.

Meanwhile the Duchess Esclaramonde kneeled down on the grass beside Rainouart, watching him with malign eyes. The ring that she had taken from Simon she placed deliberately on her left hand. Then she drew from her right a ring set with a royal ruby, and, taking Rainouart's limp hand in hers, thrust it onto the finger where the red mark showed her that he had been wont to wear the ring she now wore. At her touch the youth turned his head once or twice like a man who dreams bad dreams, and then opened his eyes heavily. He groped with his arms as if seeking some dear presence.

"Where are you, love?" he asked, faintly.

Instantly Esclaramonde answered him.

"Here, my dear lord," she whispered, passionately, and she bowed her dark head tenderly over him.

Rainouart, his senses hurriedly returning, gazed with wonder into her fair, familiar face, and for an instant deemed himself in France, in Paris, at the court of King Philip. He lifted himself a little on one arm, for he was stronger now with the strength given by deep sleep, and realized that he was in the forest, but that Esclaramonde was bending over him.

"I crave your pardon, lady," he said. "When came you here? I seek another, she who was here but now."

The dark eyes of the duchess swam in the sad waters of anxiety, and well-feigned amazement was painted on her face.

"Of what other do you speak, dear lord?" she asked. "I have been here by your side ever since those villains fell upon you."

Rainouart looked dully at her and overmuttered her words, trying to interpret their meaning.

"You have been by my side?" he asked.

The duchess wound her arms tightly about him and kissed his forehead hotly, and the kiss troubled him, for the woman was very beautiful and his flesh was strange to kisses. Esclaramonde spoke in his ear low and quick.

"I was journeying to Athens, travelling by night for my whim and pleasure, and by happy chance passed by here at the time when you were bested. The coming of my people frightened the knaves from you, and they fled, with some of mine in pursuit. We were alone together"—she lowered her eyelids for a moment, craftily modest—"and I tended your wounds."

The prince made to free himself bodily from those embracing arms, mentally from the net-work of those bewildering words. It was easy to free himself from her clasp, though he did so with all courtesy and rather as one unwilling and unworthy to be so greatly honored, but it was harder to free his spirit from the meshes of her lying tale.

"You speak strangely," he said, vaguely, wondering if this were parcel of a dream. "Surely you did not tend me? Where is she?"

His haggard eyes wandered over the moonlit space towards the darkling wood and marvelled at the solemn presence of the men-at-arms. Again Esclaramonde wound her arms around him, reluctant, and there was an agony of solicitude in the duchess's voice, an ecstasy of tenderness in her eyes, as she cried to him, clasping him tighter to her warm body:

"My lord, my dear lord, what trouble has come to you? It was but a few poor moments ago that you told me how you loved me."

The prince looked despairingly into that beautiful, sensual face, and he remembered how it had shone in its splendor over the festivals at Paris. It was very lovely to behold, alluring, commanding, yielding, insisting, but it was not the loveliness his white spirit had longed for then or the worshipped loveliness his memory longed for now.

"I told you that I loved you?" The sound of his voice was full of doubt, and yet it went hard with his knightly heart to doubt the word of a woman.

Esclaramonde's pale cheeks filled with flame.

"With words too flattering sweet for me to echo," she whispered, and she stooped, and her eager face was close to his and her dark hair brushed his forehead, and she kissed him on the mouth at once sharply and suavely, and the fire from her lips ran through his veins.

"You gave me a ring which I shall wear forever." She withdrew one clinging arm from about his neck and held a smooth hand before him, and he saw on her finger the ring that had been his own for so long, the ring that had been his mother's, that she had made him promise when she gave it to him never to part with save to the loveliest and the worthiest. "You took a ring from me." She lifted his hand a little and he stared stupidly at the great ruby.

"Have you forgotten?" Esclaramonde cried. "Can men forget so soon?" Her eyes swam in obedient tears.

The maze of the man's mind showed tragically in his eyes, and then he spoke, but rather to himself than to the woman by his side.

"Which is the dream?" he asked. "I thought when I fell that a white girl came from the woods and succored me, a divine child, the loveliest—"

Esclaramonde shifted her body a little away from him, though still she clasped him fast and he could not in courtesy release her clinging fingers.

"Dear my lord," she protested, pathetically, "my overvaunted beauty may be of little account; still it is not many seconds since you chose to call me passing fair."

The prince, looking at Esclaramonde, knew that she was very fair indeed. There was for the merely desirous no more desirable woman of all the French dames dwelling in Greece.

"You are very fair," he said, truly, "but you are not she whom I saw." And once again his anxious eyes looked longingly over the silver grass towards the implacable silence of the wood.

"She was some dream," Esclaramonde answered him, earnestly, her warm lips close to his flushed cheek, her soft breath fanning his troubled face. "She was a vision born of the quick fever of your wounds. You swooned again after our change of vows and change of rings, and in this swoon you must have dreamed this dream of another who was not I. Indeed, you murmured snatches of strange speech in your sleep which astounded me, but such delirium is common with men in your case. Will you stain your knightly faith and deny your honor for the sake of a sick dream?"

Great waves of doubt flooded the prince's struggling consciousness, overwhelming it, drowning it. Was she, in very fact, no more than a vision, that white child of the woods with her yellow hair and her haunting eyes and her perfect body? Did the help he had dreamed of really come to him from this splendid, voluptuous creature who had striven to allure him in France? Was it those insistent hands that had brought healing to his hurt? Was it those passionate lips that had soothed him to sleep? Was it those enticing eyes that had summoned love to take possession of his stainless soul? His thoughts were all a tangle, his fever burned bright as his eyes travelled vaguely from the unfamiliar ring upon his finger to his mother's ring upon the finger of Esclaramonde. One thing alone seemed plain to him where all was imbroglio. If in whatever bewildering way he had pledged his word to this lady, his word must be kept.

"If I gave you my knightly faith, lady," he said, faintly, "I may not take it again."

The eyes of the duchess were triumphant torches, success was throned in her smiling face. But the pallor of Rainouart's face grew greater, for the spiritual strife within him had weakened him more than his loss of blood, and Esclaramonde, watching him, believed he was about to swoon again. She turned and made a sign in the direction where her following stood, huddled together, a group of lances and flaring torches on the lip of the wood. The golden page quitted the little throng and ran to his mistress.

"Bring me some wine, Bohemond," she ordered.

The page sped back to the litter and returned to his mistress with a golden flagon and a golden cup. Esclaramonde took the cup and held it while Bohemond poured out red wine that glowed like dragon's blood in the moonlight. Then a gesture dismissed the page to his companions, and the duchess set the golden cup upon the grass. She was still supporting Rainouart with one arm, his eyes were closed, and his lips had lost their color. From the jewelled pouch that hung at her girdle the duchess drew with her free hand a tiny phial, and, cuddling it in her palm, drew the stopper with her finger and thumb. She poured the contents into the cup and thrust the empty phial back into her pouch. Then she lifted the cup and pressed it to the young man's pale lips.

"Drink, my lord, drink," she entreated, and her voice could implore and command with the same breath and charm the listener away from reason. She was eager that he should drink, for she knew that what he drank would make him sleep sound, and that when he woke he must needs think as she would have him think, and so she said again:

"Drink, my lord, drink."

Rainouart opened his eyes wearily and looked up. He had hoped that he might sleep, and, waking, find the coming of the duchess a fever's fantasy. But she was still with him, his imperial deliverer, and the white child only the picture of a dream. Esclaramonde tilted the cup a little at his lips, and he drank at it eagerly, sucking in surcease of memory, sucking in unconquerable sleep. It was delicious, that draught of dark and deep oblivion; the tired senses relaxed.

"I thank you, lady," he sighed, in relief, and then all knowledge slipped from him and he lay his length unconscious. The duchess called to her page, and Bohemond raced across the grass to her side. Him the duchess commanded:

"Let two of my people carry this lord to my litter. We will make sure of his safe convoy to Athens. I will ride for the rest of the journey."

Her orders were swiftly and instantly obeyed. Three tall fellows of her men-at-arms, picked by the knight who led the van of her escort, came to where Rainouart lay and carried him as easily and as gently as if he had been a sleeping child to their lady's litter. A servitor moved from the rear of the little army leading a white riding palfrey, valiantly caparisoned. As she made to mount she paused, missing something, and her quick eyes sought for Simon.

"Where is the braggart we talked with but now?" she asked, sharply, and her question proved hard to answer. The men-at-arms into whose charge Simon had been put looked at one another with dismay, for truly Simon had disappeared. The disappearance, very surprising to the soldiery, was not very surprising in itself. The fact of the matter was that Simon had decided some time back that it would be excellent well for him to be quite clear of the complication that the coming of the duchess had created. It was plain to the adventurer that the duchess had taken a fancy for the heir of Athens. It was also patent to his understanding that he himself existed an undesirable witness of that earlier passage between Rainouart and the woman of the wood, the story of which the duchess had so vehemently resented. Simon, who had something of the art of reading women's natures in their faces, imagined, not unwisely, that the Duchess of Thebes was not a woman to stick at much if the removal of a disagreeable witness might be convenient to her. Once Simon had made up his mind that it were well for him to go, he lost no time in making the experiment.

It was no very difficult enterprise. The men in whose custody he stood, occupied to their greater interest in watching the duchess's attentions to the wounded knight, though they could see little and hear less, paid scant heed to Simon, who, on his side, had done nothing to provoke watchfulness by any resistance to their guardianship. So, finding them thus indifferent, little by little he edged him away from their neighborhood, moving very cautiously and gradually as one who scarcely seemed to move at all till he backed against a tree, against which he leaned lazily for some seconds. Once in front of a tree it was but simple strategy to slip to the other side of its trunk, and this feat Simon, choosing his time wisely, accomplished dexterously and un-noticed. Had he been by misluck interrupted in his progress, he relied upon his mighty strength to overthrow any six who sought to restrain him, and to make a bolt for it into the thickness of the wood where he believed he might effectually evade pursuit. But he wished, if it might be, to glide away in quiet, and fortune favored the adventurer. A floating fleece of cloud, stray fragment of the shattered dragon that seemed to obey Argathona's incanta-tion, had again muffled the moonlight. In the gloom Simon was on his hands and knees in the brushwood and threading his way on all-fours with amazing celerity among the trees into the deep of the forest. Thus it came to pass that when the duchess demanded Simon, Simon was not forthcoming.

"He was here a moment since," one man-at-arms asserted, lying hardily, as he stared into the vacant faces of his fellows.

"Belike he has slipped into the wood," another suggested, shading his eyes with his hands and peering into the impenetrable gloom behind him.

"Shall we search for him with torches?" Bohemond proposed, briskly, while the men-at-arms looked sheepish over their blunder and wished Simon at the devil. The duchess shook her head impatiently.

"No, it is no matter," she said.

She believed that she would recognize the man again if she saw him in Athens. She was confident, too, that the man could have little power, even if he had the inclination, to interfere with her plans. The immediate need was to carry Rainouart quickly to Athens and there to work her will upon his troubled wits. She mounted lightly into the saddle of her horse, her spirits were nimble, her heart gay, her brain elated. She had taken at last a prize that she had long desired, a prize that she would not lightly yield again. All was very well with her.

"Onward!" she commanded, "onward! Athens, ho!" So she and her com-pany resumed their measured journey to Athens, a line of torches on the white highway, while the prince slept a dreamless sleep on the litter still warm with the pressure of the limbs of Esclaramonde.

10

SIMON BLOWS OUT HIS LANTERN

When Simon had made some little way into the wood he quitted the animal all-fours, irksome to one already stiff and weary, for the natural carriage of man, and made to think things over and to look about him. The latter was difficult to do, at least to any great advantage. More frequent clouds now scumbled the sky and huddled in dull clumps between moon and earth, wherefore in the dense wood the darkness was so thick that Simon felt as if he could pluck pieces out of it as out of a palpable pall or curtain. But Simon was not discomfited, Simon was not at a loss. "Here," he murmured, sagaciously, "comes in the wisdom of your philosophic lantern." Squatting cautiously in the darkness, after assuring himself by preliminary pattings of the absence of any hostile snags, he fumbled in his pouch till he found flint, steel, and tinder-box. Then after the habitual preliminary pains and failures that darkened the lives of those that sought illumination, he succeeded in getting a light and applying it gingerly to the candle in its iron house. When the wick began to burn freely he hasped the door and felt less lonely and astray. Through the thin plates of horn a pale yellow light flowed dimly, showing like some civic lamp of fish-oil seen through a fog. But it was at least bright enough to enable Simon to distinguish where he was for a few paces in any direction, and to protect himself when he started walking again from crashing with unnecessary vehemence into unexpected tree-trunks. What was less to the purpose was that the flickering wick seemed to stir from slumber all manner of moths and midges, which hustled in their myriads about lantern and lantern-carrier with a wholly unnecessary activity. But if their attentions called for a brave display of philosophy, this was all in the part of one who carried the lantern of Diogenes.

Having looked about him, Simon now proceeded to think things over. All the events that had followed upon the unexpected arrival of the duchess had passed so swiftly that he knew they had taken little time in the happening. He had not the least idea where he was or what he should do next. He wanted, in the second place, the road to Athens, but he did not know where to find it; also he wanted in the first place to see the woodland maid again, but he did not know where to find her. He was still more than three-quarters inclined to think her mad. A lonely life in the forest had no doubt unhinged her pretty wits, and led her to credit all sorts of gossamer nonsense about immortality and forgotten gods. But were she the maddest witch that ever straddled a broomstick she was as fair as fair, and it occurred to the lantern-carrier hopefully that perhaps now that her prince was thus beraped from her she might be more willing to let Master Simon from Corinth play lieutenant.

After a while he decided that the best thing for him to do was to try to find his way back to the glade whence young Athens had been carried, for thither the wood-maid was sure to come with the healing herbs for her lover, and Simon's strongest purpose was the wish to see her again. He groped his way slowly through the trees, oathing free at sundry awkward bumps and stumbles, and endeavoring painfully to retrace his steps over a soil that gave no indication of his passage. But he moved with fair confidence served by occasional glimpses of the moon, and sure that by this time the duchess would have vanished from the goal at which he aimed. Fortune rewarded him. He had not travelled very far when he caught a glimpse of a clearing through the trees, and hastening his speed he soon broke from the wood and found that he had, indeed, returned to the scene of the night's adventure. Here was the glade newly trampled with the coming and going of many feet, here were the marks of horses' hoofs on the grass, here was the slight hollow in the turf where the youth's body had lain. The place seemed strangely deserted now which had so short a while before been populous. Surely the girl would come soon, Simon thought. He lowered his lantern to the ground and humped himself beside it, resolved on waiting, and wishing he had a store of food and drink with him to cheer the waiting-time. He had not long to wait. There came a gleam of whiteness through the trees, the gleam of a white body garmented in white stuff. Another moment and Argathona emerged from the forest and came running across the grass towards him. She was holding the skirts of her smock in both hands to form a kind of sack, and in this sack she carried herbs. As she came near to Simon she shook what she carried in a heap upon the sward and leaped forward to where her lover had lain. Then she gave a great cry as she saw that Simon sat there alone.

"Where is he?" she asked, an agony in her voice.

Simon was glad to see the girl again, but sorely against his will he found himself a sharer in her sorrow, and could almost have wished young Athens back again between them to conjure away the pathos of her look. He rose up to answer her, honestly sorry for her flagrant sorrow, painfully conscious that it was not for him to bring her consolation.

"Gone," he said, simply. It was all he could find to say on the instant; it really seemed all there was to say.

"Gone!" she echoed, and it seemed to Simon as if the woes of all unhappy lovers in the world seemed to flow mournful through her lips. He nodded his head and spoke soberly, gently, weighing his words:

"In your absence there came a great lady riding by, the duchess she of Thebes, no less, with a large escort. She saw your young gentleman sprawling on his back in the moonlight, and, seeing him, seemed to know him and to show a fancy for his fair face. So when she had tickled him out of his swoon she persuaded him, as I take it, for her voice carried far and I could catch snatches of her speech in the stillness, that you were no more than the doll of a dream and that it was she, the duchess, who had tended him in his time of peril, she who had changed troth with him, she who had taken his ring which indeed lay on the grass for any chance-by to handle, she who had given him a ring in exchange, for indeed she did thrust a ring on his finger while he slumbered. I suppose in the end he gobbled her story, which seemed, on the face of it, plain and specious. Anyway, she gave him wine to drink which sent him to sleep like a baby, and so without more ado she bundled him off to Athens."

Simon paused after this patter of narrative. To his surprise the girl had mastered her instant grief, and her countenance carried its former air of sweet serenity. The tears had dried from her eyes; the fear had faded from her cheeks; only she seemed to regard Simon now with cold, accusing mien.

"Did you do nothing to stay her?" she asked, and there was that stroke of reproach in her voice which made Simon feel, he knew not exactly why, as if he had betrayed a friend. But he answered bluffly enough, putting a bold face on his conduct, for, after all, maugre her strength, she was only a slip of a she-wizard and he a bearded man little accountable to such jills.

"I am a soldier of fortune," he blustered, "and it is not the way of my trade to take sides in a squabble unless I be paid for it. But if I had been fool enough to thrust my nose into another's quarrel, there was nothing of any purpose to do, for my high-mighty lady the duchess had fifty or so stout fellows with her, more than I could tackle. I was in a kind my lady's prisoner, and if I had not contrived to slip aside into the wood while she was plying him with the wine it is like she would have carried me, too, to Athens, and indeed it was not part of my plans to travel thither in such fashion."

Argathona seemed to be listening to Simon, but in truth she was paying little heed to his surly speech. She was looking steadfastly at the white ribbon of road which skirted the glade and ran, a highway, to Athens, and her face showed only the composure of a noble hope.

"He does not love her," she murmured to herself, and her words flowed with the motion of some proud and ancient song. "It is I whom he loves, I who love him."

Simon hoisted his shoulders to his ears. These amatory flights were not to his mind, for he took himself to be in a free field, and he was mulishly set to push his own case.

"He may live content enough with his bargain," he asserted. "Lady Esclaramonde of Thebes is a great lady and a wealthy and a fair, with broad lands for her dower—a better match, saving your presence, for young Athens than a wood-wench in a wood."

Argathona looked at him now with the same air of triumphant patience.

"You do not understand us," she said. "If it were for his welfare to leave me I would not hinder him. If it made for his happiness, now and hereafter, to dwell with this woman I would not hurt his life. But I have looked into his eyes and I know that he loves me as I love him."

Simon resented sharply this harping on a single string. The Athenian prince was not the only man in the world, nor the only man in Greece. There was a stout fellow at that moment, hailing lately from Corinth and earlier from Rouen, well worthy of any maid's eye.

"Be wise," he counselled, jovially, slapping his broad chest. "The boy has gone and there is an end of the adventure. Let by-gones be by-gones, and look more favorably upon one whom war and the world have mellowed to a ripe prime. A green goose makes a sour sweetheart. Here is a trained hawk to your hand. I will abide with you in the woodland cheerfully if you give me the wink of a lid."

Simon felt that he was acting most handsomely, and he beamed. But Argathona surveyed him with very much that show of scorn which an armed and haughty amazon might have vouchsafed to some woosome, presuming satyr who dared to waylay her on a hunting morning.

"I am glad the world you serve is not all made up of men like you," she said, quietly, and then she turned her calm eyes again upon the white highway.

Simon laughed dryly, but he felt that he grinned on the wrong side of his visage, for it vexed him sorely to find the maid so stubborn.

"Alack the day, no," he answered, gruffly. "Believe me, pretty mistress, I show better than the bulk. I am but quarter bad, like a clipped coin, and such as I am it is no offence for me to cherish you."

Argathona answered him more gently.

"You are well enough when you do not fret me with foolish words. But you do not speak of a cheerful world."

Simon was perplexed.

"What a saint's name does it matter to you how the world is compassed?"

Argathona understood the drift of his question.

"I am going into the world," she said, with decision.

Simon stared into her fine face. If one of the trees round about him had taken unto itself a vegetable voice, and told him as much of its intended travels in speech familiar to his French ears, he could scarcely have been more gravelled.

"You are going into the world," he growled, and the growl in his voice was meant to make it very plain to the girl that he thought she was talking nonsense.

But the girl answered his growling with the same unchangeable voice flowing from the same unchangeable countenance.

"I am going into the world to save my lover."

Simon was now one part diverted and three parts vexed at the girl's pertinacity. It was aggressively plain to him that she made far too much of one man at the expense of another, with nothing that he could see to warrant the partisanship.

"How will you find your way?" he questioned, drolly, mocking with eyes and tongue, and he thought he had posed her. But the girl's blithe face remained untroubled in its tranquillity of resolve.

"I shall find my way to my lover," she cried, and her voice rang in his hearing like the hunter's horn at the find of the deer. "My lover needs me; my lover is in danger; wherever he is my lover is alone without me as I am alone without him. I know that it were better for both of us not to be than to exist apart."

Simon laughed lustily, venting his spleen so, and the false thunder in his lungs shook his bulk as a sudden breeze shakes the flag-iris in the sedges. When he had done crowing and could speak like a Christian again:

"I have never known any lad to speak so for the loss of a lass," he assured her.

The dryad turned her unfathomable eyes on her jeering companion, and somehow, all of a sudden, his jesting seemed to lose its savor.

"There cannot be many men like my lover," she said, with clean assurance. "You have tramped so much through a muddy world and taken such stain in your travels that you have lost the thoughts of the solitudes and the sacred places. But here is the greenwood way of it. We have changed loves, he and I; we have changed hearts, he and I; where one is the other must be, though all the seas and all the mountains lie between us. If he be kept from me by guile I must win my way to him by craft, for that I know is what he would have me do."

Simon nursed his nose thoughtfully with his finger and thumb, eying the valiant lass and pondering as to whether she really meant what she said or whether all this ecstasy were only plain proof of the madness he shrewdly suspected.

"I wish you were a more reasonable rusticity," he grumbled. "The Duchess of Thebes is a very great, dangerous lady. I heard tell of her in Corinth that she dabbled in sorcery and was so skilled in the distillation of philtres that if ever a man drank a draught of her brewing he became her slave soul and body. What can your country-side courage do against her?"

Argathona's eyes radiated pity on his ignorance.

"I am of kin with the gods," she reminded him, austerely proud.

Simon twisted his features with a whimsical grimace that meant compassion for her madness and mirth at her earnestness.

"The gods will be of no use to you in the world beyond this wood. I do not know where they have gone, and in this regard you seem no morsel wiser than I, for all your phrases; but we seem to be both agreed in this, that they have gone, and in my world men raise shrines and altars to unite other powers."

"I think I shall still find love honored in the world," the dryad replied, confidently.

Simon whistled softly the fag end of a friendly drinking-song before he spoke. He was thinking grimly of what he and others like him honored as love in the world below the wood.

"I doubt if you would know the God of Love in some of his changes," he said at last. Then he went on, remembering and correcting: "Yet, as I am told, they hold pretty parliaments of love in Athens where jolly lords and dainty ladies wrangle to infinity over touches and phrases and prove very finical in discrimination."

Argathona was not disturbed by his doubts; she sang the same song of Olympian assurance to his unwilling ears.

"My lover bears my heart in his body and I bear his in mine. I will follow him to Athens; if needs must, I will follow him to the ends of the earth."

Simon tickled at his beard, looking at her with a dismal pity while he strove to light love's candles in the windows of his eyes and to speak to her wooingly, for he still cherished a desperate, dwindling hope for himself in the venture. So he again hazarded discouragement.

"You will spare yourself many pains and aches if you stay in the forest. Why can you not listen to me?" Even as he entreated he read in her face that his wooing was vanity, and he ended angrily in a challenge.

"I believe you would listen to me if I wore a silk coat and carried a smooth face."

The dryad smiled, divinely patient of his peevish speech.

"I would not listen to you," she said, "if you wore the robe of Zeus or showed like Apollo."

She turned away from him and stretched out her white arms towards the dark wood.

"Dear forest, where I have lived so long, the time has come when we must part. Dear birds and beasts, I must say you farewell. For I follow the forest law and I go to seek my mate."

Simon looked at her with a new wonder and a new approbation in his eyes.

"You are resolved?" he asked, and the girl answered him irrevocably:

"I am resolved."

"Then," said Simon, "I think I may blow out my lantern," and on the word he swung his lantern to the height of his face and drew back its door. Pursing his lips he whistled a curfew call, and his breath puffed out the feeble light of the candle.

"Why do you do that?" Argathona asked, with the naïve curiosity of a child.

Simon turned his head to Argathona, and the look on his face was at once roguish and reverential.

"I carry this lantern," he said, "daytime and nighttime, like my old-time pattern, looking for an honest fellow-being, a thing I could not find in Corinth and doubted to find in Athens. But now I believe I have found a true woman, for I call you a woman, by your leave, though you choose to call yourself immortal. Wherefore, out goes my sceptical glimmer, and if you are willing I will go with you to Athens as your honest friend and true servant; and, indeed, I think I may prove of service, for I know something of the rough edge of the world."

"You may come if you choose," Argathona answered, "and you shall give me advice, for I am strange to men and cities."

"Faith," said Simon, bluntly, "to begin with, you cannot go as you now are. Women wear other gear in these years of grace. I cannot say that they look better than you do, but truly they look very different."

"I shall not go as a woman," Argathona answered. "I shall go as a man."

Then, seeing that Simon stared at her with the greatest amazement his face had yet worn, she went on:

"Is not a man's life a good life still to live in Greece, as it was in the ancient days?"

Had Simon been blessed with a graver temper he could not choose but laugh.

"By the rood," he swore, "a man's life is as round a dish and as full of meat as ever, but 'tis never a dish for a maid to nibble at. Why, a man's life is a bustling, brawling business, noisy and jocund. Your true man is ever eating, drinking, loving, fighting. When there be no real wars for him to break heads in, he betters the heavy peace with a tournament."

The dryad's eyes looked inquiry, and Simon, guessing what she would know, expanded his matter.

"Your tournament," he explained, "is a brave game by which knights who are weary of idleness and quiet times put on their armor and take up their arms, and bang each other lustily in an appointed place just as if they were enemies, though for the most part they are honest friends and bear no malice for thrustings and thwackings."

Argathona's eyes widened and brightened as if she desired to win a prize in such kind of diversion, and her words showed her thoughts.

"If there be such jolly sports to share yonder," she cried, "then I must play my part in them."

Simon really hardly knew whether he ought to laugh or to cry at the simplicity of the witch.

"What a devil should a slim maid, be she woman or warlock, do at a tourney?" he gaped.

Argathona laughed a little at his bewilderment, and her laughter was pleasant as the piping of summer wind among summer thickets.

"Friend," she said, "you have seen that I am no weakling. Truly I have the strength of the strongest amazon that ever drew bow, and the amazons were as strong as the companions of Theseus. And I doubt if the men of today have the strength of the fellowship of Theseus."

Simon was inclined to resent the imputation cast upon an age that he adorned, but, remembering betimes that the girl who faced him had made so little ado with his strength, he grinned weakly and held his peace on that matter. Argathona continued:

"While I play a man's part in Athens I will find a way to save my lover, if he be ensnared as you say. For if I go as a man this woman of Thebes will welcome me as a friend."

Simon wagged his red head approvingly.

"By my faith," he said, "you seem strong enough and wise enough to wander the world alone; but I will go with you and serve you, because I love you, and I can teach you something of the world's ways that may help you, a stranger. But you are wise to go as a man if you think you will look like one."

"Friend," replied Argathona, "we of the woodland can use the woodland glamour, and what we strongly wish men to see us and think us I believe you will find that they so see and think. Tonight we will rest in the forest; tomorrow we will make for Athens."

"Where is your male attire?" Simon questioned, dubiously. "For my part I have nothing but the rags I stand in."

Argathona laughed blithely.

"Let not that vex you. There are shepherds in the valley, and you shall go to these shepherds and buy for me a sheepskin suit and a shepherd's pipe and crook." Seeing a frown on Simon's face, she went on: "It may be that you have no coin in your scrip." Simon nodded bashfully. "That need not trouble you neither, for this wood holds many hidden treasures whose lurking-places are known to me, so I will find you a piece of gold for the shepherds. Then as a shepherd I will pass to Athens."

"Nay," Simon commented, gravely, "it will never do for you and me to trip into Athens at all adventure, stout man and slim maid, with no tellable tale to back them. Here is my rede, that we rest a full day in the forest while I tell you so much of the ways of us who live at the end of time as will serve you to play your part with persuasion."

Argathona nodded, wise enough to read the wisdom in his words.

"It shall be as you say," she agreed. "We will abide a day in the woodland and you shall lesson me in the ways of men of the Iron Age."

So said, so done. From the dawn of the next day to the same day's dusk Argathona sat at the feet of the soldier of fortune and listened while he spoke. He told her of the world as he knew it, a fair world made for Frenchmen to rule. He told her of its kings and its captains, and of the names and lineages and lives of those who now lorded it in Greece. Because he had a shrewd wit, with caustic words to lackey it, he made his tongue's puppets live more human than they always showed in knightly histories and monkish scripts. He painted frank pictures of great ladies, too; told truths of the customs of men with women and of women with men, and little doubting that he was doing aught to distinguish with praise, proved himself an excellent chronicler. But of the great faith of the world he spoke scantly and dully, caring for it little, understanding it less, and taking it for granted tranquilly as him seemed a soldier should. On her side, Argathona, keen to learn much about the living things she had to play with and strive against, eager to teach her age-long ignorance the game of the gray world, she had very little curiosity about the faith that had banished the gods of her infancy. And so she listened and learned much and learned little, and one more Attic day of all her wealth of days waxed and waned and left her as it found her, divinely young.

11

THE CATALAN GRAND COMPANY

From the days when the Christian faith was born in Galilee of Judea, from the days when Hellas became portion and parcel of the Roman empire, the glory of Athens dwindled and withered through the centuries for more than a thousand years. Paul preached. Nero plundered. Philopappus patronized. Hadrian adorned. Herodes commemorated the loved and lost Regilla. Neo-Platonism persuaded its followers that the lamp of the Academy was still alight. The terror of the north swept upon the city as Spartan and Persian had swept upon her, only more bloody and more merciless than both, to be beaten back for a season by the waning strength of the Roman arms. The gleaming image of Athena stayed the rage of the triumphant Alaric, but could not stay the envy of Constantinople. Byzantium stripped Athens of her riches; Byzantium silenced the voices of her philosophers. Gloom of night settled upon the sacred place for generations till, after the fourth crusade and the fall of Constantinople, Boniface of Montserrat came to turn the Parthenon from a Greek church to a Roman Catholic cathedral, and the city of Theseus into a Frankish duchy. In the dawn of the thirteenth century Otho of the Rock became grand sire of Athens, and he and the descendants of his house ruled for a century, till the time came for Baldwin to take the throne.

The French nobles who throned in Hellas in the thirteenth and fourteenth centuries of Christendom knew nothing, or next to nothing, of the old-time glories of their home. The lions of Mycenæ told the occupants of Peloponnesus nothing of the king of men and his murderous queen, and the vengeance of Orestes leaping like a bright star to his aim. The chiefs in Attica viewed with indifferent eyes the masterpieces of antiquity still standing intact or almost blank of ravage upon the Attic plain and on the Attic hill. But the French lords of Peloponnesus and the French lords of Athens had a very liberal and deep affection for the civilization which they carried with them from their sweet land of France, and for those chivalrous institutions which made life one high delight to them. The best dream of the French gentlemen was to make the land of Greece as like the land of France as might be in all the grace and all the gayeties of life. To this end they lived in Attica as they lived in Languedoc, in Lacedæmon as in Limousin, and their greatest pleasure in their Hellenic empery was to make believe that they were in Paris or Provence. In the land where the Grecian gods had been hymned by Pindar, moulded by Phidias, painted by Apelles, and caricatured by Aristophanes, the adventurous French knights, who tricked themselves out with the titles of cities of Sparta and cities of Attica, bore to the golden land they governed all the pride and pomp and color that made their France so lovely in their eyes. They strove to make their lives as luxurious and as sumptuous as if they were kings of France and not lords of Grecian duchies, and they succeeded greatly in their purpose. French of Paris, French of Provence, French of Picardy, sang of love or commanded for battle in places where Socrates had died yesterday and Atreus the day before yesterday. All the parament of chivalry paraded, a riot of color and luxury, where Lycurgus had fed a strenuous people on bitter bread and brackish water, or played its games of mimic war and held its tribunals of fantastic love in the pale presence of the theatre of Dionysos.

The narrowness of the environment made these efforts after magnificence more conspicuous than they would have been in the country they had quitted. Gorgeous garments and splendid armor adorned and defended bodies cherished with pompous banquets and royal wines. But the ease of their condition did not weaken the limbs or the spirit of the French lords. Their passion for the tournament kept them hardy for their wars with each other, stiffening their voluptuousness with that desire to shine in strife which forbade pleasure to degenerate into effeminacy. Their passion for ballads and the ballad-maker's arts refined their wild, bright life with tales of ancient days and heroic ideals. Their passion for women, growing apace in the magical atmosphere of that enchanted land where the winds seemed to whisper the songs and lisp the names of old-time lovers, was saved by their persistent chivalry, artificial perhaps in form, but with a heart behind its artificiality, from lowering into the Oriental grossness that was the weakness of Byzantium. The history of the ages has no stranger as it has no more bravely painted page than that which records the rule of the French dukes in Athens and Peloponnesus.

If Athens in the dawn of the fourteenth century was strangely unlike the Athens of the Periclean age, the contrast was rather of one kind of splendor against another than of a present squalor with a splendid past. The capital of the French dukes of Athens surpassed in luxury and comfort any European capital of the time. Their commerce flourished, their port was populous with ships, their influence was felt, and their strength unquestioned all along the Greek littoral. Many of the other French princes in Greece had pomp and power, but Baldwin, Duke of Athens, overcrowned them all for wealth and power and magnificence. He delighted to beautify after the fashion of his time the spot that once had been the loveliest in the world, and if the shade of some great Athenian could have returned for an hour to the city of Cecrops, he must have regretted, indeed, the glories of the past; but, at the same time, he must have recognized that the barbarian who held by a strong hand the land of Deucalion was not denied some measure of the intelligence that goes to the making of a fair town and a great state. Duke Baldwin was always hospitable to strangers visiting Athens, and delighted to send them away brimmed with admiration of the civilization of Athens and the generosity of Athens's duke. If he did not set a kingly crown upon his helmet, he lived like a king, and could have entertained the monarch of France or the sovereign of England with an opulence not to be outdone in Paris or in London.

There was a policy in all this opulence and hospitality to strangers. Duke Baldwin owed much of his first supremacy in Athens to the presence in Thessaly of a band of free lances. When he arrived, hissing hot with haste, in his new duchy he found that his hold over his dominion was not to be unthreatened nor his rule untroubled. A prince of Epirus here, a prince of Vlachia there, menaced his unsteady empire. Even Duke Baldwin's bull-dog courage recognized that he was not strong enough to compete with his enemies single-handed. But Duke Baldwin was a man of resource, and he saw that there was a valuable alliance at hand. The Catalan Grand Company, having fought its fierce way through Macedonia, had planted itself upon the soil of Thessaly eager for more conquests. The Catalan Grand Company was a remarkable association of rascals, assassins, ragamuffins, blackguards, and admirable captains. It was originally formed in Spain with the avowed purpose of selling the arms and the bodies of the brotherhood to anyone needing them and willing to pay the price. The Catalans had gone hither and thither serving this master and that, till at last their baleful star had led them, maugre the teeth of the Byzantine tyrant, to the land of Greece.

A new-comer to a throne who is not in the direct line and is not upon the spot when the succession falls due is never too sure of his seat, even if his authority be unchallenged, and Duke Baldwin, with enemies ready to take the field against him, deemed it prudent to enter into negotiations for the services of the Catalan Grand Company. The Catalans, already weary of acting for their own hand, were very ready to take Duke Baldwin's pay and to play Duke Baldwin's game. Their terms were large, but Duke Baldwin's need was keen and Duke Baldwin's tongue was glib. He promised them what they asked with a cheerful spirit, albeit the company asked a good deal. Baldwin agreed to pay each full-armored horseman four gold ounces a month, each light-armed horseman two gold ounces a month, and each foot-soldier one gold ounce a month. When Duke Baldwin made, or rather accepted, these terms, the strength of the Catalan Grand Company totalled three thousand five hundred horsemen and three thousand men on foot, so that Duke Baldwin found himself pledged to a pretty penny. But with Duke Baldwin the present was very emphatically the present. The immediate important thing was to tighten his grip on the pleasant Duchy of Athens, to tweak the noses of Epirus here and Vlachia there, and he genially agreed to the terms of the Catalans, prepared no less genially hereafter to bamboozle them, but in the mean time making what might have been a dubious dominion indubitable with the strength of their support.

Yet Baldwin knew too much of the world of fighting-men to think that throne stable which was mainly defended by an army of mercenaries. So he made it his business to woo and welcome to his court all gentlemen-adventurers from France, and from the neighboring little principalities of Greece, who were willing to take chivalrous service under his standard. His fame as a warrior, his open-handed generosity where open-handed generosity was expedient, and especially the beauty of the open-hearted women with whom he took care that his court was always a-quiver, attracted to Athens a great number of knights and gentlemen-at-arms, who swelled his immediate following very rapidly. He further strengthened his hand by enrolling and equipping so many soldiers that in a short while he had more than doubled the strength of his solid little standing army. He had not been many months upon his throne before he had made his duchy the most formidable state in Greece and his duchy and himself very patently independent of the Catalan Grand Company. Feeling little need for the further services of the Catalan Grand Company, he felt little gratitude for their services in the past. Duke Baldwin was not a man burdened with a too lively sense of duty to others, and though in the early days of his dukedom he had paid the Grand Company month by month their promised wage, that payment had now been suffered to fall into arrears for a very considerable period.

For the time being this mattered very little to the Catalan Grand Company. Its members were quartered comfortably enough in the pleasant plain of Attica; they amused themselves from time to time with little marauding expeditions to the north, and they had, or affected to have, every confidence that sooner or later Duke Baldwin would pay up all the moneys that were due to them. The principal leaders of this company dwelt in Athens, and mingled on equal terms with the chivalry of Duke Baldwin's court. It could not truly be said that there was much love lost between the Spanish mercenaries and the French knights, for the latter looked down upon the Catalan companions as unchivalrous freebooters, and the Spaniards knew of this feeling, and it rankled in their hearts though they betrayed no trace of resentment in their faces. But between the two parties there was all outward show of amity, all outward interchange of knightly courtesies, and the Spanish leaders shared in all the festivals, drank at all the banquets, and jousted in all the tourneys of Duke Baldwin's court. If the Spaniards themselves were to be believed, they found no such hostility nestling in the white breasts of the fair French ladies of Athens as they were conscious that the mailed bosoms of the French gentlemen sheltered. But if the policy of the duke was regarded by the Catalan Grand Company for the most part with indifferent eyes, it was not so regarded by one of their number.

Fernand Ximenes was captain of the Catalan Grand Company, so far as the Catalan Grand Company could be said to have any single captain. That turbulent, mercenary army, though strongly bound together by common love of gold, common instinct for plunder, common lust for the gratification of all greeds, and common readiness for warfare under the service of any prince who chose to pay them, was not a community over which it was easy for any single man to extend an uncontested sovereignty. Since the Grand Company marched out on its career of rapine from Spain, leader after leader had fallen victim to the heady quarrels and bloody passions of his subordinates. Chieftains old in battle, and young chieftains eager to prove themselves peers of their predecessors, had in turn swayed for their moon the angry tides of the company, and in their turn had fallen victims to the weapons of those they were supposed to head.

For a time it seemed as if to accept any leadership over the Catalan Grand Company was not merely to court but to assure a violent death. Strong as were the links of common interest which bound the savage Spaniards into a depredatory army, it looked at one hour of their wild fortunes as if their forces must needs dissolve into anarchy from the reluctance of superior spirits to entertain or from the incapacity of inferior spirits to maintain control over the body. At length it became plain, even to the most ungovernable ruffian of that lawless brotherhood, that the promiscuous slaughter of superiors, however diverting in itself, was not the surest means of attaining the ends for which the free companions had been called together. A kind of compromise was arrived at: a form of parliamentary discussion instituted resulting in the evolution of a little cluster of captains, nominally each of equal authority, and only directing the action of the company when they spoke with a common voice and struck the drum-head of council with a common hand.

Of this little body of captains Fernand Ximenes owned indubitably the ablest mind, as he owned no less indubitably the strongest body. Of a smooth and grave exterior, with something of an ecclesiastic suavity blended with the urbanity of a scholar, this outward serenity masked a spirit as ingenious in forming schemes for self-aggrandizement as relentless in their execution. Greatly gifted as a practical soldier, greatly gifted as a possible statesman, Ximenes was most graced of all in this, that he knew how to wait. He was never in a hurry; he had never been known in a life that had now well come to middle age to speak a word there was no need to speak or strike a stroke there was no need to strike. His ambition was unlimited, but he never allowed it to lead him farther than he could safely see his clear way, and he had often let some apparently bright occasion go by when to his shrewd eyes the brightness seemed fallacious. He loved all desirable things—women, kingdoms, gold, images, pictures, jewels, costly habits, costly fare. He even—and this seemed a strange thing in a leader of the Catalan Grand Company—was not indifferent to books. But he could deny himself as vigorously as the most rigid ascetic to any of these fleshly temptations if his crafty mind were convinced that the denial of a moment meant a fuller gratification later, and he had never yet found that such wise denial had gone unrewarded.

It was through the influence and advice of Ximenes—so subtly exercised and so subtly offered that it seemed to each of his colleagues as if the course of action resolved upon had been decided as a result of his individual will—that the Catalan Grand Company entered into the service of Duke Baldwin of Athens. There were some, indeed, in the little cluster of captains who had talked none too vaguely of the possibility of the Grand Company making itself the master rather than the servant of the Duke of Athens. But with infinite patience and with infinite pains Fernand Ximenes made it plain to his co-captains that they had not at their command anything approaching to the necessary strength that would entitle them to enter upon a struggle with a fairly powerful prince of Greece, who had at his command a following little inferior to their own. "So long as we are well paid," he pleaded, "we shall do very well in Attica. The duke is generous; the duke is a free liver. He will be courteous to us captains, and our comrades will grow fat. The women of Greece are fair, if less radiant than the women of Spain, and the wines of Greece are very cheerful drinking." With these and other arguments he succeeded in carrying his point, and the forces of the Catalan Grand Company pledged their allegiance to Duke Baldwin in return for the stipulated sum.

From the moment that Ximenes had entered Greece with the company his mind had been filled with the desire—and with him to desire was almost invariably to attain—to become himself a prince in Greece. The most obvious way, and also the most difficult, was to seize some principality by the sword. An easier method suggested itself to him when the old Duke of Thebes died and left his duchy in charge of his young wife. Ximenes seemed here to perceive a chance of aggrandizement. He knew that the duchess was fair; he knew very well that the duchess was faithless, for he had visited Thebes ere he entered Baldwin's service and had found favor in the eyes of Esclaramonde. Indeed, so greatly did the handsome Spaniard gain the graces of the lady that when Ximenes heard of the death of the old dotard duke he was confident that the duchess would be likely soon to wed, and he was very ready to entertain the hope that the Duchess of Thebes would be willing to take for consort a certain valiant captain of the Catalan Grand Company. He began at once to work with his usual patience towards his goal. It was the result of his suggestions that Duke Baldwin welcomed the idea of holding a tournament, to which tournament the principal potentates in Greece should be bidden. Ximenes counted on his skill at arms to distinguish himself in the tourney; he counted on his way with women to ingratiate himself anew with the supple duchess—all seemed pleasantly and feasibly mapped out, and he thought of the project as much as he allowed himself to think of anything that lay ahead closed in the folded fingers of fate. And then, lo and behold! one moony May evening the Duchess of Thebes comes riding into Athens with Duke Baldwin's son and heir dozing on a litter, and in less than no time it is buzzed abroad through all the babblesome city that Rainouart, heir of Athens, is infatuated with the lovely Duchess of Thebes, that she is nothing unwilling to unwidow herself for his sake, that Duke Baldwin is hugely delighted at this union of Athens and Thebes, and that the marriage is decided and to take place with a celerity only excusable through the ungovernable passion of the prince. All of which is galling to an ambitious captain of Catalans, who shows, however, no sign of anger, but imperturbably waits on events.

12

THE WINDING OF THE HORN

The palace of Duke Baldwin on the Acropolis was the stateliest of the many stately buildings which the French lords had made for their pleasure in Athens. All that the lessons of Western civilization could teach, all that the experience of Eastern luxury could suggest, to embellish the ducal dwelling had been accepted, and the daily state of Baldwin's existence was little, if at all, less regal than that of the monarch of France. The living-rooms were richly furnished and hung with costly tapestries. The walls of the great banqueting-hall were painted with vivid representations of the deeds of the Crusaders in the Holy Land. Vessels of gold and vessels of silver were in common use, and the jewelled pride of Byzantine mosaic filled every corridor with coloring as lustrous as the dawn and as glowing as the sunset. Whatever the arts could do to enrich and to adorn had been generously welcomed, and the people of Duke Baldwin's household moved familiarly, while the guests of Duke Baldwin's hospitality walked in wonder, amid surroundings as lovely as the liberal creation of a dream. Never had an abode been known more worthy of the presence of beautiful women, and the fair faces and shapely forms that made the home of Baldwin a wanton paradise in the minds of his knights found in every part of the great mansion a background worthy of their favor and their grace.

Duke Baldwin's palace, look at it one way, hummed like a human hive. It was full of sounds from dawn till night—servants going and coming, minstrels bowing and thrumming, the rustle of women's dresses, the flutter of women's fans, the patter of pages' footsteps running on delectable errands, merry messengers of love, the ring of noble voices, the clink of noble swords. Here, there, and everywhere Duke Baldwin's presence loomed, jovial, ferocious, vehemently alive and blithe, making love to a dozen ladies with a whole heart, drinking a dozen wines with a clear head, voluble, jocular, a brawny image of the lusts of the flesh. He was very well content with the world, and would not have it other than it was. To indulge all appetites furiously without hurt or satiety, to play the prodigal host and to read the reward of his opulence in the admiring eyes of easy women, this was Duke Baldwin's simple ideal of existence. It was the ideal of many others, but few attained it as completely as the genial, truculent duke, for few had his length of purse and fewer his strength of body.

But just now Duke Baldwin had other causes for complacency and content than gluttonizing in all the passions. The presence of the Duchess of Thebes in his palace he had at first looked forward to as an experiment in the affections, and it had never occurred to him that he might have his own son as a rival. But now this was so, as it seemed, and yet Duke Baldwin was plainly satisfied and limber of spirit over the business. For when the Duchess Esclaramonde came riding up to his gates on that memorable evening and told him her strange tale, Baldwin was well content with the way of affairs. Here was his son's life saved by this great lady and neighbor, and here was his son's heart given to, and taken by, this same great lady, which meant the welding of Thebes and Athens in a common strength and a common splendor. Baldwin thought better of his son for a sensible choice, and was quite willing to forego dalliance with the duchess in consequence, the more readily, indeed, that a number of lovely, affable ladies had newly landed from Byzantium.

The duchess was all for a speedy wedding. Her brief term of widowhood was expired; she needed, she said, the prop of a man's arm, and the duke, grinning in his sleeve, was delighted to meet her wishes. As for Rainouart, he took his good-fortune with a curious apathy, which might have puzzled his parent if that parent ever troubled his mind about people's motives so long as their actions conformed to his idea of the precisely right. Whatever the duchess said Rainouart echoed. Recovered from his hurt, thanks to the deep sleep and easeful rest on the duchess's litter, he squired her pertinaciously, patently in love to all beholders, patently under the spell of her beauty: under the spell also of her ministrations, for she must needs continue to be his leech who had begun by being his rescuer, and she slyly plied him with philtres in his drink. So it was settled out of hand that the heir to the Duchy of Athens and the dame of the Duchy of Thebes should be married on the second day following the evening of their arrival in the city, and that all the pomp and ceremony of the joustings should be regarded as incidental and obsequious to the hurried nuptials.

Fernand Ximenes was sorely displeased at the news, but he protested pleasure with the best, persistently patient. Everybody else was hugely delighted, for this sudden marriage put the perfect top to all the jollity—it was the cream on the milk of mirth, the finest feather in the cap of happiness. Of course the opinions of the gentlefolk were the only opinions that counted, but in their obscurity the citizens of Athens made merry with the rest, for the waves of great folk's pleasure always carried some flotsam and jetsam to their humble thresholds. As for those dark subalterns of St. Nicholas, Captain Fox and Captain Gander, Captain Bat and Captain Chanticleer, Captain Rat and Captain Badger, they were neck-high in delights, and drank of the best daily and nightly in popular taverns, toasting bride and groom mellifluously, and thanking their saint and their stars that they by a storm and a strange voice were stayed from slitting the weasand of the son of Duke Baldwin the Beneficent.

On the morning of the marriage-day the great court-yard of Duke Baldwin's palace was a little world of many types and many nationalities. From the gallery of the palace the loveliest ladies of the court looked down upon the flower of the French chivalry below and named their names to new-arrived beauties, and told tales of them, not always without malice. The slender fellow with the yellow hair was Sir Guy de Hainault. The gallant with the brown curls who sat apart and nursed a lute upon his knee was Sir Jaufre de Brabant. That lean, dark, strenuous figure, his visage bronzed by Spanish suns, the man with something Moorish in his garb and accoutrements, was Fernand Ximenes, chief among the leaders of the Catalan Grand Company. The portly, florid man, no longer young but comely in his prime, who carried a white staff in his hand and moved hither and thither among the knights with cheerful greeting for each, was Count Ernault of Toulouse, Duke Baldwin's right-hand man and lord-marshal of the lists. The two who walked and talked together in the shade, talking very surely of women and deeds of war, were Sir Ambrose of Blois and Sir Raymond of Provence. The two who sat and diced upon a drum-head, with faces as grave as if every cast gave or took great slices of empire, were Demetrius, the vassal prince of Epirus, and Andronicus Palæologus, the great noble from Constantinople.

So the fair told their tale to the fair, and pointed out for admiration of the strangers the two huge soldiers who stood at guard inside the great gates of the court-yard. They were veritable giants, chosen by Baldwin—feeding his greed for the monstrous and excessive in all—for their extraordinary size and strength. They leaned upon such mighty battle-axes as were the familiar weapons of the Varangian Guard at Constantinople, and their duties were to open the great gates to every summons. Outside the gate a huge horn hung for any comer to wind who desired admittance. An ordinary knight was to sound the horn once; a baron was to wind it twice; a triple summons was the privilege of princes. Such was Duke Baldwin's etiquette, familiar to all his world. So the ladies laughed and chattered, eying the bright throng through which every now and then little shimmering pages or servants in heraldic colors picked their way, carrying hawks on wrist or hounds in leash, or bearing some message from lady to lord or from lord to lady. It was all as pleasant to witness as a pageant or a play in the bright, idle morning, and the babble of women's voices floated through the pellucid air like the chatter of starlings.

In the quietest corner of the court-yard, and in that court-yard quiet was indeed only a relative term, Sir Jaufre de Brabant, whose brown curls the ladies had praised, sat apart picking at the strings of a lute and humming to himself. Sir Jaufre considered himself, and was considered by many, to be the handsomest man in the service of Duke Baldwin. It was his wish, further, to be considered the gallantest, a wish fulfilled in the consideration and complaisance of many, and one of the jewels of his gallantry was his gift of song. He had been turning words this way and that way in his brain for some time on that spring morning, and at last it seemed from the smile on his face that he had turned them to some purpose that pleased him. Now he began to sing softly to himself, accompanying his song with little gentle touches on the lutestrings that wakened a plaintive melody. As he sang Sir Ambrose of Blois and Sir Raymond of Provence first paused in their walk and talk, then came near and listened, and in a little while Sir Guy de Hainault left his place and joined them. And this is what Sir Jaufre sang:

> *"He is the wisest in the world*
> *Who rides his road with flag unfurled,*
> *With heart unfetter'd from the care*
> *That love of ladies places there;*
> *With sword that knows no master's laws,*
> *But shines and strikes for any cause,*
> *To highest bidder blithely sold;*
> *Glory is good, but better gold,*
> *And as for ladies, fair or brown*
> *He finds who sacks a captured town."*

As Sir Jaufre finished, Ambrose and Raymond beamed approval, but Guy of Hainault, the young, fair-haired knight with a face that was partly girlish and partly angelic, pierced the approbation with a sneer.

"I do not like your song, Jaufre," he said, and said it with as much sweetness as if he had been crowning Sir Jaufre with a wreath of golden laurel in the heart of hot Provence.

Sir Jaufre flushed and looked up angrily.

"That makes me no bad minstrel," he retorted, "but it argues you a fool."

Sir Guy de Hainault's face was imperturbable, his voice was placid as he answered, smoothly:

"Your music and your manners would mend with your health if I let you some fretful blood."

Sir Jaufre shrugged his shoulders.

"You talk like a barber," he said—"white and red nonsense."

Guy smiled on a gradually increasing audience, for Demetrius of Epirus and Andronicus Palæologus had quitted their dice to hear the argument.

"You sing like a screech-owl," commented Sir Guy. Stooping swiftly, he caught the lute from Sir Jaufre's hands, ran his fingers skilfully over the strings, and awakened a tender tune. Fernand Ximenes, stately as a cat in his Spanish gravity, leisurely added himself to the circle, watching the rivals sardonically. His coming seemed to stimulate Sir Guy's ambition to sing.

"Listen to me, friends," he challenged, and began:

> *"All lovely ladies everywhere,*
> > *Whose eyes are blue or brown or gray,*
> *Whose manes of black or yellow hair*
> > *Lead your poor lovers' hearts astray,*
> *Here on this mirthful morn of May,*
> > *I turn to ye and make salute;*
> *And I would kiss you all today,*
> > *Were all your lips one crimson fruit."*

Every man of the little group applauded except Sir Jaufre, who yawned affectedly behind a languidly lifted hand.

"You mew too lewdly to be true," he asserted, contemptuously. "Your sincere kiss-winner has no leisure to sing of it."

Sir Guy made him an extravagant bow.

"Suave Sir Jaufre," he said; "smooth Sir Jaufre, by that count you should write red ballads of battles."

There came a faint laugh from some of the hearers, others raised their eyebrows and drew nearer. The war of wits promised to quicken. Count Ernault, coming from the palace and conference with Duke Baldwin, spied the excited group and drew nigh. As he came near he heard Sir Jaufre interrogate his critic.

"Your meaning?"

Sir Guy, still with the same air of extravagant respect, explained, syllabling, with laborious slowness:

"I mean that if I am no lucky lover you are no famous fighter."

Sir Jaufre propped his hand on his chin for a moment as one drowned in deep thought. Then his eyes travelled slowly along the little line of listeners.

"Who can tell me the Latin for 'braggart'?" he asked, meditatively.

There was a little silence. Scholarship was not a strong point of Duke Baldwin's companions. Then Fernand Ximenes, to end or extend the embarrassment, asked:

"Why the Latin?"

Sir Jaufre made a deprecating gesture.

"That it may serve for Guy's epitaph tonight," he interpreted.

Sir Guy laughed again very softly, swaying a little backward and forward, as one exceedingly amused.

"Do you think," he asked, "that anyone will kill me tonight for killing you this morning?"

Sir Jaufre spoke again, not to Guy, but still to the constrained, attentive circle:

"I do not know the Latin for 'braggart,'" he said, thoughtfully, "but I know the French for 'fool.'"

"Why, so do I," Sir Guy agreed, instantly; "it is Jaufre de Brabant."

Every one of the hearers laughed at this, coming so crisp and pat, but Sir Jaufre sprang to his feet.

"Up sword, and out!" he cried, and drew his weapon.

Sir Guy as swiftly bared his blade, and it seemed for a moment as if to the many images of life the court-yard presented that of a battle to the death was to be added. Only for a moment, for instantly Count Ernault thrust his white staff of marshalship between the combatants.

"House your swords, gentlemen," he insisted, peremptorily. "Do you not know the day's law? There shall be no challenge taken, no quarrel honored in arms, save in the tourney and under the eye of Duke Baldwin. For today the duke's son marries the Duchess Esclaramonde of Thebes, and on such a day there may be no brawling; wherefore, close hands in amity."

Sir Jaufre sulkily calm, Sir Guy seraphically affable, extended each a hand, and clasped in sign of formal peace. The somewhat awkward silence that followed on this stifled brawl and seeming reconciliation was strangely interrupted. Outside the great gate came the clear sound of the note of a horn, which immediately attracted the attention of every man in the court-yard and every woman at the palace windows.

"What belated knight is this?" cried Ambrose of Blois, pleased at the interruption, for he liked both the disputants.

The lord-marshal shook his head.

"I thought that every expected knight was in the castle," he answered, and had hardly finished speaking when the horn was wound a second time.

"It is a baron's summons," Ximenes exclaimed, pleased to air his intimacy with Frankish etiquette, and on the heels of his exclamation came a third time, louder and clearer, the note of the great horn.

"By the Lord!" cried Count Ernault, "this is a prince's parley," and he turned to the giants at the gate.

13

THE KNIGHT OF ELEUSIS

"Open the gates," Count Ernault ordered, and the guardian giants obeyed. The great bolts were drawn, the great key turned in the lock, the great gates were flung apart. Every eye was turned towards the opening; every gazer expected to behold some splendid personage, some great prince in golden armor with his glittering retinue of men-at-arms. What the gazers saw was a tall, fair-haired youth with a shepherd's straw upon his head, with a shepherd's sheepskin bound about his body, with a shepherd's staff in his hand and a shepherd's pipe at his girdle. The knights stared in amazement as the shepherd advanced towards them confidently, with head held high and easy carriage. Behind the shepherd strode a burly, travel-stained soldier, with a huge sword at his thigh, a mighty cudgel in his fist, and a rusty lantern on his belt.

The first astonishment of the knights now translated itself into vehement laughter, which brought a faint flush to the shepherd's cheek and a deeper scarlet to the tanned face of the soldier. The amazement of the knights was as great as their entertainment, but both would have been a thousandfold greater if they could have guessed that the slender shepherd whose coming had so diverted them was in sooth a slender she-creature, a daughter of the forest. But the glamour of the woodland shone from Argathona's eyes, and the knights in the yard and the ladies on the gallery saw nothing but the simple shepherd. Argathona advanced towards Count Ernault where he stood resting on his white staff of office, and easily saluted him and his companions.

"Good-morrow, lords," she said, and the French lords marvelled, understanding her, and yet wondered vaguely how it came to pass that they did understand.

"A most sweet-voiced shepherd," Guy said to the knight Ambrose of Blois, who stood next to him.

Count Ernault answered the shepherd.

"Hail, young rustical; but we thought one of royal blood came to the tournament!"

"You thought rightly," Argathona answered. "I come to the tournament, and I am of royal blood."

Ernault looked earnestly into the beautiful face of the youth before him. Sir Jaufre de Brabant edged forward.

"Do you wrap your royal flesh in sheepskin?" he asked, with a ring of derision in his voice which did not escape Argathona.

"There be some lords," she answered, "whose best coat were the hide of a donkey; but for myself, though I walk in wool, I am of the ancientest, rarest race in Greece."

At this confident assertion, made with all the daring of youth, murmurs of surprise, amusement, and even of protest came from the listening knights. Sir Jaufre de Brabant shrugged his shoulders. Guy de Hainault moved a little nearer to the new-comer, studying the fair, unfamiliar face with whimsical good-humor. Andronicus Palæologus frowned, as it was his way to frown at any assertion of dignity which could by any means be twisted into a challenge of his supremacy. Fernand Ximenes narrowed his dark eyelids, scrutinizing the slender figure of the audacious youth, and estimating his possible value as a fighting-man to the Catalan Grand Company. The Prince of Epirus, whose vassaldom to Athens always galled him, gave something like a smile of greeting to the stranger who came at least unbidden to the court, and might in so far be taken as an enemy to Duke Baldwin. The French knights were, for the most part, frankly diverted by the defiance of a shepherd boy, but Count Ernault, always courteous and debonair in dealing with any man, king, captain, or shepherd boy who spoke him fair, addressed the youth with civility.

"Young sir," said Ernault, seriously, "that is a grave assertion. Within the walls of this palace are assembled all the high nobility of Greece. What claim have you to set your shield—if, indeed, you have a shield—among us?"

Argathona flung back her head, and her fair hair shone in the sunlight.

"You are great lords in a strange land," she said, proudly; "but my race have ruled in yonder woodland since the dawn of time, and Athens was built but yesterday in the history of our race. We keep apart, we princely foresters, but we are none the less proud. You may call me the Prince of Eleusis."

The courtly marshal was puzzled. Proud of his French descent, and indifferent to the ways of the people his master and his master's peers had come to govern, he knew nothing of the Grecian folk, and it very well might be that some lines lingered in those mountains which had, in their own estimation, the right to call themselves noble. Anyway, it mattered very little in so general a jousting, and there was no harm in flattering the vanities of a conquered people.

"The Prince of Eleusis? It is a sounding title. Do you come as a knight-challenger?" he questioned, urbanely.

Argathona nodded.

"Even so. I heard of your purposes from this valiant." She pointed to Simon, where he stood apart weighing with appreciative eyes the chivalry of France against the mercenaries of Spain, and appraising the giants at the gate. "Liking your purposes, I trudged to tussle."

Jaufre de Brabant pushed a little way ahead of the knight-marshal.

"Sans arms, sans armor," he drolled. "Will you batter us with your bare fists, shepherd?"

"Or conquer us with your pipe," Guy insinuated, "as Joshua's trumpets tumbled Jericho?"

The dryad smiled back into the smiling faces of the jesting knights, and held out her hands in an appeal of comradeship.

"I come unarmed, it is true, for my race have known no need of arms for ages, but I fling myself on your chivalry. Will you not make me up an equipment among you?"

It was a curious sight for the ladies on the balcony, this sight of the white shepherd standing thus alone and fearless in the midst of a ring of knights, while around them the capacity of the court-yard was filled by the curious of all kinds, free companions, pages, men-at-arms, all keenly interested in the audacious new-comer. The lord-marshal glanced with a smile round the circle of faces.

"Most magical modesty," he said, "that invites us to arm him against ourselves."

All who heard him laughed as at an exceeding good joke. It seemed prettily preposterous that this stripling from a Greek wood should come to Duke Baldwin's tournament and demand, not merely the privilege of tilting against glorious shields, but also an outfit of arms and armor. Argathona understood the laughter, and answered, swiftly:

"Nay, I ask nothing for nothing. I know it is the world's way to bargain in this iron age, and that none will give save for value. But I am wise in the earliest wisdom—I can tell you tales, sing you songs, read the secrets of the stars, the signs in your hands. I will tell any man here his fortune if he will pay for fate with a part of my armament."

A buzz of interest hummed among her hearers, and Jaufre de Brabant sprang eagerly forward.

"Can you do this?" he asked. "What are the signs in my palms?" and he thrust his strong hands out to the shepherd.

The dryad turned to the lord-marshal.

"Lord," she said, "I pray you to beg of these gentlemen that they give me a little space. A man's fortune is for his own ears."

"The lad is right," said Ernault. "Room, friends, room," and with a sweep of his marshal's wand he widened the circle about him to the evident discomfort of the crowd outside, who were thus forced rudely against the wall or uncomfortably out of ear-shot and eye-witness. Argathona, thus left in a sense alone with Jaufre, though many eyes were curiously fixed upon the pair, took the hands of the knight in hers and peered into his palms.

"Glory," she began, "glory, glory; a lifetime shining like a star."

"I will give you a sword for this glory," he said, and paused; then he asked again, quickly, "And what of my death-time?"

Argathona looked no more into his hands; she looked steadfastly into his wild eyes.

"I think you will sink like a star in the peace of old age."

The face of Jaufre clouded.

"I would have picked a fiercer finish," he sighed; "but you shall have the sword."

"I thank your valiancy," Argathona said; and Jaufre, turning from her, rejoined his companions. Before Count Ernault could signify which knight should next have speech with the shepherd, Sir Guy de Hainault had sprung from the marshal's side and approached her.

"Read the page of my palm," he cried, pushing out his fine, white hands impatiently.

Argathona held them for a moment, glanced at their smooth surface, and let them fall with a sigh, looking gravely at the girlish face of the knight.

"Speak!" cried Sir Guy. "Why do you hesitate?"

Argathona spoke in a low voice.

"Death is near at hand," she said.

No change came over the delicate face of the knight.

"How?" he asked, as quietly as he might have asked the hour for supper.

"Bravely—in battle," Argathona answered.

Sir Guy struck his hands together exultingly.

"You merit a princely gift for that promise. What will you have of me?"

"Will you give me a helmet?" asked the shepherd.

"You shall have a golden helmet," Sir Guy promised. "What is your crest?"

And the shepherd answered, remembering with a smile the heraldic wisdom of Simon:

"An oak-tree with acorns."

Sir Guy saluted Eleusis and turned and joined his fellows.

Others were eager to take his place, but this time the staff of the lord-marshal restrained impetuosity.

"My turn, I pray you," Count Ernault said, and, advancing, faced the seeming shepherd with extended hands.

"Don't tell me of battles," he said, "or how I shall come to my death; death is the handman of Heaven. Today I live, and to live is to love. Read my love-riddle."

Argathona looked steadfastly at the hands that many women had held with passion, for Count Ernault was the well-beloved in every land where he had wandered.

"Many women will love you," she said, slowly, and Ernault gave a sigh of joy, for he was no longer in the hot of his youth and he dreaded love's twilight. She went on—"but never the one woman."

Ernault's passionate eyes clouded for an instant, for all the world knew of his passion for the lovely Duchess of Corinth and the implacable chastity of the lady. Wherefore she and her husband came not as guests to Athens. Then his eyes widened again and he smiled. "Well," he said, half sadly and half laughing, "I must make the best of the many, if I show the worst with the one. I will give you a blank shield, brother-in-arms. Tell me your device for my squire to paint."

"A golden acorn on a green field," Argathona answered, again profiting shrewdly by the lessons in heraldry that Simon had given her during the long day in the forest.

"A golden acorn on a green field," Count Ernault repeated, committing the new device to his courtly memory. He turned away from the shepherd and addressed the expectant knights.

"Come, friends," he said, "our knight-challenger has now sword, helmet, and shield; he still needs body armor and battle-axe, horse and lance. Who is for having his fortune told that will pay this price for the tale?"

A multitude of hands were lifted, and Count Ernault contemplated with assumed dismay a forest of waving fingers. Then he shook his head in depreciation.

"There is no time for all," he said. "The sun climbs high, and our guest needs no more than a single equipment, wherefore I will trust to the ordeal by chance."

He lowered his lids till his eyes seemed closed, and then struck lightly, and apparently at random, with his white staff among the knights nearest to him three times in succession. But it was characteristic of the courtly and politic marshal that the touch of his white wand fell on the shoulders of those whom, for one reason or another, it was expedient to please. Fernand Ximenes, maleficent captain of free companions; the vassal Prince of Epirus, always a thorn in the Baldwin flesh; and Andronicus Palæologus, eminent, pompous exile with an eye to a great succession, were the chosen three. Fernand Ximenes, on whom the first lot fell, advanced to the shepherd and tendered his steady, lean, brown hand. Argathona regarded it for a breathing space in silence, then she said:

"You dream strange dreams suspected of none. It is well for you that none suspect. Your dreams will come true."

No change stirred the impassive face of the Spaniard as he listened to what seemed, indeed, the speech of a seer. With untroubled voice he spoke.

"I had a suit of armor wrought in Toledo, steel and gold; it were a privilege for any prince to wear it. I have it no longer; it is yours."

He saluted the prophetic shepherd with the dignity inherent in his race, and rejoined the circle of knights. His place was promptly taken by Demetrius of Epirus, the prince with the furtive eyes and the fine, false voice. Argathona looked at his hand and whispered:

"Faith and treason quarrel in the cup of your fingers. If faith win, faith must fall soon in honor; if treason triumph, treason will flourish long in dishonor to end on a high place."

The pale lips of the Prince of Epirus twitched.

"I will give you a battle-axe," he said, thickly, for he knew what path he would choose when the chance came, and he had grace enough to feel some shame at his knowledge. He turned and pushed his way through the circle of knights into the crowd beyond, as a man might who wished to hide his face from keen eyes.

Andronicus Palæologus moved forward, ostentatious of port, gorgeous of apparel, and extended his beringed hand in arrogant condescension to the stranger. Argathona gave a quick glance at the plump, sensual palm.

"You will wear the crown of Cæsar," she promised.

Andronicus flushed the imperial red in spite of himself, then he said, urbanely, for, indeed, he was very pleased with the oracle:

"I will give you a horse as white as the moon and as fleet as the wind. I will give you a spear as sharp as desire and as tough as hope," and so he turned and joined his brother knights. Even as he did so the air was stirred by the sweet sound of a silver trumpet, and there was immediately a sign of great bustle and commotion among the ladies who thronged the gallery. The lord-marshal lifted his hand.

"Friends all," he said, "the sun of beauty shines upon us in the pride of noontime, for her grace the Duchess of Thebes is coming on the great gallery to take the air. Let those that are her slaves attend upon her."

Immediately the fixed circle of knights dissolved into its units, and the crowd around them parted to give passage as the cavaliers made eagerly for the stately stairway that led to the great gallery. Argathona caught Count Ernault by the arm as he turned away with the others.

"Pray you, tell me the laws of this day's tourney?" she said.

Count Ernault, looking with much approbation at the shepherd knight, answered:

"Today our lord's son, Sir Rainouart of Athens, will proclaim to all and sundry that the Lady Esclaramonde of Thebes is the fairest she in Christendom. Those that challenge him set the fame of their lovers in jeopardy, for Duke Baldwin's son is an unconquerable jouster."

"What would happen," Argathona asked, "if he were to be overthrown?"

Count Ernault laughed gently.

"It could scarcely happen," he asserted.

"But if it did happen?" the shepherd persisted.

Count Ernault looked about him and saw that he and the shepherd stood alone, for the press of knights was thronging the great stairway.

"I think," he said, softly, "that the lady of Thebes would never forgive him."

"Is she so imperious a queen of beauty?" the shepherd questioned.

Count Ernault laughed compassionately, as the well-informed laugh that instruct a stranger in a strange land.

"She will suffer no man to wilt from allegiance to her will. She is the most insatiable fair, and would have all men for her lovers."

The shepherd looked at the courtly marshal with a strange smile.

"Would she condescend to a shepherd?" Argathona asked.

Count Ernault distorted his smooth face with a grimace.

"'Tis very likely," he answered, "none better being by; but when you ride radiant in coat-armor in the lists we shall see if she will pick you out. Till then, farewell, Knight of Eleusis."

He turned from the shepherd and joined the mounting crowd to pay his respects to the Lady Esclaramonde where she stood patent in beauty upon the gallery. Argathona looked about her for a place where she might see unseen. In the court-yard stood an ancient image of a god, headless and armless, which had been set up there in indifference, if not in derision, by those who had dug it up when the court-yard was a-making. Behind this image Argathona stationed herself, and Simon, who had kept apart in the crowd outside the knights, now came to her side. Argathona looked up at the gallery, where, above the bowed heads of obsequious lords, she could distinguish the dark, imperious loveliness of the Duchess Esclaramonde. Simon whispered confidentially in her ear, behind his big hand:

"There stands your fair foewoman."

Argathona still looked at the duchess with unchanged face.

"If I were a man," she said, slowly, "I would not be her lover."

Simon grunted.

"Many have loved her, and all have sorrowed in the loving. While I stood in the throng but now I heard strange tales of her from some of those Spanish rascals and some of the duke's people. They say that when the Duke of Thebes lived, whose unweeping widow she now is, she would send him to sleep at nights with a drugged draught, and then"—he coughed a little behind his hand, as if apologetically, and resumed—"and then entertain company."

Argathona's eyes were still set steadfast upon Esclaramonde where she smiled upon her flatterers.

"It is blasphemous to wear a fair face and hide a foul heart; but if she be as base as you say, she may help me well if I win in the tournament."

Simon whistled.

"Pray God you may win," he said; "but if you thrust your body where hard knocks are going you must not pule at bruises."

"I do not think I shall come to hurt," Argathona answered. "But I shall fight fair, trusting to my strength as the others trust, and using no more woodland work than this, that my spear is invincible against all false lovers."

14

THE TRIUMPH OF THEBES

The Lady Esclaramonde held a little court upon the gallery. Leaning against a pillar and playing with her fan, she summoned this lord and that from the throng of knights now mingled with the brilliant swarm of women, and gave each a few gracious moments of her sunshine ere she dismissed him from her side. Count Ernault had his turn, and the flash of their glances was always alive with intimate memories. Jaufre de Brabant came and Guy de Hainault, and pompous Andronicus Palæologus and the others; none was forgotten; each beamed with the conviction that the duchess preferred him above his fellows. The last that Esclaramonde called to her was Fernand Ximenes, and when the Spaniard was by her side she turned to look into the court-yard, and he following her example, none could hear their speech.

"You have not been brisk to wish me felicity," the duchess complained.

Ximenes shrugged his shoulders.

"I do not think you have made a good shot for fortune," he answered, frankly. "The boy is a fool, and you might have had a man for a master."

The duchess's eyes mocked him under lowered lids, and she patted his hands with her fan.

"Such an one as a certain soldier of fortune?" questioned Esclaramonde. "But I believe I do not desire a master, and, besides, this boy-fool will be Duke of Athens, whereas—"

She left her sentence unfinished, provocatively. Ximenes stared impassive into her defiant face.

"I say you have made a bad shot," he replied, firmly. "You might have chosen better; but I dare say you will be content enough, and, indeed, I hope so."

And with that he bowed very stately and left her, knowing well that his words would rankle uncomfortably. Which indeed they did, for the duchess bit her lip and picked at her fan, brooding over troublous fancies. She thought as well of Ximenes as it was possible for her to think well of anyone, and she knew that she held her betrothed by lies and guile. But she had always desired to win him since the first time that her eyes had entreated and his eyes had denied, and it seemed to her a great thing to conquer his scorn. While she stood thus moody there was a flutter among the women a-nigh, and then knights and ladies made a lane down which came the burly Duke Baldwin arm in arm with his son.

Duke Baldwin, sturdy soldier of fortune, with bright eyes ever fixed on the main chance, was all for keeping the young couple together. Enthusiastic about the match, he had confided to his intimates that he thought it the most sensible act his son had ever undertaken, far more sensible than he could have hoped for from a youth who wasted precious living-time in the reading of foolish books. But if Duke Baldwin understood and approved of the alliance, he did not altogether understand or approve of the conduct of his son on the preceding day. In the duchess's company Rainouart appeared to be the very proper image of a perfect knightly worshipper; he had no eyes but for his lady, and his voice echoed with a fair show of passion the endearments of which the duchess was amiably prodigal. But apart from her the youth seemed, in his father's words, to mope. He walked apart with head bent like a scholar pursuing some tangled thread of thought rather than like a soldierly lover hugging his heart at the capture of a fair prize.

This was not an attitude Duke Baldwin admired. Love-making with him was a brisk business, alien from melancholy, sunning itself lustily in the company of the beloved; and as Rainouart seemed to stand in shadow when alone, Duke Baldwin made it his business to see that he should sun himself as much as possible in the duchess's company until the marriage ceremony was over and Thebes and Athens indissolubly linked. So it was that but now having found his son walking apart in a quiet colonnade, Duke Baldwin had rated him for a sluggard lover, had thrust a strong arm within his, and haled him neither willing nor unwilling to the great gallery where he knew that he should find the duchess.

That conduct in the son which had so perplexed the father had not escaped the notice of those knights who were the nearest companions of the prince. These thought him changed, thought his meditative moods strange; but for the most part they set it down playfully to moon-calfishness. "It is the young candle burning overhotly with its first love, and guttering with every draught of fancy," was the comment of Jaufre de Brabant. Guy de Hainault, more sympathetic, if not less cynical, had his doubts, and tried to answer them with friendly questions to which he got no satisfactory answers. Certainly he saw that the prince when in her presence seemed devoted to his imperious mistress, walked loyally by her side, listened reverently to her speech, and seemed to thrill at her frequent caresses. Yet Guy de Hainault said to Count Ernault, who bade him keep his thoughts to himself, that to his eyes the young prince seemed more like a man in a dream than a man in love, and Guy de Hainault had dreamed enough and loved enough to speak with authority.

On one point there was no quarrel: there certainly was no doubt of the duchess's free and full devotion to her lover. She had not even for form's sake made any diffident protest against so swift a wedding, the swiftness whereof came so largely from her own suggestion. Indeed, it seemed as if with shining eyes and sugared tongue she spurred her young lord to protestations and entreaties. The court, for the most part, however, entered into no niceties of discrimination between the conduct of the youth and the lady. It sufficed for those jolly spirits, male and female, that there was to be a wedding, for a wedding meant festivals, and the sight of a wedding, too, had a way of spurring laggard gentlemen into proposals and prompting ladies that would be coy to come to directer terms. Wedding calls for wedding, as blood is said to call for blood.

The genial duke made his way with his son through the rapidly formed alley of retiring lords and ladies to the place where Esclaramonde leaned against a pillar of the gallery and fanned herself languidly, watching their advance with bright eyes.

"Here," said the duke, cheerfully, "is one who would not be denied to come to your presence for all that I could do to occupy him with other matters."

He gently urged Rainouart forward as he spoke, and Rainouart, under the influence of the eyes of Esclaramonde, moved with what seemed to the spectators a lover's eagerness to greet her. The duke smiled a vast smile on all around him.

"I was like that once," he said, with a leer, pinching the chin of the nearest pretty woman and clipping another round the waist. "Come, friends, come; let us leave the young people to themselves. They have little time for courting and must make the most of it." And so with a laughing baggage under each arm Baldwin led the way from the gallery followed obediently by a merry retinue of knights and ladies. The place was swiftly quiet that had been so lively, and for the moment Esclaramonde and Rainouart were left alone. It was, indeed, to be their last occasion for wooing in solitude. The day was all laid out: first the tournament, then the wedding ceremony, then the banquet; the next time this pair were to meet alone it was to be as man and wife. The youth and the woman leaned over the balcony looking down into the almost deserted court-yard. Neither heeded how in a corner, wellnigh concealed from view by an ancient image, a shepherd was standing with a sturdy fellow by his side. Indeed, there was little need to heed, for but a moment after the princely pair were left together the shepherd lad had touched the soldier on the arm, and the two passed quietly out of the court-yard and went their way together in the direction of the tilting-field. When they were gone, Rainouart, who had neither noticed their presence nor their departure, still kept silence for a while, but it was with a strained silence of one who seeks to remember what it was that brought him to the place where he stands. The duchess was silent for a while, with the serenity of one who triumphs and wears her triumph with delight. So a few seconds sped, and then Esclaramonde placed her hand on the hand of her companion where it rested on the marble, and Rainouart's flesh and blood tingled in response to the warm clasp.

"Dear lord," she said, with that caressing voice which always ran like kindly fire over the nerves of those she sought to conquer—"dear lord, your father reminds us that we stand alone as lovers for the last time. You are happy, dear lord?"

Though her words had the form of a question, something in their utterance seemed to sound like a command. The prince turned to her as if he obeyed a summons, and fixed his eyes upon her face—eyes at first indifferent, but which began to glow ardent from the moment that they met her gaze. He put his hand to his forehead and brushed away his hair as a man does who seeks to dissipate perplexing thoughts. It seemed to him as if he had lost his way in the rose-garden; as if, though his heart were still the quivering target for the shafts of love, the living presence of the god were veiled and his voice obscure; as if the noble rose were still afar. He sought in vain to frame the face of Esclaramonde with the mystic petals. But her words sounded imperious and sweet in the halls of his ears, and he took them for the behests of love.

"Surely I am happy," he answered, and the duchess smiled at his speech.

"You love me very much?" she said again, and again her voice was blended with the two notes of interrogation and command.

"Surely I love you very much," he answered again, still in the same smooth, measured manner. It was not very ardent, but it seemed to satisfy the duchess that she could make him say what she pleased.

"When we meet again," she murmured, "you will be the hero of the tournament, yet I think you peril your fame and jeopardize your judgment to proclaim me most fair."

Her words and her eyes stimulated him to the measure of her intention.

"Are you not most fair?" he asked, wonderingly, and his look was compelled admiration and his voice paid the demanded homage.

The duchess smiled provocatively.

"Some have said so, and I smiled at their little wit, but when you assert it my fond heart leaps to believe what my honest mirror denies."

She held out both her hands as she spoke, and Rainouart caught them in his own obediently. It seemed rather that she drew him nearer to her than that he drew her nearer to him.

"The mirror were wicked crystal that showed you other than most fair," he declared, "but there is no such lying glass in the world."

The duchess shook her head, and a cherub wind that was playing along the gallery caught a free lock of her dark hair and blew the tresses against his cheeks, and his cheeks burned.

"I should be proud," she said, "to count myself fair for your sake, for you are the fairest of men and the bravest."

Even while she spoke her spirit seemed to laugh within her, for she remembered to whom she had last said those words, and she wondered to whom she would say them next. But the prince's eyes glowed as if with the exaltation of strong wine.

"Your words are sweet to hear," he vowed. "I will do my best endeavor to merit some little of their grace."

She bent her head forward as if to kiss him on the lips. There was no one to see her—at least no one that counted; no page or servant loitering in the court-yard mattered, and even before a larger audience the duchess would scarcely have denied herself. But even as Rainouart waited for her kiss the quiet of the noontime was broken by the shrill call of a clarion, the call that warned all knights to hasten to the lists and make them ready for the tournament. Rainouart stooped and kissed the white hand of the duchess.

"Farewell, fair lady," he said; "I must go to my tent."

"I will watch your triumph from the gallery," Esclaramonde said, and he turned and left her with no other word, and went down the stairway into the court-yard.

Esclaramonde waited a little while, watching him depart and thinking Thessalian thoughts. He was under her spell; he had forgotten what she willed him to forget; he should never remember while she was by his side. That he was only her lover through the make-believe of her philtres and her will troubled her nothing. He was her lover, comely and young, and she saw herself Duchess of Athens, and her heart leaped and she laughed at times. When Rainouart was out of sight and she was tired of her thoughts, she turned to the far end of the gallery, where her immediate women waited, and summoned them with a gesture to follow her to her appointed pavilion by the lists.

15

THE CHALLENGE OF RAINOUART

Rainouart walked slowly down the sacred mound through the long lines of soldiers that made a lane for the gentry all along the winding road and at the foot of the hill. He went as he always went after parting with Esclaramonde in these few fantastic hours—like one in a feverish day-dream who found himself unfamiliar amid familiar surroundings. The realities of life distorted themselves into unrealities; your simple soldier standing on guard in his rank loomed monstrous as a giant; your habitual building chose to enlarge and radiate door upon door and gallery upon gallery into infinite, meaningless space. Rainouart walked airily, for his physical condition seemed strangely light; he walked warily, because his mental condition seemed strangely heavy. He was troubled at he knew not what; he wondered, he knew not why; he thought ceaselessly of Esclaramonde, and yet the thought of her seemed always to tease his drugged memory with a desire for some face, some voice, that were not the face and voice of the Duchess of Thebes. So, like a man that walks in sleep, he came from the Acropolis to the meadow at its foot, heedless of the mass of folk, heedless of the clamor and the flapping banners, the eager mien of knights and the radiant faces of ladies, only conscious that his duty in life was that day to sustain in arms the fame of the Lady Esclaramonde.

As he passed through the wicket into the lists and found himself in the vacant space behind the galleries, he was accosted by a young knight, partly armored, whose words and gesture invited him to a halt. The young knight was Argathona, daintily boyish in her man's armor. When she and Simon had made their way to the tilting-field they found that a pavilion had been allotted to the Prince of Eleusis by order of Count Ernault, wherein were placed the arms and armor promised by the different knights, while the white horse of Andronicus Palæologus waited in the stables to carry its new burden. Simon of Rouen, as the strange prince's esquire, helped his seeming master to arm swiftly, and thus Argathona was ready to meet Rainouart as he entered the enclosed meadow. Rainouart did not recognize her face, for it was the woodland will of the dryad that she should seem unfamiliar to him. The aura of the immortals was about her, and mortal eyes must see her as she pleased. But there is a power higher even than the wills of such immortals, and the young prince, looking into the face of the youth who stopped him, found his strange stupor troubled with new torments of striving to remember the unrememberable. He could not assure himself that he had ever seen the stranger's face before, and yet the sight of that strange face, with its gleam of golden hair beneath the silken cap, with its haunting suggestions of sea wave and lake water and forest fountain in its blue eyes, troubled him with an aching desire and the yet more aching knowledge that he knew not what he desired. If he had loved some woman in his boyhood, some woman long dead, this might have been her brother come upon him unawares, at all adventure, with some trick of the old love's look in his eyes, of the old love's carriage in his gait. But he shook himself impatiently, for there was no such memory in his life, and he was vexed with the blind, maimed memories that would never take shape and color. Through the dull hum of his confused thoughts he was conscious that the stranger knight addressed him.

"Rainouart of Athens, are not you today the general challenger?"

Rainouart saluted him mechanically, looking into his eyes and only finding there unanswerable mysteries.

"At your service, sir knight," he answered, and the sound of his own voice seemed as meaningless to him as the thin sighs of spirits heard in dreams, and yet he knew that he had spoken and that his hearer had heard and understood. Through all the entanglement of his senses he was conscious dimly of a curious surprise at his own ability to understand the stranger's speech, and his wonderment seemed to hark back to some other time, some other age, perhaps some other existence, when in some way he had heard one speak to him whom he understood and yet marvelled to understand.

"What are the terms of your challenge?" the stranger knight asked him. The prince answered, slowly:

"That my Lady Esclaramonde of Thebes is the rose of the world."

There was a moment's pause, and the prince made to resume his journey, but again the stranger stopped him with a question:

"You love this lady?"

The prince looked wonderingly at the fair, perplexing face.

"I wed her tonight," he answered, and still the stripling persisted:

"You are very sure you love this lady?"

The prince hesitated, then said, sharply:

"You question somewhat rustically. I wed her tonight."

Again the strange knight interrogated, pertinacious:

"You have left no other love for her sake?"

The prince drew back and set his hand to his sword.

"Sir," he said, angrily, "if you question my honor I will answer you to your hurt!"

The bearer of the name of Prince of Eleusis came a little nearer to Rainouart, and her voice was as plaintive as summer rain on forest leaves.

"No maid weeps for you in the greenwood?"

The prince shifted his hand from his sword-hilt to his brow, for his head ached with confusing, formless memories; but the troubling thoughts fled elusive through his brain, leaving no more behind them than the blackened spaces left by a forest fire.

"The greenwood!" he echoed. "The greenwood! It was in the greenwood my lady found me." He paused again, ever seeking to remember the unrememberable, then ended, rapidly, "The Lady Esclaramonde, whom I love, and whose love makes me invincible."

Infinitely sad the eyes of Argathona shone upon her lost lover's sadness. Against the spells of the subtle sorceress her simple immortality seemed compelled to surrender. Were she to declare herself now, she might fail to quicken the wit that was crippled by the incantations of Esclaramonde. Only Esclaramonde could undo what Esclaramonde had done, and to bring this about Argathona must trust to herself—she, the immortal, alone in an unfriendly world. Argathona had lived but a few hours in the company of men, yet she had lived with them long enough to pity all, to mistrust most, to love one with a love as abiding as her gift of ceaseless life. But her unstained spirit read clearly and swiftly the lessons of the world's law, and she hoped to overthrow the guile of a woman with the guile of a girl.

"You are very proud of your love and your lover," she said, gently, for her heart ached to see him so astray. Rainouart answered her with a kind of resentful defiance, as one that sought to convince himself, and he echoed her words:

"I am very proud of my love," and so far his voice rang clear and bright as a battle-call; then he ended, more heavily, "and of my lover."

He turned from her with a courteous salutation and went towards his tent, and Argathona went her way to her own pavilion and made an end of her arming, thinking upon many things.

16

THE TOURNAMENT

Captain Fox and Captain Gander, Captain Bat and Captain Chanticleer, Captain Rat and Captain Badger had thoroughly enjoyed their visit to Athens. The first day of the tournament had come and gone and left them very substantially the better in paunch and pocket. On this, the second day, they hoped, and with reason, for still fairer fortune, and severally, and as a corporation, made liberal vows of wax candles to St. Nicholas if their hopes should come true. They moved at ease through the assemblage outside the lists, clad in the disguises that time had taught them to be best suited to each man's individuality. Captain Fox, who had a persuasive tongue, went as a mendicant friar and vended relics. Captain Gander, because he could sing a catch at random with some volume of voice, jigged and whistled, minced and ambled as a wandering minstrel. Captain Bat was a lame beggar, arm in sling, patch on eye, a maimed hero, victim of wars, voluble of sorrows, and eloquent in appeal. Captain Chanticleer skipped hither and thither as a glib-lipped fortune-teller, and fumbled dirty pieces of wood that were painted with pips and points and dots of mystical meanings. Captain Rat and Captain Badger, who had each some skill in tumbling, clowned to the crowd as itinerant mountebanks, and paraded alternately one on the other's shoulders inviting the world to see wonders.

So dexterous were all these gentry in their assumed occupations that their legitimate receipts represented a very fair proportion of the day's earnings. Therefore, as Captain Fox pithily observed, they did very well both as honest folk and as rogues. But while their hands were busy in emptying the pouches of others to fill their own, their eyes were not idle or indifferent to the pleasures which Duke Baldwin provided for knave as well as for knight. Experience of camps had made the gang of rascals acquainted with the bearings of many warlike lords, and they were able to blazon with confidence to a gaping crowd about them most of the coats displayed upon the shields that hung before the pavilions in the lists.

Thus said Captain Fox to his audience: "The black pale on a silver field proclaims the Prince of Epirus. The red bend on the gold enriched with three laurel wreaths on the field is the bearing of Andronicus Palæologus, who longs to wear the imperial laurels of Constantinople. The six gold lozenges on purple are the arms of Sir Jaufre de Brabant. The three boars' heads of silver on the black field assert Sir Ambrose of Blois. The golden stag at gaze on a green field stands for Sir Raymond of Provence. The golden dolphin on the orange field represents Sir Guy de Hainault. The shield divided per pale green and silver and charged with a scarlet castle, from whose summit emerges a black dragon, belongs to Fernand Ximenes, the aspiring Spaniard." Only one cognizance baffled the garrulity of Captain Fox that day. There was a shield bearing a golden acorn on a green field that was as unfamiliar to him as to his hearers. So he looked mighty wise, gabbled some patter about mysteries that might not be revealed, and went on to explain, what everyone of course knew, that Prince Rainouart carried a golden shield with no charge upon it, and that the lord-marshal, Count Ernault, carried potent blue and silver. Of many another knight that day, of many more armorial bearings, Captain Fox discoursed learnedly enough to such as would listen to him, and generally succeeded while his tongue wagged in impoverishing his hearers of some jewel, purse, or button, dexterously nipped by his thievish fingers. But at least the plundered person, when he discovered his loss and Captain Fox had vanished into the sea of human beings, might console himself with the reflection that he had moved, as it were, for a season in a kind of intimacy with the great, and that this pleasure, like all others, had to be paid for.

The place which Duke Baldwin had appointed for the holding of the tournament was excellently well chosen. One of the greenest meadows of the Athenian plain facing the sea, with the Acropolis for a background, had been enclosed with great hoardings of painted wood, red and white, the duke's own colors. Under the shadow of the Acropolis a great gallery had been erected, glittering with gilding and brilliant with silk, to form a bower from which the Duchess of Thebes and the fair ladies of Baldwin's court might witness the encounters. Behind these, still within the enclosures, were two pavilions set apart, one for the use of the Duchess of Thebes and the other for Duke Baldwin, who took no part in that day's sport save as on-looker and arbiter. The pavilions of the knights were ranged inside the lists, and at the door of each a page in some fantastic habit stood holding his master's shield. Here and there in the wooden barrier encircling the lists were apertures guarded by mighty men-at-arms, brothers in size and strength to those that wardered the door of the ducal court-yard. At each of these doorways a herald was stationed to make sure that none entered the lists unprivileged.

The Duke Baldwin was a great stickler for custom, past-master of punctilio. He knew all that there was to know of the laws that had hitherto governed the gentle art of tourney, and thinking that nothing in the world exists so good that it could not be bettered, especially by Duke Baldwin of Athens, he had devised many novel regulations in gracious methods for mimic combat, which pleased him highly the more they rendered complicated and intricate the laws of the royal sport. He rejoiced to invent some new rule for the disqualification of a combatant who might to the unconcerned eye of the actual spectator appear to be the victor. His opponent might, indeed, lie sprawling on the grass, fairly pushed from his horse by the heavy impact of the blunt-headed spear, but if that spear had not struck in precisely the right place permissible at that very moment of the play, according to the laws of Duke Baldwin, or had struck in some place not permissible, again according to the laws of Duke Baldwin, it was the sprawler on the ground who received the laurel and not he who rode his horse victoriously amid the cheers of the multitude. It followed, naturally enough, that Duke Baldwin's regulations were not always and altogether popular with the knights who encountered under his eyes. But the duke was so deeply versed in the whole history of his sport, and always so readily recited precedents from this great tournament here and that noble jousting there, that it would have been difficult, even had it been profitable or even advisable, to argue a point with him, and as he was autocrat of Athens, strong of hand and choleric of nature, few ever did venture to argue with him.

On this occasion Duke Baldwin had taken special pains over the whole paraphernalia of the tournament. He had examined with his own hands and eyes the great barrier that ran down the middle of the lists to divide the encountering knights and prevent their horses from colliding. He had made sure by personal interrogation that each of the heralds was well acquainted with the arms, titles, lineage, and deeds of each of the nobles who offered themselves to take part in the combat. He saw to the pitching of the pavilions, the comfort of their furniture, the lodgings of the squires. He visited the stables where the horses were to dwell, the stithies where swarthy smiths were to wait ready with bellows working and fires burning for the mending of shattered mail, and he was at pains to see that the pavilion of the Duchess of Thebes was adorned with all the luxury that even a lovely woman could desire.

Duke Baldwin was so well satisfied with himself and with the world in general that he allowed himself the relaxation of idleness in one particular. He left to his lord-marshal, Count Ernault, all that belonged to the personal arrangement of the tourney, to the order of the encounters, and to the degree of those who might be permitted to take part in them. Thus it came about that when the hour struck, and the trumpets sounded for the beginning of battle, he knew nothing of the existence of a Prince of Eleusis to whom Count Ernault had given promise to ride in the fight.

All the meadow-land round the lists was thronged with a fantastic congregation of folk. Every square inch of standing room a-nigh the red and white palings was occupied by eager spectators hotly arguing the merits of their favorites, and when they could afford it going so far as to stake silver piece against silver piece on the issue of the conflicts. On the fringe of this multitude the speculative had erected a veritable village of wooden booths, wherein all kinds of foods and drinks, gross and dainty, were to be had for the asking and the paying by those whom the thoughts of martial prowess made hungry and the spring sunlight stung to thirst. Travelling glee-men, penniless enough, pushed their bold, sunburned faces hither and thither, ready at any moment for coin or cup to sing to the interested some song of the deeds of heroes—Charlemagne and his twelve peers, Arthur of Brittany and his knights of the Table Round, or the fortunes of the lord of Orange. Every tree in the meadow bore its load of human fruit; scarce any bough seemed too high or too slender for some adventurous spirit to assail, obtaining thereby a view of the tournament at greater peril to life and limb than any run by the knightly combatants.

In the delicate air of Athens, where sound travels far, the chattering of all this swarm of human beings came to the ears of those in the pavilions like the humming of a hive of monstrous bees, or the chattering of an incredible army of starlings, or the slappings of an angry sea. Inside the sacred enclosure the scene was less crowded, but more brilliant and many-colored. On the silk-swathed galleries which had been set up for the benefit of non-combatant courtiers and the ladies of the palace, the gallantest gentlemen vied with the loveliest women in the magnificence of their apparel. Cloth of gold and cloth of silver, all the dyes and jewels of the East, all the plumage of the brightest-hued birds, glittered and twinkled in the strong sunlight in a manner dazzling to the eye. Outside the lists the common folk chattered and gabbled. Inside the lists the noble lords and ladies chattered and gabbled, too, until, as Simon said to himself, it seemed as if the world might very well fear to be talked out of existence. But when the great trumpets sounded which told to every eager ear of all those thousands that the time had come and that the game was afoot, there fell upon the plain a silence as deep and still as the clamor had before been plangent. In that awful silence Duke Baldwin lifted his mighty bulk in the golden throne which groaned under his weight, and, raising his sceptre in his right hand, gave order, in a voice which would have honored a bull, to the lord-marshal that the sport might now begin. The lord-marshal in his turn spoke to the heralds. Again there came a blare of trumpets, and then again a silence pierced by the voices of the heralds calling upon the earliest combatants to begin the fray.

The first part of the tournament consisted of a series of single combats on horse between the allotted pairs of knights. Sir Jaufre de Brabant and Sir Raymond of Provence were the first to ride, and the episode was brief, for in the first encounter Sir Jaufre unhorsed his adversary and cantered to the end of the lists triumphant, while Sir Raymond of Provence scrambled to his feet and regained his tent with as much dignity as he could master under the pitying eyes of the ladies who liked him, the smiles of such lords as misliked him, and the grinning faces of the diverted multitude. Sir Guy de Hainault rode next against Sir Ambrose of Blois, and though Sir Guy looked as slender as a girl in armor and Sir Ambrose a thing of bulk, Sir Ambrose went down at the first push before the well-planted thrust of his adversary's lance. Fernand Ximenes rode against Demetrius of Epirus and overcame him. Andronicus Palæologus overcame Sir Gaston of Nîmes. Many knights rode, gaining good fortune or bad, and the praise or pity of ladies. The inquisitive may seek for their names and their bearings, and their share of that day's fame and shame, in the painted chronicle made later at Count Ernault's cost, from Count Ernault's memory, and now preserved in the University of Madrid, to which Fernand Ximenes presented it. Those who beheld the jousting averred loudly that it was the best and bravest that had ever been seen. In their hearts they were well aware that it was patently like all other tournaments that had ever been held under the laws of honor, and that all the tourneys that would follow through the years would be of like pattern for chance and valor, strength and skill, success or failure—ay, and would be witnessed by eyes as lovely, whether shining with the pride of triumph or shining through the mist of tears.

When a certain number of these courses had been run, then came the great business of the day, the general challenge of the Prince of Athens to all and sundry that were true knights to contend in arms against his declaration that his lady, the Duchess Esclaramonde of Thebes, was the rose of the world. As the prize of this contest he offered a wreath of golden violets, a glory of the goldsmith's art, which the victor was to offer to his queen of beauty, and which Esclaramonde was very confident to receive from the hands of her betrothed.

17

THE ROSE OF THE WORLD

A tumult of applause went up as Rainouart entered the lists, riding a black charger given him by Esclaramonde, and glittering in arms, while his handsome head, still unhelmeted, inclined to right and left in recognition of his greeting. For though Rainouart was too newly come to Athens to be very generally known of the populace, and though report, ever busy with talebearing from great places, had whispered something sneering of his bookish ways and his distaste for light ladies, he had endeared himself with the fickle Athenian public by his deeds on the preceding day of the tourney, when he had ridden from victory to victory. At the close of the first day there had been a general assault or mêlée between five-and-twenty Frankish knights, champions chosen by Duke Baldwin, and five-and-twenty of the picked chieftains of the Catalan Grand Company. The struggle was as fierce as brief. It seemed at first as if the Moorish-looking warriors from Spain were destined to gain the day under the angry eyes of Duke Baldwin, but Rainouart's individual deeds of prowess and the gallant manner in which he rallied the French force at the last redeemed the honor of Athens, and forced the Catalans from the field. Duke Baldwin's joy had been unbounded, and he had expressed it as exuberantly as he could to the young man who always listened so gravely when he spoke, and while he listened thought upon his mother's wrongs.

Now the heralds cried the challenge of the Prince of Athens, and as they did so, Rainouart, gripping his horse with limbs of steel, felt as if the brisk wind of battle blowing in his face drove from his senses something of that lethargy under which they had lain supine. His tormenting, denying, mysterious memories troubled him for the moment no more; he was just for that moment a good knight on a good horse, with a good lance in hand ready to do battle with all the world for the sake of a woman. Scarcely did he recall the familiar features of Esclaramonde; in his mind, as in his challenge, he was fighting for the rose of the world, but the rose was the rose of the lovely legend, the unfound flower.

Now knight after knight came forth from his pavilion and mounted his horse to do battle, and knight after knight went down before the conquering lance of young Athens. Guy de Hainault, Jaufre de Brabant, Ambrose of

Blois, Gaston of Nîmes, Raymond of Provence, Demetrius of Epirus, and Andronicus Palæologus, each had his own fair lady, star of his life or star of the hour, to tilt for, and each in turn sustained defeat, and Rainouart remained invincible. The populace huzzaed, courtiers applauded demonstratively, Duke Baldwin grinned like a pleased hyena, the ladies of the discomfited tried to smile through tears, and the face of Esclaramonde shone with pride, for she had snared a rare mate. As for Rainouart, he thought not of her; his thoughts were only of the joy of strife and the delight of victory. He was fighting for an ideal; he could not give it name, but it seemed to fill the air with the scent and the color of roses.

Brimmed with the wine of exultation, he waited at his end of the lists after the overthrow of Andronicus Palæologus to see if any other champion would stand against his challenge. There was only one knight left of all the chivalry then in Athens who could hope to contend against him. That knight was Fernand Ximenes, and Rainouart hoped to see him advance. But Fernand Ximenes kept his tent, for he had his own thoughts and purposes concerning the Duchess of Thebes, and he wished to whisper later in her ear that he could not for the life of him challenge her supremacy. So Rainouart waited for a little in his place, a splendid image of steel upon a splendid horse, unquestioned master of the lists. All the spectators, gentle and simple, believed that the day was over, the field fought and won. Rainouart, thinking as they thought, was about to ride forward to receive the wreath of golden violets from the hand of Duke Baldwin when a great shout from the crowd without the barriers, and a murmur that ran along the galleries, stayed his purpose. Then he, with all the rest, became aware of the presence of a new challenger in the lists. A knight in gilded armor, with an acorn for his device, had emerged from a pavilion at the farthest end of the field, and after mounting a white horse which was held in waiting by a burly squire, had ridden slowly to the challenging station. The new-comer's visor was raised, and the spectators beheld a little of a young and beautiful face, very noble in an unfamiliar fairness of feature, of a pale favor delicately colored. But what most won all were the stranger's eyes of lively blue, which made many a woman wish to see her own countenance mirrored in them.

Duke Baldwin leaned forward on his throne in some surprise at the sudden presence; his rugged, bull face flushed with wonder. Count Ernault, after reading the new-comer's shield, whispered to a herald, and the herald proclaimed that the Prince of Eleusis desired to break a lance with the Prince of Athens on the question of his challenge. At this unexpected announcement Esclaramonde, who had bent forward to look at the new-comer and noted how slight he seemed, and youthful, leaned back again with a disdainful smile, though her ready senses quickened at the sight of the youth's beauty. Sympathetic smiles rippled all along the galleries, and many in the crowd beyond laughed derisively, though none that could see the stranger's face denied its marvellous grace. Duke Baldwin called to Count Ernault, who approached his throne.

"Who is this strange knight?" he said. "I have not heard of any Prince of Eleusis."

"Sire," the lord-marshal answered, "this is a young stripling of Greece who claims descent from an ancient Grecian line. For my own part, I know little or nothing of the race which it pleases your grace to rule, yet because he seemed of gentle blood and carried himself so fairly, I saw no reason to deny him a presence in the lists. Your grace, however, who, knowing all things, doubtless knows intimately the genealogy of every Greek his vassal, will be able to set me right if I have erred in this instance, but for myself I thought it better to stretch a point rather than perchance in denying to attain undoubted gentility."

Duke Baldwin frowned. His son was thus far the victor; the Lady Esclaramonde thus far proclaimed peerless. One never could tell what might come of an unexpected challenge. Yet Duke Baldwin, who, in spite of the omniscience attributed to him by his flattering marshal, was well aware in his heart that he knew nothing whatever about the people whom he held subject by an iron hand, was very unwilling to infringe courteous chivalry in the case of one who might be a gentleman of old descent. So with the ferocious distortion of countenance which was Duke Baldwin's conception of a smile, he approved the lord-marshal's action.

"It were shame," he declared, "if ever noble gentleman were denied to ride in lists opened by me. But here I think decision must rest with our son. If he elect to meet this stranger knight, your Prince of Eleusis has our willing leave to joust in this tourney. But tell our son that as he has fought today only with knights of known lineage and bearings, he is free if it please him to deny this Grecian, and to remain the unquestioned victor of the day."

The lord-marshal hastened to where Rainouart waited, and made him aware of the conditions under which a new player had come into the game, and of Duke Baldwin's decision in the matter. Rainouart answered instantly that he was in no way breathed or weakened by what had gone, that it would be strange, indeed, for him to deny any challenger, and that he would take the stranger's word for his gentility. Straightway Count Ernault sped to where Argathona waited, mounted on her white horse, and, after acquainting her with the cause of the delay, made her free of the duke's permission to tilt.

Nobody in all that vast concourse had watched these parleyings with more interest than the Duchess Esclaramonde of Thebes. Her heart had been dancing all manner of joyous measures at the success of her betrothed. As knight after knight went down before Rainouart, her eyes brightened and her spirits sang, for all was in her honor, and she knew, rejoicing in her knowledge, that every woman present envied her. The sudden apparition of an unexpected challenger could not affect her triumph. The cavalier who had so triumphantly overcome seven of the gallantest knights in Duke Baldwin's gallant court was scarcely like to have his supremacy menaced by a stripling of Greece. Yet in spite of herself, this apparition of this unexpected challenger, unknown to her, unknown to Athens, unknown to Athens's duke, seemed mysteriously to threaten her confidence, and her cheek burned with anger against the fair-faced stranger as she watched the preliminaries of the combat.

The trumpets sounded, and instantly the opposing knights rushed one against the other, swift as warring winds. In full centre of the tilt-yard the white horse and the black horse came wellnigh head to head. Rainouart's spear was aimed a thought too high as it seemed, and slid over the shoulder of his opponent while the lance of Eleusis struck fair and square at the breast-plate of the Athenian prince, and the next moment the black horse was sweeping riderless down the lists, and Duke Baldwin's son was lying on the grass. While a great groan came from all beholders at this fall, the Knight of Eleusis, galloping to the end of the lists, turned at the barrier and rode back again to draw rein with visor exalted in front of the royal pavilion.

When Duke Baldwin saw his son fall, he gripped his sceptre in both hands so fiercely that it bent in his fingers as if it had been a waxen candle, and his whole soul groaned in travail because he could think of no oath horrible enough with which to express his mortification. Esclaramonde for her part hid her burning face behind her fan and dreamed incredible tortures for the victor. However, there was nothing for it but acceptance of the result of the combat, and, while assiduous squires helped the fallen prince to his feet, Duke Baldwin took from the cushion held by a page at his side the golden wreath, and extended it to the Knight of Eleusis, who received it on the point of the lance. Hardly articulate, Duke Baldwin gasped out that the wreath was the victor's, and that his was the privilege to crown whom so he pleased in that presence queen of the day. Immediately the stranger, shifting a little in the saddle, extended the lance dexterously poised so that the golden wreath swung just in front of the face of Esclaramonde. A little sob of joy came from the duchess's lips.

"Why, this is better than best," she murmured, and with something almost too eager in her action she caught at the golden wreath and placed it on her head, while the whole arena now rang with applause at the chivalrous act of the victor. The moment the duchess had taken the wreath, Argathona turned her horse's head in the direction of her pavilion. Duke Baldwin rose in a towering fury from his throne. "This comes of the reading of books," he muttered to himself, and, quitting the gallery, he entered the lists to make inquiry as to the condition of his fallen son.

Argathona, slowly riding down the field on her white horse, was yet some distance from her pavilion, when a page, running breathlessly to her side, informed her that the lord-marshal desired speech with her. Immediately reining her horse, Argathona turned round and advanced to meet Count Ernault, who told her that the Duchess Esclaramonde earnestly entreated the favor of some speech with the victor who had crowned her queen of beauty.

18

AN APPLE OF GOLD

Following the lord-marshal, Argathona came to the silken tent which sheltered the Lady Esclaramonde. At a sign from Count Ernault the pages in attendance drew back the curtains, and Argathona entering found herself in the presence of the Duchess of Thebes. The Lady Esclaramonde was reclining upon a pile of many-colored cushions, playing with a mirror and talking to her women. She propped herself on one elbow and smiled first at Sir Ernault and then at the fair face of the victor.

"I thank you," she said, and there was that in the tone of her voice, and that in the look of her eyes, and that in the deep of his own memory which made it plain to him that the duchess desired to be left alone with the young knight.

Gravity reigning in his face, irony rising in his mind, Count Ernault bowed and left the presence. At a sign from Esclaramonde the duchess's women withdrew into a further apartment of the pavilion, curtained off from the place where Esclaramonde now lay, who looked up alluringly into the impassive face of the youth. For to her, as to the others, with the glamour of the woodland will upon her, Argathona seemed no more than a handsome lad.

"You joust well, youth," she said. "Who is your true-love?"

"I played for a lady's sake," Argathona answered, "whom I maintain very fair."

Esclaramonde leaned forward a little on her silken couch, resting herself on both hands, like some beautiful wild beast about to spring.

"Who is this lady?" she asked, steel in her voice and steel in her eyes, for she could not bear to think that any man could find any woman fair while she was by.

A smile rippled over the dryad's face.

"I dare not say her name," she said, "yet, if you choose, you may see her."

Esclaramonde's dark brows met in a frown.

"Is she one of my women?" she asked, suddenly, and the sound of her voice boded ill for that one of her women whom the champion might name.

Argathona shook her head.

"Indeed no. She is not an inch below you in rank nor an inch above you in stature. Her eyes shine with no less than your brightness; her lips smile with your lively red. Here, if you please, is her image."

Stooping a little, Argathona caught up the mirror with which the duchess had been playing and held it deftly in front of the beautiful, cruel face. The red blood raced into Esclaramonde's cheeks and ebbed again, leaving her strangely pale.

"Am I your lady-love?" she cried, with that joy in her voice which conquest always brought her.

"You are she I rode to see," Argathona answered, enigmatically.

Esclaramonde gave a little sigh of dissatisfaction.

"Your heel needed a sharper spur; you are a day too late. I am to be married this evening."

Argathona laughed.

"Love you, lady! I am a fellow of adventure, and would never make a hearth-haunting husband. I am here today and gone tomorrow. My love is the child of a night."

Esclaramonde's eyes widened and dwindled like a cat's. She was thinking of many times and many nights and many comely men, and she was loath to admit that this stripling should slip through the net of her desires.

"Why, we may find a time by-and-by," she sighed, all enticement.

Argathona shook her head.

"I ride from Athens tomorrow," she began, slowly; then swiftly, with the imperiousness of victory, she ended, "Give me tonight."

The duchess laughed, but the duchess was pleased at the vehemence.

"You are a mad rascal. Am I not to be married this evening?"

Argathona answered her, in a lowered voice:

"There is an old tale of the Theban country, how a beautiful, open-hearted lady would send her lord to sleep in the sipping of a spiced wine, and then talk in the starlight with some lighter, brighter body."

As Argathona spoke a frown grew and deepened on the face of Esclaramonde.

"What are you saying?" she whispered.

"An old tale of Thebes," the dryad replied. "You know not such notions. Yet 'tis a pity. Here is your lord, the unhorsed knight, will be your fellow forever and a day, while I, who overtumbled him, must willy-nilly be gone tomorrow. If he were to sleep tonight how should it harm him? He would not hear us speak in the starlight."

The duchess waved her hand impatiently as if in dismissal.

"You are a mad lad; ride where you will."

"As you please," Argathona replied, "yet I have a toy here I would give to any fair who was gentle with me."

If the duchess was greedy of love, she was greedy also of lovely things.

"What toy?" she cried, eagerly.

Argathona put her hand to her girdle and held out on extended palm a small, perfectly fashioned apple of pure gold.

"This golden apple. See, it is pure gold, and see, writ on it in the Greekish script, 'To the most fair.' This was the globe Paris gave to Venus and set Troy burning. She who has it will ever be deemed the loveliest in the eyes of men. I will give this to you tonight if we talk together in the starlight."

The duchess propped her chin on her palm and meditated. There came before her mind a diverting picture of her late lord, the ancient Duke of Thebes, dozing hoggishly in his corner while she talked with another in the starlight. The young knight of Athens was fair, but very surely this young knight of Eleusis was fairer, and, after all, if he rode away tomorrow there would be an age-long time to pass in the company of Duke Baldwin's son. She decided quickly.

"Well, have your will if I win the golden apple. Come to the west postern of the palace tonight. I will see to it that the door is ajar. Mount the stair when I show a light from the window. Be very sure you bring the apple with you. Farewell."

She extended her hand, which Argathona took and feigned to salute. Then, swiftly, the wood-nymph turned and passed from the silken tent into the meadow. As the dryad came into the liberal air she breathed a great breath. It seemed to the daughter of the forest as if she had escaped from some strange place where subtle poison guising like sweet odor saturated the atmosphere and murdered all wholesome thoughts. She stretched her arms joyously, as one released from cramping labor, and, smiling to think that so far the woodland guile had triumphed, she moved towards her own pavilion. Instantly she was aware that the field which she had expected to find deserted still presented a scene of animation. Duke Baldwin with a little cloud of knights and courtiers about him was slowly tramping towards his palace with an angry gloom upon his countenance, which was reflected in varying shades of obsequious sympathy upon the faces of those who followed him. A little removed from these a gigantic soldier moved slowly across the field, his vacant, honest face overcast with melancholy. Still farther off she could see Simon standing in front of her pavilion, carefully counting gold pieces from one hand into the other and whistling blithely to himself. By the time she had reached her squire Duke Baldwin and his courtiers had disappeared from the field, the gigantic soldier had vanished, and the lists were vacant save for herself and Simon.

19

SIMON THE STALWART

When Duke Baldwin, leaving the gallery in no good-humor with the world to ask after his vanquished son, entered the field, he found that his son had arisen and gone to his tent. Rainouart left with Count Ernault the assurance that he was unhurt, that he had been fairly overthrown by the best-planted blow he had ever received, and that his fall was due to no fatigue on his part, but solely to the greater skill of his antagonist. As Duke Baldwin listened frowningly to the phrases of the lord-marshal, he caught sight of a brawny fellow who was lounging in the lists at a little distance from the duke and the courtiers who accompanied him. This was Simon of Rouen, who, seeing that Argathona had been summoned to the pavilion of the Duchess of Thebes, thought he might as well while away the time by stretching his legs over the trampled turf. Even in a bad temper Duke Baldwin had an appreciation of a fine figure in a man, and the sight of Simon's proportions brought a sudden gleam of interest into his angry eyes. He cherished a taste for collecting giants, and he surveyed Simon with the eager appreciation of a possible purchaser. It never occurred to Duke Baldwin to doubt that any man-at-arms could be other than rejoiced to enter his service, just as it never occurred to him to doubt that any lady would be other than pleased to accept his homage.

"Yonder stands a tall fellow," the duke grunted into Count Ernault's ear; "stands he taller and broader than the pick of my body-guard?"

Count Ernault was not enjoying himself. The duke was in a beastly mood and hard to manage, and Count Ernault's elastic urbanity was strained to extreme tension. Desirous to gratify his master, he answered suavely that the fellow bulked big enough, but that he doubted if he surpassed, from toe to top, or from shoulder to shoulder, the mightiest of Duke Baldwin's giants. Duke Baldwin growled uncourteous disbelief in Count Ernault's skill in gauging height and width, not because he really disagreed with him, but because he was in the mood to contradict anything said by anybody, even a compliment to himself. He made his way to Simon and stared critically at him, and Simon supported his gaze composedly, looking into the duke's fierce eyes and longing to try a fall with him, for the duke was a mighty fellow.

"How tall are you, man?" the duke asked, and Simon answered:

"Six feet four, your grace."

"Are you as strong as you look?" was the duke's next question, and Simon smiled as he answered, somewhat ambiguously:

"I don't know how strong I look in your eyes, but whenever I look in a mirror I never take the plain face I see there for the face of a weakling."

Duke Baldwin was hugely strong, and he would have liked nothing better than to make a personal trial of Simon's vigor, if Simon had only been of gentle birth, or if, indeed, the two had been alone. It would not do, however, for Duke Baldwin to indulge in physical competition with a mere man-at-arms in the presence of the nobles, his courtiers, and guests. For an instant the idea came into Baldwin's mind to confer knighthood and title upon the unknown soldier for the sake of indulging his whim, but a moment's reflection warned him, unwilling, that this course would probably be found too eccentric in the eyes of his illustrious companions.

"Bid them send for Harald Haraldson," he said to Count Ernault, and while Count Ernault gave the order to a page, who sped like a greyhound to execute it, Duke Baldwin went on questioning Simon.

"Tell me, friend," he said, "have you seen the pygmies who serve in my body-guard?" Simon grinned.

"I have seen some of the laddies," he answered; "they may grow tall if they live long enough."

"There be some there that are taller than you," the duke answered; "do you think you are strong enough to overcome the smallest and the slightest of them?" Simon shrugged his shoulders.

"I should not like to hurt your gracious play-things," he answered, amiably, "but if you have, as you say, one among them that is taller than I, and broader of breadth, I will be heartily pleased to try a fall with him for the honor of Rouen."

"You have a good conceit of yourself," said the duke, grimly. "My giants are the pick of Europe, but if you will stand by your vaunt, here is your chance," and he pointed to where the little page came skipping back, followed slowly by a man who seemed, indeed, a monster in size and strength. The new-comer, with the fair hair and blue eyes of a Norseman, was, indeed, some four inches taller than Simon, and seemed broader across the shoulders. Simon eyed him approvingly as he came slowly to where the duke stood. The duke spoke with the Norseman.

"Harald Haraldson," he said, "here is a strange soldier who thinks he may prove as strong as you."

A suggestion of a smile for a moment disturbed the bland calm of the northern giant's face, as he answered in execrable French to the effect that the stranger must be a madman. Simon said nothing, and the duke, looking at the pair, felt his confidence in his own soldier swell within him and trumpet triumph.

"Will you try a fall with my partisan?" Duke Baldwin asked, clapping the northern giant confidentially on the shoulder and eying Simon sardonically.

"With all the pleasure in life," Simon answered, briskly.

"I take you at your word," said Duke Baldwin—"at this place, on this instant."

The lists were almost empty, the crowd outside had for the most part dispersed. Captain Fox and Captain Gander, Captain Bat and Captain Chanticleer, Captain Rat and Captain Badger, prowling at the heels of the departing multitude to pick up any little trifles that negligence might let fall, were among the few who noted signs of renewed animation in the enclosed space, and, noting, came again to the barriers and leaned upon them to see what might be towards. Their curiosity found its reward. Duke Baldwin had explained to Harald Haraldson that the French adventurer was willing to try a fall with him, and the Norse giant had looked pityingly upon the French adventurer, who, for his part, was brisk in getting him ready for the coming scuffle.

On the spot the Norseman stripped off his body armor, and in a few seconds the two men stood in their jerkins opposite to each other, while Duke Baldwin and the nobles with him watched hard by in a little group that gradually swelled its numbers as knight after knight emerged unarmored from his tent and joined it. All who were with Duke Baldwin were trained students of men, and to all it appeared patent that the French adventurer was over-matched, not merely in patent height but in no less patent breadth. Duke Baldwin, seeing the two men quiet and silent, waiting to begin, felt some uneasiness of mind. He knew, of course, that his man must win, and he would not have had it otherwise for much, and yet he was sorry to think that a countryman should be bested by the northerner. He again asked Simon if he persisted in his wild challenge, and, on Simon reiterating that he did, the duke, with a scowl of pity for his foolhardiness, gave the signal and the struggle began.

The two men linked their arms each round the other's body, and stood so for some seconds motionless, wedded pillars of mighty flesh. As they waited thus there came into Simon's mind the thought of the last time he had so clasped an adversary, and of his brief contact with the soft flesh of the wood-maiden, and of his unparalleled overthrow. Then the Norseman, obviously surprised by the strength of Simon's clasp, made a strenuous effort to lift Simon from his feet, and found that he might as well have attempted to lift a pillar of the Parthenon. Frank astonishment reigned in the faces of all the spectators, who had been confident that, though the Frenchman showed a sturdy fellow enough, he would be little less than a plaything in the hands of the northern Goliath. But their astonishment deepened into marvel when Simon, striving in turn with no palpable exertion of force, plucked his gigantic adversary from the ground, and, wrenching himself free from his clasp, flung Harald Haraldson heavily to the earth. The Norseman was up in an instant and ready to renew the tussle, but the duke, in a very ill humor, forbade it. This was his second discomfiture that day, and he chafed at it.

"No more," he said; "go your ways, Harald," and as the defeated northerner withdrew, the duke turned again to Simon and offered to take him into his service. Simon shook his head.

"I cannot serve two masters," he said, "and I will not leave the master I serve now."

"Whom do you serve?" the duke asked, and Simon answered:

"I serve the Prince of Eleusis."

For the second time that day the name of the Prince of Eleusis had been associated with the defeat of Duke Baldwin's wish, and it was very plain that his rage longed to interpret itself in furious speech. But the Prince of Eleusis was the conqueror of Rainouart, and under the conditions not to be spoken ill of by Rainouart's father, so swallowing his rage as well as he was able, Duke Baldwin thrust a number of gold pieces into Simon's ready fingers and stamped sulkily away in the direction of his palace, followed in discreet silence by his courtiers and his knights.

20

THE PROMISE OF RAINOUART

When Simon of Rouen saw Argathona speeding towards him across the meadow, he stopped counting his gold pieces and turned to counting his heart-beats. With every new occasion now of seeing the girl, were it but a few minutes since a parting, his heart must needs drum the same foolish music, to his vexation, yet to his greater vexation he knew that he would not have it otherwise. He had forgotten her mad fancy of immortality; he could never forget her glorious beauty and her glorious strength, and at times the slow thought was forged in the patient stithy of his wits that if in his youth he had met such a mate, Simon of Rouen might now have shown another man than Simon the soldier of fortune with his body soiled with the world's mire and his lips stained with the world's wine. But he kept such thoughts to himself, partly because he would have found it hard to throw them into words, but chiefly because he dreaded that they might peril a friendship which he cherished as his breath. Now as the girl neared him he rose to greet her in a rapture, shovelling Duke Baldwin's gold pieces into his pouch that he might have both hands free to applaud her.

"You have done well, lad," he cried, as she came a-nigh, then hurriedly would have mended the matter, adding, "I should say, you have done well, lass."

Argathona set a finger to her lips and smiled protest.

"You must think of me as a boy, friend," she entreated; "the girl of the greenwood has forgotten her girlhood while she wears this golden gear."

Simon looked contrition for his slip.

"How in Heaven's name did you do it?" he questioned. "You are amazing strong for so slim a strip, but it takes more skill than strength to overtumble a practised cavalier that had just upset no fewer than seven gallant gentlemen."

"I have little joy in my victory," Argathona answered, sadly, "but the thing had to be, for my lover is bewitched, and it will be hard to win him to his wits again, for as I think none can unspell him save she that has cast the spell."

"That seems a grim task," said Simon, "but in the mean time you have won his horse and armor."

"I build some hopes on that," the girl answered; "help me to disarm," and she passed into the tent, followed by Simon. Scarcely had she begun, however, to peel off her steel when a voice was heard without calling for the Prince of Eleusis. Straightway Simon went into the open, where he found the page of Rainouart at the tent's door, and the heir of Athens standing a little way apart in the meadow. The page bade Simon tell his master that Sir Rainouart, Prince of Athens, was without and desired speech with him. Simon returned to the tent and delivered Rainouart's message, whereupon Argathona bade admit him, and Simon brought Rainouart to her and left her with the young man. Rainouart's eyes were downcast, and it was plain that, strive as he might, he was dejected at his most strange, most unexpected defeat. He broached his business immediately.

"Knight of Eleusis," he began, "you have won the toss, and by the rules of the tourney you have the conqueror's right to my horse and armor. As for the armor it shall be carried to your tent, but for the steed, it was a gift to me from one whose gifts are dear to me"—he sighed a little as he spoke, and Argathona was angry with him and pitied him. "If you will let me ransom it at your hands, I think there is nothing you can ask that the treasury of the Duke of Athens cannot amply answer."

The little red flame of rage that threatened for a moment to sear the heart of Argathona was instantly drowned in a great wave of sorrow for the gallant lad so tragically beguiled. All her womanhood longed to clasp him in her arms and kiss him tenderly, and tell him the truth and her name and renew their loves. But she knew that she would speak in vain. Her clear spirit saw that his eyes were purblind, that his soul was swaddled with sorceries, and that only she who had set the spell upon him could unspell his senses. Sad and frank she addressed him:

"Fair lord, I do not think I could ever have overthrown you if you carried a true heart in your body. Somewhere, I think, some maiden calls you false."

Rainouart's brows clouded.

"It is enough to have overthrown me without finding such shameful reason for my fate. You are my conqueror, with whom it were dishonor to quarrel while my defeat is unredeemed. But when I am quit with you and a new sun reigns in heaven, I shall be very glad to give you the lie. So if you will take ransom for my charger, I pray you to name your price, and I will pay it were it all my estate and all my credit."

Argathona answered the loyal disloyal with an anguish in her voice which he did not understand, being too busy with his own humiliation.

"Prince of Athens, will you promise me by your knightly chivalry to grant me, in lieu of golden ransom for this horse you cherish so dearly, whatever favor I may pray of you?"

Rainouart stared at his antagonist with a surprise that was almost a suspicion, yet even his thickened vision could see nothing but candor in the brave face opposed to him.

"I will grant you whatever favor you may pray of me," he promised, "that is consistent with the laws of honor and the conduct of a chivalrous knight."

"Is there anyone in the world," Argathona asked, "so bold as to entreat Rainouart of Athens to infringe in the least the laws of honor, or to smirch with the slightest stain the conduct of a chivalrous knight? Have I your promise?"

"I give you my promise," Rainouart declared, holding out his right hand, that Argathona clasped in hers; "it is ask and have."

"It is a little thing," said Argathona, slowly, still holding the hand of the prince, "yet it may come to carry a great meaning. All I demand of you is that when you are alone tonight with your bride, if she offer you a draught of wine to drink you do not drink it, but feign to do so, and feign to fall asleep."

The young prince looked angrily into the frank eyes that made him think, he knew not why, of forest fountains, and marvel why the thought made him sad. Suddenly a ray of light shone on his darkness, for his old memories of Esclaramonde, and of all that men and women once said of her, rekindled in the gray ashes of his enchantment, and his spirit was vexed with bewildering suspicions.

"That is a strange request," he said, "for it meddles with my lady, who has nothing to do with our parley."

"It is a request that you are bound to answer," Argathona insisted, "for, by my faith, it offends not against your chivalry. If the Lady Esclaramonde offers you to drink tonight you will not drink. She may not do so; then you are absolved. But if she do you will not drink, but you will feign to drink and you will feign to fall asleep."

"And what then, if I do this?" Rainouart asked. He felt that he must obey, he felt that Esclaramonde had someway ensnared him. He felt all this dimly, incoherently, but there was a kind of hope in his heart.

"If within a little piece of time you are not glad of your feigning," Argathona answered, "why, you may put it by and all is well, and your black horse neighs in your stable. Have I your promise?"

Her eyes were fixed intently upon his. She felt that she was struggling with the spell that numbed his real self. Her spirit commanded him to obey. He yielded to the strong influence. Bitter distrust of Esclaramonde struggled against her sorceries and justified him in entertaining the test.

"I have given you my promise," he said, gravely, "and will not gainsay it."

Argathona repeated her demand: "If the duchess offers you to drink to-night you will not drink, but will feign to do so and will feign to fall asleep."

Rainouart saluted her and passed out of the tent, and she listened to his footsteps dying away over the grass. Then she called to Simon, and told him she was full of cheer, and bade him see that the prince's horse was surrendered to his page. When Simon was gone on this errand, Argathona fell on her knees in a corner and began to cry, just for all the world as if she were human.

21

THE WINE OF ESCLARAMONDE

Duke Baldwin had devoted the fairest rooms in his palace to the Duchess Esclaramonde of Thebes before her arrival, when he thought of her only as a visitor whom he might—and the rumors of her encouraged the thought—persuade with no great pains to an intimacy of friendship. The best part of the left wing of the palace was consecrated to her use, and its spacious rooms that looked upon the plain of Athens were furnished and adorned in the most noble manner that the age could compass. Duke Baldwin loved to be prodigal of pleasures to others when the prodigality enforced an almost aching sense of gratitude, and probably any woman in the world, with the exception of the Lady Esclaramonde, would have felt at least a little grateful to Duke Baldwin. All that gold and silver and bronze and ivory and ebony and silks and furs and jewels could lend to make her rooms a little paradise of luxury had been done under the duke's orders by those who knew better than the burly duke how to grace the haven of a fair dame. Money that would have paid twice over the outstanding demands of the Catalan Grand Company had been squandered with a free hand to make a fitting background for the imperious beauty of the lady of Thebes. In fulsome compliment that might have been flagrant irony, the mosaic walls were hung with exquisite arras, upon which the cunning hands of many craftsmen had woven amorous images from every passionate tale of love.

All this the bluff duke had done, and done cheerfully, when his only thoughts concerning his comely visitor were of a personal nature. But when the duchess rode to his gates on that May evening, bearing his son's inanimate body with her, and, while that body still lay inanimate, told the lord of Athens that her troth was plighted to his son, Duke Baldwin's cheerfulness dwindled no whit. His palace hummed with ebullient compliance; he would have no lack of consolation, while his foolish son had done a wise thing unawares. So Duke Baldwin resigned without a sigh all thoughts of his fair Theban neighbor, save as a daughter-in-law, and chuckled inwardly at the little less than prophetic instinct which had led him to prepare so fair a nest for her homing. As for Esclaramonde, who had started upon her journey in a spirit of perfect willingness to entertain with complaisance any homage that the Duke of Athens might lay at her feet, she now readily dressed her temper to accept his paternal caresses, while she smiled significant appreciation of the duke's ostentatious care for her comfort.

On the evening of the day when the great tournament had been fought and won and lost, four of the duchess's favorite women, delicate dissolute minions, waited for their lady's coming in her dimly lit dwelling room. Amicia and Hildeletha, Yelette and Aveline, were huddled together in the alcove of the window, looking out upon the moonlit plain and listening to the sounds of revelry in the rooms below. They had left those rooms, they had left that revelry a little while agone, daintily flushed with wine, daintily prodigal of love-promises, that they might be sure that all was ready for their mistress when she rose from the royal feast. Now they were busy disentangling the imbroglio of their assignations, pitting lover against lover, and trying to remember times and places of meeting, lightly agreed to, and no less lightly forgotten or confused with other trysts.

It had been a wonderful day for the merry girls. There was the tournament in the morning with its unexpected end. Then there was the solemn ceremonial of marriage in the afternoon, when the Archbishop of Athens pronounced his benediction on the heir to the dukedom of Athens and the wondrous widow of Thebes. Then came the splendid banquet stretching through the hours. Now in a little while the bridal pair would be conducted in triumph to the duchess's apartments, and speedily thereafter Amicia and Hildeletha, Yelette and Aveline, would be free to pick their paths in pursuit of love. Meanwhile they babbled with bated breath of the duchess, and her old lord, and her many lovers, and of her fire-new groom who seemed to dwell in a dream even while he knelt at the altar. But they marvelled most over the stranger knight, the Prince of Eleusis, the victor of the lists, who came to the banquet habited in white and gold and sat between two of the fairest ladies of Duke Baldwin's court, and while he himself spoke little, listened to their chatter with a bright, indefinable smile. All the women, it seemed, thought him handsome as the day, and the men swore that he was a comely youth, and those that were nigh enough to see noted that he ate no food but fruit and drank no drink but water, and wondered how such meat could feed such vigor. Each of the gossip girls would have been glad to see the conqueror at still closer quarters, for their places at table were far from where he sat. They were experts in the points of men, and would fain have compared him with their immediate lovers. But they watched him closely, and thought that he seemed both merry and sad at the prattle of his companions, and they agreed that if Sir Rainouart kept his eyes ever upon the face of his bride, their Lady Esclaramonde shot many a glance of an admiration they knew well how to interpret at the grave face of the stranger. And therewith the talk swayed lightly back to their lady, the duchess, and the fair heads pressed together and the sweet voices chuckled over the echoes of many scandals.

Suddenly the sounds of revelry beneath them dwindled, and the minxes heard the swell of joyous music and the tread of marching feet. They sprang to their feet in haste, ready for obeisance, ready for service. The mirthful music and the marching feet came nearer and yet nearer, filling all the stairways and corridors with joyous noise. Then the great entrance door swung open, and a little cluster of golden pages entered bearing scented torches that flooded the room with yellow light. These in turn were followed by a train of fair maidens in white robes, who scattered white roses on the floor and sang to the music of a band of lutanists, the epithalamium which Sir Guy of Hainault had composed in honor of the bride and bridegroom. And this was the song they sang:

> "Lo, the lovely pair are wed,
> > Making one
> Gallantry and goodlihead,
> > Moon and Sun:
> Now we bring the bride to bed,
> > Wedding done;
> Flesh to flesh divinely led,
> > Bone to bone.
>
> From the pillows where her head
> > Lay alone
> Weary solitude has fled,
> > Wisely flown.
>
> She must share her wine and bread,
> > Share her throne,
> With the lover, dear and dread,
> > All her own,
> Till the one for other dead
> > Maketh moan.
>
> All is sung and all is said:
> > Loose her zone!"

As the last words of the song, the last notes of the music, sobbed away into silence, the singing maidens made a lane from the door like two lines of tall white lilies, and through the doorway adown the lane came Duke Baldwin in his bravery holding the Duchess Esclaramonde by the hand, while beneath the heavy tramp of the knight and the light tread of the lady the crushed white petals of the scattered roses suspired a haunting perfume sickly sweet.

Even to the familiar cynical eyes of her women, Esclaramonde at that moment showed radiantly fair. Flattery had fanned her cheeks to their loveliest color; triumph had lighted her eyes with their brightest fire; passion mantled her body with its atmosphere of flame.

In an instant Rainouart followed, escorted by Count Ernault, and it seemed to the keen eyes of the dainty waiting-women that his bearing showed less mazed than of late, and that his look was keener than it had seemed since his misadventure in the wood. "Marriage will make a new man of our mooncalf," Yelette whispered into the ears of Aveline, with a sauciness that was partly resentful, for she remembered with a sting how, in spite of her allegiance to her mistress, she had wasted her witcheries on his indifference on the morrow of their arrival at his father's court. "We may have our turn yet," Aveline answered, mockingly, for she, too, was one of the tempters who had failed to tempt, in which particular the two girls from Thebes wore the same kind of shoes that were worn by every delectable dame of Duke Baldwin's court. Then "Hush," cried Hildeletha, as through the doorway thronged those who interested the damsels more than their predecessors.

These were the knights of the court and the knightly visitors—Sir Guy of Hainault, Sir Jaufre de Brabant, Sir Raymond of Provence, Sir Ambrose of Blois, and the rest of Duke Baldwin's chivalry; Andronicus Palæologus, Prince Demetrius of Epirus, and the other noble visitors, squiring and gallanting smiling women. After these came the leaders of the Catalan Grand Company, with Fernand Ximenes at their head, gravely insolent to the ladies they attended, watching the vivid scene with impassive faces, indifferent to the merrymaking of the man who owed them their pay, but not indifferent, with the keen eye of your practised bandit, to the delightful possibilities from the bandit's point of view, if only Athens were to sack. And so the great room filled with light and color and laughter, and through all and over all, immeshing all in slender threads of melody, ran the tender wailing of the lutes.

Duke Baldwin bowed the Duchess of Thebes to the high seat on the dais, and paid her some compliments at once florid and full blooded, which must have embarrassed a maiden, and at which the duchess, with no little difficulty recalling far earlier memories, affected embarrassment. Then the lord of Athens, suggesting that the young couple had liefer be left alone, reminded the assembly of brilliant men and beautiful women that supper was still towards, and so with many smiles and salutations and good wishes the bright company faded in music from the room. A glance and a gesture from Esclaramonde sent Amicia and Hildeletha, Yelette and Aveline, tripping at their heels, and so the bride and groom were left alone together, face to face in the place that swooned with the scent of trampled roses.

The man and woman stood opposite to each other for a while in silence, Esclaramonde thinking inscrutable thoughts, Rainouart gazing at her like a man who wakes from sleep-walking and wonders why he has come to such a spot and how. Esclaramonde was habited in a robe of many reds, subtly blended, for she wished through the richness of these shifting tints to recall some royal rose imperial in its wealth of crimson petals, yet still a tender pink at the core. Indeed, Rainouart thought of a rose as he looked at her: his thoughts had been all of roses since he saw her so clad at the ducal banquet, and because of the rose his heart was full of care and travail. While his senses spurred him to woo such voluptuous beauty, enigmatical memories cried out to him strange forest cries; it was as if soft voices were calling at his ears, asking, "Is this the rose of the guarded garden, is this the noble rose of the world?" But her witchery was potent over his wits; his spirit seemed tugged this way and that inexplicably; he was bewildered; he would and he would not. At last he found voice under the spell of those lamping eyes that lured his pulses, and he stretched out his hands to the wonderful woman.

"To my arms, fair wife!" he cried, and though his voice sounded unreal in his ears, as if it were an echo of speech whispered to him by other lips, it rang real enough in the ears of Esclaramonde, and almost she regretted for the space of half a second that she could not answer promptly to the call. But swiftly she thought of the golden apple, swiftly she remembered that her lord would be no less loving when the night was a little older, and his senses had rekindled from unremembered sleep. She lifted her hand for a moment as if to stay his vehement advance; then she moved to the table, where a golden beaker stood circled with golden goblets, and she saw that the beaker was brimmed with wine. Dexterously and unseen of Rainouart she drew from her girdle a tiny golden phial, jerked the contents into one of the goblets and slipped the phial out of sight. Then she poured two full cups of wine, and held out the treasonable cup in her white hand to her lover.

"Pledge our health and happiness," she said, and her voice and eyes commanded, though voice and eyes seemed only to entreat.

As a shaft of sunlight suddenly pierces a mist, so suddenly did Rainouart's promise to the Prince of Eleusis drive its dart through the dark web of desire that enveloped his mind. Through all the wedding ceremony, through all the later festival, overcrowed by the magic of Esclaramonde, he had forgotten that pledge to the knight who had conquered him. Now it lived again with the duchess's proffer and beat furiously at his heart. He took the cup from his bride's hands and looked eagerly into her eyes, luminous and cryptic as the eyes of a sphinx.

"To your health, Fidelity," he murmured, half in idolatry, half in irony, as he lifted the cup to his lips.

The words "feign to drink" now buzzed in his ears imperative, and he seemed to see that in the glance of Esclaramonde which accentuated their meaning. He carried the cup to the open window and looked out over the wide plain of Attica. He was conscious that the duchess was watching him curiously, and the words of the stranger knight seemed to scourge his numbed intelligence into vitality. Looking steadily at Esclaramonde, he tilted the cup, but no drop of the red wine rippled over his lips. Then he set down the cup on the window-ledge and moved towards his consort. "Feign to sleep" hummed in his ears, and he moved sluggishly, obedient to a will that proved stronger than the will of Thebes.

"Is not the night warm and heavy?" he asked, and his lips and his lids seemed drawn with desire of sleep. Turning towards the casement he pointed at the Athenian sky blazing with its myriad eyes. "The stars swoon and fall from heaven!" he cried. He moved towards her with a reeling gait. "Shall I catch you a handful," he gasped, and so, struggling towards her with out-stretched palms, he stumbled to the table and fell across it with his face between his arms, a seeming heap of sleeping flesh.

The duchess, who had sipped prettily at her cup while she watched him, now set the vessel down upon the table, and bending softly over Rainouart, touched him on the shoulder, and whispered his name to him, wooing. But Rainouart of Athens lay inanimate, making no sign, and the lady of Thebes smiled malignly.

"Sleep sound, my prince," she muttered, "and dream content, and wake fresh and credulous. My boy-lover is fairer than you, and he woos with a golden apple."

She turned away from her motionless lord, and took up a little golden lamp that stood burning on the table hard by the beaker of wine. Going to the open window, she leaned out into the blueness of the night, and held the lamp high above her head, and its tiny flame burned steadily in the still air. The enchanting beauty of the Athenian plain, steeped in moonlight and starlight, haunted by a million divine memories, said nothing to Esclaramonde. She was thinking only of a golden toy which she desired to own, and of a youth with golden hair whom she desired to kiss. After a little while she came back to the room and set down the lamp, and walked about slowly hither and thither as a cat walks, crooning to herself the burden of an ancient song:

> *"Dwelt a queen in Nineveh*
> (*Take my heart, Semiramis*),
> *Fairer than the dawn of day*
> *In the strength of summer is;*
> *Falser than the Moon of May*
> *Mirrored in the black abyss*
> *Of the stream by Nineveh,*
> *Where the bodies drift and sway*
> *Of the lords who loved amiss,*
> *Of the drowned who died for this—*

Once to hold a queen at play,
Once her crimson mouth to kiss;
Tigris bears them to the bay,
Far away from Nineveh
        (Take my heart, Semiramis)."

22

REMEMBER THE GREENWOOD

She had scarcely finished the verse when the arras at the side of the window was drawn back, the little door of the turret-stair closed, and Argathona came into the room. She was habited in white, with a silken tunic girdled with a golden belt, and she looked like a noble youth. She entered so quietly that Esclaramonde did not know of her coming till she turned in her pacing of the floor and saw the slender, beautiful figure facing her.

Esclaramonde moved eagerly to the new-comer, with out-stretched hands and eyes bright with cupidity.

"You are welcome," she said, quickly, and indeed she was pleased to greet the radiant youth, but her hottest thought was for the promised toy, and she added, "Give me my gift."

Argathona came a little way down the room, looking steadfastly at the man who lay across the table with his head between his extended arms.

"Is your lord asleep?" she asked, and the duchess made a grimace as she answered:

"He is never my lord, though I be ever his lady. Where is your toy of the gods?"

Argathona was still looking at the recumbent figure, and she questioned again:

"You are sure he is asleep?"

Esclaramonde clasped and unclasped her fine fingers impatiently.

"You tease like a peevish child," she protested. "I blended his drink with such syrups that the trump of Jove would not wake him for an hour to come. Quick, my gift."

Argathona slipped her hand into the pouch that hung from her girdle, and let her fingers rest on the golden apple that lay there. She felt that she trembled as she touched it, and that her heart was beating to a most unfamiliar time. For now she was face to face with her enemy, now or never she must prevail upon her enemy to unspell the spell that had been cast upon her lover. She spoke again, while she still kept the apple hidden.

"You remember the terms of our bargain? If I give you the golden apple you give me your love."

"Yes," Esclaramonde cried, angrily, "yes, fretful. Why do you waste time thus?"

Now Argathona drew out the golden apple from her pouch and showed it in the hollow of her hand. That golden apple was a wonderful toy, for while it had all the shape and semblance of the living fruit, it glowed on the white palm of the dryad as if its precious metal had been steeped in the essential sunlight, in the essential starlight, and forever gave off something of the glory of the sun and stars. The duchess glowed a lively red as she saw the splendid idol, and instinctively, for an instant, shielded with her fingers her eyes against its brightness, while she gave a little animal cry of admiration. But she swiftly lowered her fingers from her face and made a clutch at the marvellous image, but Argathona avoided her, and Argathona's hand shut over the apple.

"What will you tell your lord when he wakes?" she asked, still gazing at young Athens where he lay.

The duchess banged her hands together, and her eyes blazed with frustrated covetousness.

"If you call him my lord again," she cried, "I shall hate you. He is my servant, my slave, my puppet; he shall believe what I please when he wakes. Why, he will not know that he has slept at all, and as for this trinket, how can he know what riches I hold in my treasury at Thebes? Give me my gift, sweet minion."

Argathona looked straight into the face of Esclaramonde, and her eyes were bright and stern.

"Do you love this man?" she asked, and she pointed with the hand that held the desirable apple to where Rainouart lay huddled on the table. Esclaramonde made a face of disdain.

"Love is a word of many meanings. He is a prince and he is rich; he is young and he is comely. He is different from the others I have loved, and for the time he pleases me."

Argathona's face was set and her voice was cold as she spoke again, asking the fateful question,

"How did you come to care for this man?"

The duchess gave a little laugh that brimmed with malicious memories.

"I knew him first a while ago in France, when he was counted a cold monster, and indeed I failed to melt his ice, though I tried my liveliest. Then fate flung him at my feet the other day in the haunted wood."

"And he loved you at once," Argathona asked, "loved you with all his heart and soul?"

Esclaramonde flung back her crowned head and laughed mockingly at her questioner.

"Am I not comely enough to be so loved?" she retorted, and Argathona, seizing sudden chance, bent her head in acquiescence.

"If he love you so well," she sighed, "were it not shame for us to do him wrong? Let us part now in honor, and when he wakes you will rejoice to be worthy of his loyal love."

And Argathona made as if she would go from the room, but she was cunning, and the golden apple gleamed through the net of her fingers. Rage flamed hotly in the eyes and cheeks of Esclaramonde.

"You question like a cold priest," she complained, "when you should clasp like a warm lover. But you can go if you please when you give me the trinket."

And she held out her hand imperiously, but Argathona still kept the apple. Now Esclaramonde was very loath to lose her lover though she professed indifference, and she was firmly determined to gain the apple.

"Nay," said Argathona, craftily, "I am a Greek and give nothing for nothing. But I would your lord were not so single-hearted a lover, for my vows deny me to wrong him."

Esclaramonde clinched her hands so tightly that the nails of her fingers hurt her palms.

"You are a precise fool," she raged; "but you can send your fastidious conscience to sleep. For though my husband loves me now and thinks he never loved other woman, he gave his great heart like a baby to some country girl in the woods."

Argathona held out the globe of gold alluringly, just out of reach of the duchess, while she asked, "Are you sure of this?" and Esclaramonde, her hungry eyes fixed on the apple and her hungry senses fixed upon the youth, answered vehemently:

"Most sure, for in truth it was not I who saved him from the robbers. When I came he was senseless on the grass, and a tall fellow that stood by told me a tale of some forest girl who scared away the thieves, and to whom my love-calf promptly gave his heart. Indeed, when he came to his senses I had much ado to persuade him that this girl was the trick of a fevered dream, and that I was his rescuer, I his promised wife."

The dryad watched her with firm, unchanging eyes. So, long ago, her mother in the woodland might have watched unfearing the dangerous presence of a snake.

"Why did you do this?" Argathona asked. "Did you love him so very dearly?"

The duchess laughed impatiently, for the apple proved harder to win than she had deemed, and the telling of the tale vexed her a little.

"I love very dearly the gift that he can give. Though I be a great lady he makes me a greater. It is much to be Duchess of Thebes today; it is more to be Duchess of Athens tomorrow."

There was a little pause, and Argathona's eyes travelled from the duchess to the man at the table and back again.

"Come," cried Esclaramonde, "are you content? Think nothing of him. I will wear him as the rich cloak of my loves."

The duchess was looking eagerly at Argathona, and Argathona, glancing aside, saw that the man at the table stirred and seemed about to move, and she saw that the prince's fingers were gripping the hilt of his dagger.

"I am content," Argathona answered, and tossed the golden apple to Esclaramonde, who caught it in the cup of her joined hands joyously. "Yet I think there were a better gift for you."

"What is that?" Esclaramonde questioned, greedily, and as she spoke the young Prince of Athens sprang to his feet, and came towards her with his drawn dagger in his hand.

"A true blade in your false heart," Rainouart said, and raised his weapon on high.

Esclaramonde fell at his feet and grovelled on the floor, letting the apple roll away. It was as horridly amazing to her that her bridegroom could rise from the cup she had qualified as it would have been horridly amazing if her old spouse had risen from the dead. Both were catastrophes of nature too appalling to understand, and her courage went from her in a breath and her blood was as water. She could do nothing but crouch upon the ground and moan to her master not to kill her.

Rainouart looked down upon her abjection with a sick spirit, and slowly lowered his weapon.

"You have a woman's body that must be pitied," he said, in sorrowful scorn, "but the devil it shelters must be hid. We will find cloisters for you. But you must give me back my ring."

He bent and caught at her up-stretched, appealing hands, and drew from her finger the ring that had been his mother's. He plucked from his finger the ruby that Esclaramonde had set there and cast it at her feet, while he set his own ring in its old place. Then he turned from her sprawling to Argathona, where she stood impassive with folded arms. He was all himself again; the woman's confession had unspelled him; his spirit seemed like a clean mirror waiting to reflect the face of a liberated memory. He would see the face soon, he was sure of it, the face of his beloved, but in the meanwhile there was knightly work to do.

"You are a man," he said. "You have unsealed my soul, but you have snared a woman to her shame. We fought today in sport; we fight tonight in earnest."

Argathona moved a pace nearer to the angry prince, looking straight into his eyes.

"Oh, Phœnix of knighthood," she said, smiling, and tenderly reproachful, "where is your fidelity? Think of the greenwood, knight; think of your vows of love, and tell me where is the maid who heard them. Think of your proffered ring, and tell me where it should be now."

Rainouart looked at her in amazement. Though he knew now that he had been deceived, the shadow of that deception still lay heavy upon him and he saw as in a mist. The woman on the ground, freed for the instant from her fear of death, lifted her head unheeded by the others and listened intently with a growing hope in her eyes. But even while she cowered and listened she snatched greedily at her ruby and put it quickly on her finger. The apple lay out of her reach.

"Who are you?" the prince cried, in a great wonder, and let the dagger fall clattering from his hand upon the floor. Argathona came near to him and put her face close to his.

"Look in my eyes, lover, my lover. Though I wear a boy's coat, it covers a girl's heart that was given to you in the greenwood the night you fell among thieves."

She caught both his hands in hers as she spoke and pressed them fondly upon her bosom, and so he was very sure that it was a woman who spoke to him.

"Remember my face," Argathona chanted. "Remember the song of the forest. Remember the greenwood dappled with the moonlight. Remember my face bending over you."

It was to Rainouart as if a curtain had been drawn aside and he looked through an open window on the rose-garden of his dreams.

"I remember the greenwood," he cried; "I remember you. I thank God for my memory. My eyes were sealed so that I could not see, but the spell is lifted from my spirit and my vision is clear. Can you forgive me, my love?"

Argathona looked into his beseeching face with infinite tenderness and infinite love.

"What is there to forgive?" she whispered. "You were snared; you were betrayed; you believed me no more than the sweet-seeming of a dream. But because I was sure that you loved me, who loved you with all my heart, I came to set you free."

"Dear love," said Rainouart, "you are the bravest and the fairest of women, and I worship you with my soul. Your life is mine, my life is yours from now to the end of ends."

"Come from here," wooed Argathona softly; "quit the desecrated city, quit its shameful, shameless citizens. Come to the sweet, clean greenwood, my lover, for there we shall dwell together, free from ache and care, skilled in the secrets of the seasons, the promise of spring, and the gladness of summer, and the rapture of autumn; and the sun shall be our comfort by day, and the stars shall be our torches by night, and the green grass shall be our couch, and the leaves our curtains, and the free air our friend. And when winter comes with its snows and its rains, and its fury of winds, we shall hide in caves or the ruins of temples, and build us fires to warm us, and I will sing you songs of the world before the flight of the gods, and tell you tales of the days of gold. And we shall feed on the fruits of the earth, and all the beasts and birds of the forest shall be our companions, and the glory and the holiness of love shall be our inheritance for all our days."

Now while she spoke it seemed to the charmed senses of Rainouart that his spirit had achieved its best, and that he had passed forever from the mystic rose-garden holding the noble rose to his heart. And the rose of the world was a maiden, and her face was the face of Argathona.

"I will come with you to the greenwood," Rainouart answered, exultant. "Honor and truth and purity and the simple life abide there, and there we shall live and love till our pulses cease to beat. I love you forever."

And Argathona echoed him, radiant, "I love you forever," and she forgot that he was mortal and she immortal, and her face was near to his, and the lips of the lovers met. Them seemed they were already in the greenwood; them seemed they were alone; in their joy they had forgotten Athens; in their joy they had forgotten Esclaramonde.

Slowly the woman on the floor had edged her way nearer and nearer to the pair, and now her fingers closed upon the hilt of the fallen dagger. Argathona, her first kiss taken and given, released herself from her lover's clasp, and holding him by the hand turned and made to lead him towards the turret door. At that moment Esclaramonde gripped the dagger, and, leaping to her feet, sprang forward and stabbed the Prince of Athens in the side. Rainouart, taken unawares, under the impact of the duchess's body flung so fiercely against him, reeled, and, making to turn, tripped and fell towards the table, striking his head against it and dropping thence to the ground. Esclaramonde stooped over him to repeat her stroke, but she had not time. Argathona was upon her, eagle-swift, eagle-fierce, eagle-strong. She plucked the dagger from the duchess's clutch, and flung her across the room to fall in a heap by the door. Then Argathona, paying no more heed to her enemy, bent over Rainouart. He was unconscious from the head stroke; his wound was bleeding freely, and Argathona busied herself to stanch the flow, making little moans over him the while, like a mother over an ailing child. Their second meeting, like their first, was stained with blood. As for Esclaramonde, when she found herself unheeded she crawled to her feet and beat furiously upon the gong.

"Help! help! help!" she cried, and the sound of her screaming voice and the sound of the beaten brass reverberated horridly through the night.

23

SIMON'S CHARGE

While the duchess was hammering at the gong and screaming furiously for help, and while from the rooms below, where revelry was toward, came now the noise of answering cries and clamor, the arras that masked the door of the turret was dashed aside and Simon sprang into the room. From where he waited for Argathona, below in the shadow of the tower, the shrieking of the duchess had reached his ears, and he lost no time in leaping up the turret stairs to see what had happened. In a moment his eyes took in the scene—the blood-stained weapon on the floor, the duchess screaming and beating on the gong, the young Lord of Athens stretched his length in blood, and Argathona bowed in care above him. Simon sprang to her side.

"Heaven's pity, maiden," he said, anxiously. "How are you betrayed?"

Argathona looked up at him with calm, melancholy eyes.

"My love is wounded," she answered quietly, "and he has swooned from his fall, being still weakened by the onslaught in the wood, but there is no fear for him."

The dryad had to speak close into Simon's ear, for the continued calling of the duchess and the growing clamor in the now aroused palace made it hard for him to hear.

From her bosom she drew a handful of leaves, and pressed them into Simon's palms.

"These are leaves of the herb of healing," she whispered. "I have set some on his hurt to stop the blood. Renew them soon, bruise them in his drink, and he will be whole within a day. I think it may prove that I cannot wait here, so you must tend him."

"I have sworn to serve you and stay with you—" Simon began, but Argathona stopped him.

"You serve me best in serving him," she remonstrated, "and when he is hale you must bring him to me safe and sound in the greenwood."

Simon promised with his heart, and would have promised with his lips but there was no time to say more. The billows of sound in the palace had swelled to a mighty rush and trampling of feet, and in another instant the door was flung open, and many knights came into the room—Count Ernault,

Sir Guy, Sir Jaufre, Fernand Ximenes, and others who had been tasting the duke's cheer.

"Who calls for help?" Count Ernault asked, looking around him in amazement.

The Duchess Esclaramonde was standing full height with her hands extended in appeal.

"I call for help," she cried. "Where is the Duke of Athens?"

Count Ernault sprang forward to where Rainouart lay with Argathona and Simon supporting him.

"What ails the prince?" he asked, and as Simon growled back, "The she-devil from Thebes has stabbed him," Ernault turned to the knights who were hot upon his heels and bade them keep back and let the prince have air. The gentlemen of Thebes among the throng separated themselves from the others and ranged themselves behind their duchess, questioning her and whispering together. Fernand Ximenes was already by her side.

"Fear nothing," he said, softly, "I am your friend," and then he stood apart, silent and watchful. Along the corridor came the thunder of heavy feet.

"Here is the duke," cried Jaufre de Brabant, and even as he spoke Duke Baldwin staggered into the room. He had been eating hugely, he had been drinking deeply, he was flushed with meat and wine, and furious at the interruption which had taken him from table. He glared around him like a baited bull, seeing little at first, for his eyes swam with the drink he carried and the confusion of the shifting lights.

"What is the matter?" he bellowed, his raging face turning from one to other of those about him. Then catching sight of his son upon the ground, and the duchess standing apart, and the blood-stained dagger upon the floor between them, he veered to her in a hot fury.

"Woman, what have you done?" he vociferated. Esclaramonde fell on her knees and stretched out her hands to him, but her voice was full of menace, though her words were words of entreaty.

"Justice, great duke," she shrilled, "justice on my false lord. Although he is your son, he is still your subject, and amenable to all the laws of chivalry and honor."

The duke moved upon the kneeling woman, lifting his great hands as if to strike her, whereat there was murmur among the Thebans and many hands set to sword-hilts.

"Woman, what have you done?" he asked again, and again she answered him defiantly, conscious of her backing, conscious of the neighborhood of Fernand Ximenes, conscious of the chivalry of the duke.

"Justice," she answered again, "justice on my false lord, who sought to drug my senses on my wedding night that he might entertain his paramour."

The duke stood instantly still, rigid as an image. "His paramour!" he echoed, glancing round the room, for to him, as to all the others, the only woman present was the Duchess of Esclaramonde herself, and by his son he only saw as all the others saw Simon the soldier of fortune and the young knight of Eleusis. The duke strode to where his son lay.

"Is my son dead?" he asked. Argathona, kneeling by Rainouart's seeming lifeless body, whispered to Count Ernault that he was little hurt, although stunned by his fall, and would soon recover, and Count Ernault, turning to the duke, repeated her message.

"Bear him to his chamber and summon my physician," the duke ordered, and in a moment the strong arms of the young prince's friends—Guy, Jaufre, Ambrose, and Raymond—lifted him unconscious from the floor and bore him to the adjoining room and laid him on the marriage bed. Then glaring round him with the face that all men feared who saw it so, Baldwin commanded:

"Tell me what has happened?"

Esclaramonde rose to her feet and pointed at Argathona, who was standing, now tranquil, with Simon by her side.

"That is a woman," she cried. "That cup contains the wine of sleep. It was poured that I might drink it and might sleep while he gave his false love the kisses due to me. But I was warned and did not drink, and when this woman came I stabbed him in her arms to avenge my honor."

Baldwin turned to Argathona.

"Are you a woman?" he asked, with wonder in his drunken voice. Argathona answered him calmly:

"I am no man, great duke."

The duke clinched and unclinched his great fists. He was sobering rapidly in his rage. "Are you my son's lover?" he questioned.

The dryad answered simply:

"I love him as a maid should love her bachelor, true heart and true soul, and he loved me ere he was stolen from me."

"Do not listen to her," Esclaramonde clamored; "she is a filthy witch and she has ensorcelled him."

Duke Baldwin lifted up his hand to command silence. Drunk or sober he was the master here. Whatever had happened he was the judge. If his son had sinned his son should suffer, but it was for Baldwin of the Rock to sit in judgment. Some dim memory of an ancient tale of Brutus, a Roman, troubled his muddled mind. While Esclaramonde was speaking, Fernand Ximenes had moved a little nearer to her and lightly touched her on the arm with a touch that meant reassurance, a touch that convinced her of a friend.

"Silence, lady," Baldwin ordered, not uncivilly; then he turned again to Argathona: "Boy, woman, witch," he demanded, "whatever you be, what is your story?"

Argathona answered him as tranquilly as if she were telling an old tale to old friends in the forest. Simon gaped in wonder at her, with his hand ever at the hilt of his sword to help her.

"Your son was wounded by robbers in the wood. I tended his hurt, and we changed loves and vows. While I went for healing herbs, in my absence this lady came and bore him to Athens, persuading his sick senses that it was she who had succored him."

The duke frowned horridly. "A strange tale!" he thundered. "A lying tale!" the duchess cried eagerly. Then Simon came forward and faced her, and in a clap she knew that he was the man that had escaped from her in the wood, and she went pale for an instant and caught her breath.

"It is a true tale, by your leave," Simon asserted, "for I was by from first to last."

The duke waved woman-interrupter and man-interrupter impatiently aside, and still addressed Argathona.

"How came you here?" he asked, and again the dryad answered him as calmly as if she had been singing a country-side song.

"In a boy's coat I came hither; in a man's mail I rode in the jousts, and afterwards wooed and won that lady with a golden apple to send her lord to sleep with a drowsy draught and welcome me as her lover tonight." She stooped and picked the apple up as she spoke.

The duke's grim frown grew grimmer. "Why did not my son drink?" he asked.

Argathona answered: "I warned him not to drink, but to make believe, for I wished him to know the worth of the woman he had wedded."

The face of the duke was an ugly sight to see, as he glanced from the slender girl in the boy's garb to the woman who had married his son that day and striven to murder him that night.

"This is a tangled tale," he snarled, "and some here are lying their way to hell at a hand-gallop, but this is no hour and this no mood for judgment."

He pawed at his forehead with his huge hands as he spoke, as if he hoped by physical effort to dispel the sudden troubles of the night. Then he turned to Esclaramonde:

"Lady," he said, "if it be proved that my son has wronged you, you shall have justice, for no man is son of mine who swerves in aught from his knightly fealty, but it may prove that you have slandered my son, in which case I shall deal justice upon you."

The duchess went pale anew at this threat, and those of her following standing near her made speed to ease their swords in their sheaths, seeing which act the partisans of Duke Baldwin did the like defiance. Fernand Ximenes sidled to the duchess and breathed quickly in her ear, "Defy him; I stand by you." And Esclaramonde chose defiance. With a bold and angry countenance she made a step towards the Duke of Athens.

"Baldwin of Athens," she said, haughtily, "I am a sovereign prince even as you are a sovereign prince, and you hold no right of judgment over your peers. I ride hence tonight, I and my people, and from this hour, in the name of my flouted womanhood, Thebes declares war upon Athens."

At this belligerent speech those of her company fell to drawing their swords and calling out "Thebes! Thebes!" furiously, while the huge duke grinned at them like a boar at bay.

"Are you so brave?" he raged—"then I begin the war by making you my prisoner. Count Ernault, your duty." And he looked fiercely at the lord-marshal as who should say, "Take this woman into your custody."

All was now in an uproar. The Theban knights were a line of lifted steel by the side of their lady, crying the name of their city, and behind Duke Baldwin the Athenian nobles shook their swords and hurled back their battle-cry of "Athens" against the "Thebes" of their antagonists. Argathona, standing apart, and for the moment forgotten, watched the turmoil with pitying eyes, and Simon beside her stared indifferent, resting upon his great sword.

To Duke Baldwin the Theban menace seemed meaningless; for he knew very well that the duchess had but a handful of knights and men-at-arms in her service within his city, and that he could crush them all at a blow as easily as dance handy-dandy. And indeed the menace would have been meaningless if the duchess had no more help to rely on to carry her out of Athens than the escort she had brought with her from Thebes. But it seemed that she had much more to rely on, for now beneath the angry arch of lifted blades Fernand Ximenes advanced slowly and addressed the duke.

"Magnificence," he began, blandly, smiling into the astonished face of Baldwin, "surely you wrong your honor if you attempt to restrain the departure of the Theban lady. She is, as she says, a sovereign prince, over whom you can claim no shade of vassalage."

This unexpected intervention amazed Duke Baldwin as much as if a miracle had taken place. Here was a leader of his hirelings, a man of the Catalan Grand Company, presuming to advise him, Baldwin of the Rock. He tried to speak, but the words choked in his throat, and he glared inarticulate at Fernand Ximenes, who went on with his speech in perfect composure.

"By my advice she shall be suffered to go free hence, as she came free hither, and if war ensues between Athens and Thebes thereafter, then may Heaven defend the one that best deserves the defence of Heaven."

As Fernand Ximenes ended his ambiguous speech, Duke Baldwin found his voice.

"You are over ready with unasked-for counsel," he shouted, "but here in Athens I follow my own rede."

"Surely, surely," Ximenes answered, with unchanged tranquillity of face and bearing, "a man can do no more, however big he be, and for my own part, little as I am, I can do no less. But I say my mind and in saying it I say the mind of the Catalan Grand Company."

As he spoke he drew his sword very softly from its scabbard, for all the world as if he were no more than curious to look upon its shining blade, and when it was naked in his hand he employed it to no other purpose than the tracing of imaginary lines upon the floor between him and the duke. But all his comrades of the company that were in the room drew their swords too, and ranged themselves with the fellowship of Esclaramonde of Thebes.

Duke Baldwin saw that he was trapped and baffled. He could not defy Ximenes out of hand, glad as he would have been to do so, for he knew that the games and festals had brought every man of the Catalan Grand Company into the capital, and that to provoke a conflict with their leader just then, however confident he might be of his superior forces and of the inevitable result, would be the very top of foolhardiness, while to start strife now in the crowded palace, where the opponents would be wellnigh man to man, would turn the place into a shambles. He made a great gulp of his discomfiture.

"Friend," he said to Ximenes, with a suddenly commanded dignity that well became his bulk, "you remind me betimes and wisely."

He turned from the enigmatical Spaniard and faced the duchess, paying her a grave salutation.

"Lady, Athens accepts your challenge. Go your way in peace till we meet again in war. Look to the walls of your city, for in a week they will need rebuilding."

He made her another reverence, throttling his choler, but Esclaramonde laughed at his anger and his gravity.

"Thebes has no fear of Athens, great duke," she answered, mockingly. He paid no heed to her, but, turning to Ernault, bade him see that the duchess and her people were suffered to quit the city unopposed. Ernault instantly left the room. The duchess smiled at him as he passed her, but she won no answering smile from his grave face. Esclaramonde made the duke a bow.

"We thank you for your reluctant courtesy," she sneered. Then, turning, she moved slowly from the room with her head high and a triumphant smile, followed by her Theban knights. Fernand Ximenes sheathed his sword, saluted the duke with changeless visage, and followed quietly in her wake. As he passed out his quick eye noted the pale face of one that stood on the fringe of Duke Baldwin's fellowship, gazing eagerly at him, so as without ever showing to attract his attention. The Catalan leader exchanged a glance with Demetrius of Epirus, and knew that Thebes had another adherent in the league against Athens. Ximenes was very well content to understand this, and Demetrius of Epirus was very well content to be understood. And so Ximenes went his way.

There was heavy silence in the room as the Theban party passed out, and the silence brooded over the room for a while as the footsteps of the seceders died away along the passages and down the stairs. Already, below in the great court-yard, could be heard faintly the bustle of men and horses where Count Ernault was taking orders for the departure of the Duchess of Thebes. The knights in the room sheathed their swords and stared into one another's faces, marvelling at these untoward events and the shifts of fortune. As for Duke Baldwin, he stood quite still for a little, stupid with fury to be thus bearded and deceived. But presently he remembered another enemy, and turned fiercely to Argathona as to one on whom he could safely ease his spleen.

"As for you," he shouted, "you woman out of a wood, who claim to love my son and to be loved by him, it seems very sure that you have by some manner of sorcery bewitched the boy, and to practise sorcery is to covet death in Athens. Wherefore I shall this now clap you into prison, and tomorrow will hand you over to Mother-Church, who will know best how to deal with a witch."

Simon made ready for the swinging of his great sword. Ere any one of them all should lay hands upon the damsel there would be a headless duke in Athens. But Argathona's face remained as changelessly grave as befits in danger one who claims a kinship with the high gods, and she spoke out loud and clear.

"Aliens of Athens, you live hateful lives, you live shameful lives, and my spirit is weary of you. I came a stranger into the ways of men, and I go hence very grateful to be stranger to their ways to the end. For you cannot hold me here against my will, and of my own will I come not again to your borders. Fear, for there is a curse upon you; fear, for you have polluted the beautiful city, and dreadful is the vengeance of the gods."

All the while she was speaking to the astounded hearers, a high wind seemed to be rising in the night, and even as she made an end of her speech, a great squalling gust rushed through the open window, and in a clap every torch and candle in the great room was puffed out, and for the space of a moment all was heavy blackness. When lights were found, and the room bright again, there was no sign nor trace of the girl from the greenwood who had fought in the lists as the Prince of Eleusis.

24

THE HONOR OF THE ROCK

When Simon saw that Argathona was clean gone from the room where the others were blinking at the change from light to dark and from dark to light again, he guessed that she had slipped away by the turret-stair, and he knew that it would not take her long, with her cunning, to get clear of the city. Yet, to make assurance surer, he set his back to the arras that masked the turret-door, and stood there with his sword bare waiting composedly for the trouble that seemed very likely to ensue.

Indeed, the trouble came quickly, for as soon as Duke Baldwin had winked his eyes clear of the dazzle and saw that Argathona was gone, he was very wroth with Simon for shielding her retreat, calling him a companion of witches and other ill names, while he bade those about him fling the rascal from the path. But Simon silenced him with words few indeed, but fiercer and fouler than even the duke could compass, and the duke's orders were so incoherent that none knew, or, indeed, greatly desired to know, what he wished. For while Simon stood there at vantage, with his back against the door, with his mighty sword before him, there were few of those by Duke Baldwin's side that liked the looks of him well enough to covet a closer acquaintanceship without need. For though they were valiant knights all, they remembered Simon's play with the Varangian, and esteemed him no less terrible than the giant Fierabras, with whom Ogier combated in the tale of Ogier the Dane.

Now while they stood aloof, uncertain what to do, Simon shouted anew at the duke:

"Duke of dotards, duke of donkeys, you are a foul-lipped fool to call your own son's sweetheart a witch, for she shows as one of God's angels before the sluts and trulls you cherish. So if you have the pluck of your bulk, you will fight this quarrel out with me, sword to sword or fist to fist, I care not which, and we shall see who is the better man and who serves the better kind of woman."

Outside in the court-yard, and beyond on the high-road down the hill, could be heard the rattle and clatter of the men and horses of Esclaramonde's escort starting on their departure for Thebes. In the room a silence like a stupor fell on those that heard their great duke so flouted by a common man-at-arms. But the great duke himself, whose moods veered like the vane, was only tickled with Simon's insolence, and he laughed a wild laugh, for he prized courage in others as much as he prided himself on his own courage, and he was mightily minded to try a fall with the big man.

"Now, by the beard of King Philip," he shouted, "I have a mind to meet your wishes. I had an itch to come to grips with you this morning, and I cherish no desire to deny myself twice in the same day."

The duke was volatile for all his obstinacy, and already the thought of a bout with Simon had dissipated much of his chagrin at preceding discomfitures. Duke Baldwin always charged headlong at any whim, as a bull charges at red temptation.

"On your knee, fellow," he commanded.

"Nay," grunted Simon, "I have nothing to kneel for."

His simplicity missed the duke's meaning, and when the duke saw how he missed, he grinned, for his purpose was to make a knight of the giant.

"Nay, man, on your knee to take the accolade. I cannot cross weapons with one that does not wear the rank of a knight. When you are knighted we will test your mettle."

Now Simon, seeing what the duke would be at, housed his sword, and, coming forward, bent his knee, while those of the duke's party, familiar as they were with their master's vagaries, stared in amaze to find him, after the passing of such great matters, so mightily taken up with so small a thing. But nothing ever seemed small to Duke Baldwin that jumped with his immediate humor. The duke drew his sword and was about to raise it when he bethought him.

"Stay, what is thy name, fellow?" he questioned; and Simon answered, readily enough:

"Simon the Strong, of sweet Rouen city."

Again the duke lifted his sword, and again he lowered it.

"Tell me, friend Simon," he inquired, "have you any broad lands to your name?"

Simon bethought him of his mother's cabbage-garden out in the suburbs of Rouen, a narrow patch enough where a gaunt goat tugged at its tether. It was many a long day since he had seen it, but it came very vividly to his memory now, and made him feel qualmish for a moment, with a spasm of home-sickness.

"In sooth," he answered, slowly, "I have a trifle of property at Florency, but it is no great matter, truly."

"Never care for that," said the duke, cheerfully; "small or great it will serve the turn well enough to help you to gentility."

Then he gave Simon a clap on the shoulder with the flat of his sword and cried out, "Arise, Sir Simon of Florency," and so straightway Simon arose and marvelled a little in himself that he seemed no different for his new honor.

"Now, friend," said the duke, sheathing his sword and stretching his great arms apart, "see if you can spill me as you spilled my tall soldier this morning."

Simon was willing, everyway. He was as eager to try the duke's strength as the duke was to try Simon's, and, win or lose, the struggle meant time gained for Argathona, though he had little fear for her safety. Then, as none of the knights present had the right or the courage to protest against the strange encounter, the two strong men were about to set to in good earnest when their purposes were interrupted by Jaufre, Guy, Ambrose, and Raymond, who came from the bedchamber to tell the duke that his son desired to speak with him.

The duke was vexed at the interruption, for he had set his heart on a bout with Simon, and with him the immediate impulse was ever peremptory to the exclusion of all other thoughts and needs. But he could not very well deny his son, though he cherished some rancor against him as being the cause of the knight's trouble and muddle.

"Sirs," he said to the knights, "these jars must not mar our festival. There are other women in the world, and will be other weddings, but in the mean time you will do well to return to the banqueting-hall and continue your cheer."

Sir Jaufre, Sir Guy, and the others quitted the room. The duke bade Simon stay where he was and went into the next room, where he found Rainouart stretched upon what should have been his marriage bed. The duke's physician was by his side, but he left the room on the entrance of the duke, after assuring him that the wound was slight, as being the work of an unpractised hand, and would soon heal.

Rainouart was very pale, less with the loss of blood than with all the dear and grievous emotions that had pillaged his heart so fiercely that night, but his spirit was high and bright in his eyes, and he spoke to his father with a firm voice.

"Where is my sweet lady?"

"If you mean the lady of Thebes," said Duke Baldwin, "she has gone hence in a great rage."

"I do not think of her," Rainouart said. "I think of the girl from the greenwood, the girl who saved my life once, and now has saved my honor."

Duke Baldwin grinned maliciously, for he was vexed with his son for being such a fool as to get tangled up in his love affairs and thereby bring people to loggerheads untimely.

"Why, she has gone, too. There came a squall of wind that blew the lights out, and in the blackness the valiant lass slipped away, with none to stay her."

At this news Rainouart's heart was wrung with such anguish that even the dull duke could read his misery in his eyes, and even Baldwin's tough composition felt something that was distinctly akin to a pulse of pity, and he added:

"The Jill-o'-lantern left her giant squire behind her."

Rainouart lifted himself eagerly on his elbow.

"I would see that squire at once."

"That may be easily done," said Duke Baldwin, "for he waits in the next room."

Therefore Duke Baldwin raised his voice and trumpeted loudly for Sir Simon of Florency, and instantly Simon lifted the curtain and came into the room and looked with some compassion at the young knight on the couch. Rainouart recognized him at once as the squire who stood by the pavilion of the Prince of Eleusis.

"Where is my lady?" Rainouart asked, feverishly. Simon answered him leisurely:

"She has gone back to the forest, being a little disheartened with your city and its citizens, but she left you these leaves for the healing of your hurt, and this message, that you are to come to her in the greenwood."

As Simon said his say, he drew from his pouch the leaves of the herb of healing that Argathona had given him, and laid them on the bed. Rainouart took them tenderly in his hands and kissed them fondly, while the duke smiled sourly at the folly that leads a man to the lipping of weeds.

"I will go to her in the morning," Rainouart declared; but here Duke Baldwin shook his head.

"That may not be, son," he said, emphatically.

"May not be," Rainouart flung back, hotly. "I tell you it must be. She saved my life and I loved her, and we swore our mutual troth. Then I was practised on by magic, and I forgot my true-love, and went in bondage to a false faith, and from this shame my true-love has saved me now as before she saved me from death. I am bound to her in honor as I am bound to her in love, and on my honor and by my love I will go to her with the dawn."

Again Duke Baldwin shook his head, and again Duke Baldwin answered as before.

"That may not be, son." Then seeing the anger shine in Rainouart's eyes, and the stubborn look on Rainouart's face that seemed to mirror his own native obstinacy, he went on in a voice that for him was gentle.

"Hear me out, son Rainouart, for your honor is as near to me and as dear to me as my own, and against that I think no tongue has ever wagged."

Rainouart's face darkened, for he thought of his mother, the gracious lady so basely abandoned, and he thanked God in his heart that his honor was not as the honor of Duke Baldwin. But Duke Baldwin was not skilled to read either his son's face or his son's heart, and he went on, bluffly:

"As for love, why, I am a jolly lover, too, though you and I read in the book of love at different chapters. But you cannot go to your lass yet awhile, for your very honor's sake."

"Why not?" Rainouart asked, with such a frown as might have wrinkled his father's forehead, and the big duke, who liked his son's manner best when most it resembled his own, went on very amiably to explain. He told how the Duchess of Thebes had declared war upon Athens, at which tidings Rainouart laughed contemptuously; and how Fernand Ximenes inclined to her, and would in all likelihood whistle the Grand Company to her cause. At this Rainouart's eyes shone and his pale cheeks flushed ruddy, for if this were so, it promised a fight that would be worth the fighting.

"Therefore," the duke went on, "your sweetheart must wait awhile till this little brawl be over, for I am sure that no lass who played the lad so gallantly as your fancy would have her lover lag aloof from a battle."

He smiled somewhat sourly as he spoke, for he had no great confidence in the martial constancy of knights that plied their books and fell in love with country wenches. But he read Rainouart's answer in his eyes before he got it from his lips, and it reassured him.

"While Athens is at war," Rainouart said, simply, "I ride and fight with Athens. When Athens is at peace I will marry my true-love."

Simon nodded his head approvingly, and the duke for his part applauded in his heart. He liked the lad's belligerent spirit, however little he relished the nonsense about the witch in the wood. Duke Baldwin's affection for his son, never very vehement, had waxed when he had returned as the betrothed of the Duchess of Thebes, but had dwindled to insignificance with the shattering of that alliance and the chance that his son might die by a stroke from a woman's hand. Indeed, the jovial duke, alarmed by the sudden possibility of an heirless duchy, had even in the last few minutes begun to revolve again in his mind a project that he had abandoned with the coming of the Duchess of Thebes. He had up to that time been so much disappointed with his son that, although as a general principle much averse to marriage as an institution, he was seriously thinking of wedding again. He loved to have about him none but such as were jolly eaters, jolly drinkers, jolly lovers, jolly soldiers, and when he observed the difference between his son and himself and those he cherished, he shuddered over the thought that such a puling, mulish reader of books might one day rule in Athens. Baldwin was still in the prime of life, with every right to hope for an heir, and he began to reconcile himself to the thought of a state which he had always regarded as bondage, though when it existed for him before he had allowed it to bind him but little. In such case the young prince might be clapped into a monastery to doze away his life over tomes of nonsense, while the jolly duke would see to it that the son-child of his dreams should be brought up to a very different purpose.

Now, however, the readiness of Rainouart to obey the call to arms made Baldwin more content with his son, though he frowned at the foolish words about marrying his true-love. However, with the gain of a little time Rain-ouart's mind might change, though that did not seem likely, or he might be prevailed upon to take a less high-flown sense of his obligations to his lovely amazon, or, at the worst, the girl might be got rid of some way or other.

"Well," he said, cheerfully, "you must wait a while ere you can talk of marriage to a maid. For you are married, lad, hard and fast, married to the lady Esclaramonde of Thebes, for a marriage is a marriage though it be but a marriage in name."

Rainouart gave a groan at the duke's speech, and Simon, who had not thought of this dilemma, scratched his chin and scowled. The duke nodded sagaciously.

"Only our Holy Father the Pope can set you apart now, for even when we take Thebes it would scarcely chime with the chivalry of the Rock to kill the baggage, however much she deserve it. But I will send an envoy to Avignon to put our case before the pontiff. By the time he returns we shall have taken Thebes, and then you will be a free man to go a-wooing in a wood."

"And till then," Simon added, "I will be your esquire, if you agree, for such was the wish of your dear lady, whose humble servant I am very proud to be."

Rainouart stretched out his hand and clasped the hand of Simon.

"We will be brothers-in-arms," he vowed, "as we are brothers in ser-vice." Then he turned to his father.

"Sire," he said; "your son is your soldier till there be an end of the war and till the pope makes me a free man again. And then, by your leave, I will take my troth anew to the greenwood, and humbly pray my sweet love to forgive me."

The duke said nothing, for he had nothing pleasant to say to such vaga-ries. But Simon tugged at his russet beard, and muttered:

"I think she will forgive you."

25

CEPHISSUS

The dawn was as pink as a peach, and through the pellucid air the city of Athens looked her fairest. The Parthenon, topping her holy hill, glowed like amber in the young sunlight, showing the same fine lines of perfect symmetry to the nobles of France that it had shown to the Roman soldiers of Mummius and to the Athenians of the great war. Within the sanctuary the gold and ivory image of Athena, fashioned by Phidias, had given way to the pale face of Our Lady, Mother of the Holy Child, and the grandiloquent Latin of the mass rolled its volume through the hall that once had echoed to the sonorous Greek of the Palladian hymns. The gods had gone, great Pan was dead, Christ had arisen, and still the Parthenon in almost unaltered beauty crowned the Acropolis. But the chivalry of France paid little heed to the Parthenon or the past of Athens as they rode briskly out on that radiant morning to annihilate the Catalan Grand Company. Their thoughts were with the vivid present, with the pleasure of coming battle, with the pride of certain victory, with the promise of the swift return, flushed with triumph, to find praise and welcome smiling in their ladies' eyes. It was but the second day since the night of the ruined nuptials, but Baldwin was brisk on war business, and his chivalry and his fighting-men were quick to move. The foot-soldiers had taken the field for the march to Thebes on the previous day, and this day, this glorious day of peach-colored dawn, the duke and his knights were to ride to the undoing of the Catalan Grand Company.

The Catalan Grand Company had confirmed the menace of Ximenes, and justified Duke Baldwin's doubts by going over as one man to the cause of the Duchess of Thebes. But their defection did not trouble the bluff duke. On the contrary, it furnished him with a full-blooded excuse for exterminating the mutinous mercenaries and wiping out his debt to them with a wet sword. So he and his chivalry rode to their assured victory, and made their march a gala-day.

Simon had never seen a braver menace of war. The sunlight gleamed on coats of many-tinted silk, on armor rich with gilding, on shields whose gayly painted spaces were so many brave pages from the armorial of France. Iris was outvied. Cloth of gold and cloth of silver glittered; stuffs of flame color, sea color, corn color, blood color dazzled the day; even the Athenian eyes, inured to vivid pigments seen in full sunlight, ached in the play of hue. All the knights were clad as for a tournament, save that they did not carry on their helmets the huge and grotesque crests which made the mimic fight fantastic, for these, though skilfully fashioned of light wicker-work and painted leather, would have proved too cumbrous and too bulky in the hour of actual combat.

Duke Baldwin rode at the head of his knights, with his visor exalted, and his companions, the Knight of the Fish, the Knight of the Lizard, the Knight of the Griffin, knights of all conceivable creatures that blazoners and crest-builders had taken into their whimsical kingdom, rode in Duke Baldwin's train and cried their war-cries into the ears of a delighted audience. The Athenians, then as ever eager for new things, and rejoicing in show, lined the streets and applauded lustily as the pageant of war passed by. The knights rode to the fight as to a feast, full of mirth. On every side jest challenged laughter and laughter answered jest. Sir Guy, Sir Jaufre, Sir Ambrose, Sir Gaston, Sir Raymond made merry one with another, and blew kisses to such girls as had fair faces among the gazing throng. It was true that some lords were missing from Duke Baldwin's following. Andronicus Palæologus, pompous exile, had asserted that the quarrel was none for him to meddle with and had taken shipping for Nauplia; Demetrius of Epirus had stolen away by night to Thebes to lend such dignity as his name could give to the Catalan rally. But no one seemed to remember or to regret the fugitive or the traitor, and no one seemed to think any but mirthful thoughts or to speak other than mirthful words.

Simon marvelled somewhat at the knightly mirth. There was nothing so wonderful in the crushing of such an uproar as that of the Catalan Grand Company. Yet Simon's own spirits were high, and he found snatches of old songs bubbling from his lips as he rode close at hand to his master. Rainouart seemed once again what he had been before the fatal coming of Esclaramonde. Thanks to the herb of healing, thanks to his native health, he had wellnigh recovered from the wound that the ill-directed stroke of a woman had dealt him. What was of far more moment, he had wholly escaped from the spell of Esclaramonde's magic, and rode with clear eyes and clean spirit. If he were not now as blithe as his fellows, he had never displayed a noisy humor of mirth. But while the others carolled and babbled, he rode quietly with a bright smile on his face, for he thought of the girl in the greenwood, and all the world was fragrant with the perfume of the noble rose. His carriage cheered Duke Baldwin greatly, wherefore he rode lively enough at the head of his knights, and did not trouble himself much about the amorous folly of his son so long as that son rode in arms like a gallant gentleman against the enemy.

The peach tint of the dawn flushed into rose and glowed into gold as the morning grew, and soon the sky was all of the liveliest blue above the heads of Baldwin and his companions. They knew some hours of blithe riding through a blithe country, now open as they traversed the Attic plain, now enclosed as they came to the hilly places and fringed the forest—and here Simon looked wistfully at the wood, but Rainouart rode steadily with his gaze fixed straight ahead—and then again open as they began to enter the Theban plain. Here Duke Baldwin found his foot-soldiers encamped, and here he heard that the opposing forces had marched out of Thebes and taken up their position in an encampment on the plain to await the Athenian invaders. Here the knights made a halt for rest and repose, for the morning was still very young, with the air exceedingly cool and sweet. The horses were fed and tended, the knights ate and drank, but sparingly, as befits those about to give battle, and their brief leisure was as mirthful as their march. When all were refreshed, man and beast, the march was resumed, and a little time brought Duke Baldwin and his friends in full view of the enemy and of the destined battle-field.

Simon looked curiously at the stirring scene before him. A great space of land lay between the Athenian forces and their enemies—a space vividly green with young corn that flourished on the plain of Thebes as on all the plains of Greece. On the other side of that spreading area of soft shoots the men of the Catalan Grand Company were drawn up in open array of battle, with the gaudy banner of the Duchess of Thebes floating over their ranks side by side with their own flag and the treasonable pennon of Epirus. Simon marvelled on looking to see them waiting there so composedly for the formidable onslaught of the Frankish chivalry. The bowmen were resting by their strung bows as unconcernedly as if a holiday were toward, and the armored leaders moved hither and thither leisurely among the ranks. It seemed as if the following of Baldwin had but to spur only a few yards across the soft, bright corn to brush these foemen out of existence. Nine hundred of the finest knights in Greece, swathed in steel, rode with the Duke of Athens and filled the summer air with their war-cries, eager to sweep over the field and chastise the insolence of their contemptible enemies. Behind them now tramped a well-equipped army on foot, strongly armed, admirably marshalled, inured to war, and eager for the engagement.

Simon was puzzled if no one else was. The odds against the Catalan Grand Company showed tremendous, even when such reinforcements as were afforded by the adherents of the Duchess of Thebes were taken into account, while Demetrius of Epirus brought no more than his small personal following and the cheap dishonor of his name. It looked as if none might survive the skirmish to mount the gibbets which Duke Baldwin so uncompromisingly promised to the rebels. Suddenly an idea came into Simon's head, and he slapped his leg with satisfaction. That is it, he said to himself, convinced that he had found an answer to the problem that perplexed him. The dogs knew that they must die, one way or another, by sword or by rope, and they meant to make a good end of it, soldier-wise, and at bay. Something of pity stirred in his heart for the stout fellows so soon to be butchered and waiting so soldierly for the end. They were truculent ruffians, those Catalans, but at least they knew how to play a losing game with courage and dignity. Another little hour and how many of those bearded faces would show any hot blood in the cheeks? The fortune of war, Simon reflected, composedly, and settled himself in the saddle for the obliterating charge which he guessed must soon be made, for Duke Baldwin had reined in his horse, and with him the army halted, a splendid patch of steel and color upon the plain. Duke Baldwin turned in his saddle and smiled upon his chivalry, while he pointed to the Catalan Grand Company and the forces of the lady of Thebes.

"There lie the rebels," he shouted, his great voice rolling like a drum-call over his host, "and here ride we that shall wipe them out of the field. It is but poor sport I offer you, gentle friends, to slay the jacks of a jade, but it will soon be over, and we shall scour the land of Greece clean of these cozeners."

As he spoke he swung his sword forth from his scabbard, and held it stretched in menace against the enemy, while the knights behind him thundered cheer after cheer, and settled themselves firmly in their saddles for the charge across the shining plain. Baldwin lifted his great blade to heaven.

"Saint Denis for Athens!" he cried, and stuck his spurs into the sides of his mighty charger.

"Saint Denis for Athens!" echoed his chivalry at his heels, and in another moment the splendid mass of men-at-arms was in motion. Simon's spirits were at the top as he gave his horse the rein and felt the morning air stronger against his face. But he kept a watchful eye on the young prince who rode beside him, and it gladdened him to see that Rainouart sat so stiffly in his saddle and held his lance so well. "A plague upon love and lovers," he grumbled in his heart; "what have they to do with a gentleman-at-arms?" and then he had time to think no more for the swift exhilaration of the charge. On the knights came, Baldwin leading, the young Prince of Athens close behind him, and Simon by his side, the rest thundering in open order with levelled spears. A few minutes more now and the Catalan Grand Company would be very decisively disbanded. But even as Simon charged his horse caught a hoof in a hole, and, coming heavily on to its knees, shot Simon out of his stirrup, and Simon landed sprawling on the ground. Now Simon was a heavy man, and Simon, as befitted the knight of Florency, was in full armor, and Simon, though he tried his best, found it as hard to rise as if he were a capsized turtle. But Rainouart riding ahead saw his mishap, and, reining in his black horse, came back to Simon.

"Nay," cried Simon, "ride to victory, and leave me to shift."

But Rainouart would not have it so. He might be out of the first bright wave of battle, but he could not leave his brother-in-arms in distressful plight. And there was, indeed, but brief delay. Rainouart dismounting soon got Simon to his feet, and Simon mounted his horse, which was little the worse for its stumble, and together they spurred to catch up with the charging cavalry. But the time, short though it was, had allowed a great gap of green field to grow between the riding knights and their two pursuers, and it took some strenuous seconds to bring their horses' noses to the tails of their predecessors.

Even as they who had been in the vaward now at length joined themselves to the rear, suddenly Simon saw Duke Baldwin's great charger stagger and reel and plunge unaccountably, and the next moment Simon found that his own horse was striving to make its way through ground as muddy and pulpy as a swamp. Water was squelching and oozing and bubbling over his horse's fetlocks; the young prince's horse was in the like stress; and, looking rapidly to left and right, Simon could see that all the extending line of knights had found the same difficulty in the way of their progress. It is some ditch, Simon thought, which can soon be passed, and he urged his steed with a spur to a progress that became momentarily more difficult. Duke Baldwin was floundering and struggling in the ever-increasing bog, and Simon could hear him cursing furiously as he strove to advance. Simon's own horse and the horse of the prince were now knee-deep in the horrible morass in which by this time all the knights were floundering. They could, indeed, advance a little still, but every step was harder than the last, and every inch of way seemed to find no firmer earth, while black splashes of water spurted from the puddled soil at every pace, and little pools sucked and gurgled ominously round the legs of the frightened horses.

There must be dry land somewhere, Simon thought, too much bewildered by this singular obstacle to wonder how such a ditch as this could have remained unknown to the Athenian leader. Across the green corn he could see the Catalans still composedly standing at gaze, while on all sides of him now the heavily armed knights and the heavy horses were sinking deeper and deeper in the treacherous marsh. Duke Baldwin ahead was up to his horse's middle now in the clinging mud, and was vainly essaying with oaths and curses to urge the beast a little farther. Like flies glued in honey seemed all the chivalry of Athens, plunging and struggling to extricate themselves from the fatal fen, and then Simon saw how some of the men of the Catalan Grand Company began to move. First, the bowmen lifted their bows and drew arrow to ear, and then a cloud of shafts came over the entangled knights, who could neither advance nor retreat, but were limed helplessly in the imprisoning slime. Then swift Spanish soldiers came running nimbly towards them, picking their way easily over the sump in which the Athenians wallowed an inextricable mass of men and horses, and as the Spaniards ran the sunlight glittered on the long knives they carried in their hands.

In an instant of agony Simon realized that all was lost, that the flower of the Athenian army was snared in that mysterious marish, and that there was little chance for any man among them to come out alive. Already the Spanish knife-men were thick and busy among their victims, paddling easily where horse and armor sank, and dealing death wherever they came with their terrible knives. Already Duke Baldwin was down with twenty men upon him. Hardly a dozen yards away Simon saw the girlish face of Guy de Hainault for the first time writhen with rage. He had lifted his visor to see more clearly what had happened, and he wielded his sword in vain against his unreachable assailants, and then a dozen men were on him from behind, and a dozen knives met in his body, and he went down and Simon saw him no more. The black slush was everywhere reddening with blood, as knight after knight perished ingloriously, helpless to evade the stings that slew them, and unable to strike a good stroke in defence of his life and of Athens.

It all happened so quickly, so unexpectedly, that Simon caught himself staring at the bloody work about him in a kind of unconsciousness, a kind of indifference, such as a man might wear who came unexpectedly upon a puppet-show in a village square. Above him the sky, to which his eyes travelled unawares, shone as brightly blue as it had shone in the hours of their merry march, since the peach color of the dawn had faded. The bright Greek world was the same, and yet the bright Greek world was all different, a mud-stained, blood-stained slaughter-spot, where brave knights were being murdered. Then, in the midst of the butchery all about him, Simon thought suddenly of the greenwood and a girl with a face like a god, and of a noble youth who rode at his side and strove to force his way over the morass. Instantly a great resolve came into Simon's mind that he would save the boy Rainouart for the girl Argathona.

Long afterwards, happily settled in Rouen, Simon, when he thought over the events of that whirling hour, used to remind himself that then, for the first time in his life, he devoutly gave God thanks for having made him so strong. In those after days in peaceful Rouen, he knew the cause of the catastrophe. The subtle genius of Fernand Ximenes had prepared an amazing trap for the Athenian army. He had turned aside the current of the river Cephissus into the cornfields of the Theban plain, and so flooded them, the quagmire thus created being completely concealed by the green standing corn. It was into this swamp that Duke Baldwin had ridden to his death, and it was in this swamp that Simon was now to struggle for his life and for the life of his lord.

Now when in an age-long instant Simon saw how things stood, and how certain were the Athenian chivalry to perish before the eyes of their enemies in that slough and snare, he caught at the bridle of Rainouart's horse, so that though the beast trampled and stumbled sinking in the mud, it could at least go no farther.

"In God's name," Rainouart cried at him, "why do you hold me back? Ride on. Athens, Athens!"

He strove hotly to urge his struggling horse farther into the field of carnage, but Simon would not have it so.

"My lord," he shouted—for the din was so great with the neighing of frightened horses and the cries of dying men that it was hard for a voice to prevail above it even in a neighbor's ear—"my lord, all is lost; we are all trapped rabbits; turn your rein and we may escape."

Rainouart turned on him in a red rage of despair.

"You are mad," he screamed. "We can ride and die with our fellows," and he gave a heavy groan.

"You can do nothing," Simon answered. "Come with me if you would ever see the greenwood again and the face of your girl."

"A coward's call," Rainouart shouted. "Good-bye, love. Athens, Athens!" and again he strove to urge his horse a little farther in the sucking sludge. But the horse could scarce stir for all his plunging, and though Simon's hand was still on the bridle, it was not Simon's hand that stayed advance.

"Few men have called me coward with comfort to themselves," Simon grumbled, inwardly. "Yet I will take it from this man for the maid's sake, and save him if I may. This quarrel is none of mine, and I care not a rap for Athens, and it argues me no dastard to fly from a hopeless fight."

Nimbly the thoughts skipped through his brainpan, but now Rainouart, seeing Simon's hand still on his bridle, menaced him with his sword, and shrieked at him through the din that he would kill him if he did not let go his hold. Simon's thoughts were still furiously busy, furiously swift, and they ran to this intent: "Since you think it a coward's part to fly, then you were a coward in flight. But if I, that feel no shame in escaping from such a shambles, pluck you hence willy-nilly, all is well."

By now Rainouart, beside himself with wrath at sight of such a massacre, had lifted up his sword to strike at Simon, but Simon did not give him time to strike. Swift as an arrow Simon's right arm straightened, and heavy as a blacksmith's hammer Simon's right hand, a huge and cruel fist in steel, delivered the young prince a giant's blow upon his helmed head. Under that mighty stroke Rainouart's head rattled in its iron case as a kernel rattles in a nut. Courage and consciousness alike were silenced, and Simon caught in his arms a senseless man as Rainouart reeled helpless from his saddle.

"It was high time to be making up our minds," Simon grunted, as he addressed himself to the terrible attempt to extricate his companion and himself from their desperate peril.

He leaped off his horse on to the squashy earth, and, though his great weight drew him deep over ankles into the loathsome slush, he was nearer to the edge of the terror than the main of the cavalry, and better able to move and act. With carnage raging ahead of him, Simon, as coolly as if he had been in a tent at a tournament, stripped most of the mail from the body of his unresisting lord, taking care to leave him his sword girded about his middle. Then, with a like composure and a like rapidity, he ripped the armor from his own limbs, and, picking up Rainouart from the slough where he lay senseless, flung him on to his shoulder as easily as he might have lifted a woman. Even in that moment, however, he showed his campaigning spirit. Knight or no knight, Simon had a fine appreciation for the merits of a ripe old wine, and, as fighting was ever hungry work, he had not thought it beneath his new dignity to make a filled wallet and a leather bottle of red wine part of his equipment. Now he snatched both from his saddle-bow and hooked them to his belt before beginning on his desperate enterprise of escape from the mouth of the pit.

The mouth of the pit was like the mouth of hell. There were little lanes of oozy earth running in all directions behind him, green with trampled corn and red with Frankish blood. In front of him the bog he had crossed spluttered and gurgled, and across its treacherous surface he essayed, at all adventure, to reach some firmer soil. Up to this time Simon's doings had passed unchallenged. All around him the morning was made hideous by the screams of the dying and the shrieks of the triumphant Catalans as they drove home their pitiless knives, and knight after knight of those that had been the glories of Duke Baldwin's court went unprepared on the path to paradise. If any of the enemy noticed Simon at his work they may, seeing one man stripping the armor from another, have taken him heedlessly for one of themselves, who, having slain, was prompt to plunder. But now some five or six of the Catalan stabbing rabble, having worked ahead of their fellows, and seeing a man with another man on his shoulders wading through blood and mud towards the dry land, where the main strength of the Athenian army was still standing, came rapidly to head him off, running quickly and securely on the ridges familiar to them that divided the different fields of wheat and barley, or wading through the bog itself with ease in their nearly naked condition.

They chose their prey unwisely, for Simon had his great sword bare in his hand, and, as the rascals came at him, Simon, wielding his terrible weapon, struck off head after head of his assailants till none were left to face him, and then made use of their bodies as convenient stepping-stones to help him a little farther to his desired haven, while such others as were tempted to join in the chase, seeing the havoc he wrought upon their comrades, turned with alacrity to less-resisting victims.

Little by little, inch by inch, through what seemed an eternity of effort, Simon struggled with his burden, every muscle of his great body strained, every vein in his great body throbbing as he strove inch by inch to gain a firmer foothold. At last, with the shrieks of the dying and the cries of the triumphant well behind him, he felt his heels tread upon a firmer foothold. A little more, and, with the sweat raining off him like a deluge, he staggered to sound earth, and stood dripping and stained and aching, but free. He paused for a moment to draw breath and to see what lay before and behind him. The view either way was disastrous for the future of Athens. Behind him, as it seemed, every man of the gorgeous company that had ridden with Duke Baldwin from Athens that morning had fallen a victim to the cunning and the fury of the Catalans. Before him the bulk of the Athenian army was by now in ignoble flight towards the city. Dismayed by what it saw, puffed by a panic terror and spurred by a conviction that the Catalans must be irresistible, the war-used army of Duke Baldwin fell asunder like a pack of frightened children. The road to Athens was free for the Catalans to march on; the city itself was free for the Catalans to deal with as they pleased.

Not far from where Simon now stood, a great war-charger wandered quietly and bit unconcernedly at the sweet grass. Doubtless it had unhorsed its rider in the first struggle in the concealed wash, and had made its way back again instinctively to the firm soil it had just quitted. Simon, still carrying his unconscious load, advanced towards the horse, holding out his hand, and trying to speak to it caressingly, and it startled him as he did so to find what a thin thread of a voice came from between his burning lips.

The horse did not start or shy, but went on cropping the grass unconcernedly until Simon was close beside it, and then, with no show of fear, it allowed Simon to seize its bridle. In another moment Simon was astride the saddle with the young prince lying limp on the saddle-bow. In yet another he had turned the great horse's head to the west, and was making at the best speed he could compel for the woodlands.

26

THE ANCHORITE

In a waste and desolate place of the Eleusinian wood, aloof alike from highway and byway, there stood a little shrine, with a little hut hard by it. The shrine was rudely shaped of heavy stones, piled one upon another with scant skill but with great pains, evidently the handiwork of an untrained but persistent artificer. All day the shrine enclosed a goodly image in wrought silver of our Lord upon the tree, the which image was always carried reverently at nightfall within the shelter of the hut. This hut was the habitation of an anchorite who had dwelled there for many years in little less than absolute solitude, and the place where he abode so lonely was reputed of great sanctity. The travellers were rare who passed that way by mischance, for it neighbored no pathway leading directly anywhere, and was far from the beaten path of trade or travel or use. But such as, passing, paused and prayed before the shrine that sheltered the silver image were wont to aver that they renewed their journey with a strange exaltation of the spirit and exhilaration of the flesh.

The beauty and the value of the image had, according to country-side gossip, on more than one occasion tempted the cupidity of thieves, but each essay to steal the sacred emblem had resulted in the discomfiture of the would-be plunderers. For on each occasion the hermit, whom the robbers hoped to take unawares abed and asleep, issued from his dwelling as the enemies came creeping up, and made such strange manifestations of physical strength and spiritual influence as effectually scared the sacrilegious rascals into flight. Now there was no thief in Athens bold enough to renew the enterprise, and the holy man was left to his loneliness, while weeks and even months passed without a living human creature passing by his hut. This loneliness seemed to be to the liking of the ancient man.

No one knew who the hermit was, and those few who ever had speech with him and sought to question him gained little by their pains. Even Duke Baldwin fared no better than the rest. For Duke Baldwin once rode that way by chance, a-hawking on a summer day, and some one of his company telling him of the recluse, the duke condescended to halt for a moment and hold speech with the holy man. But he found that his questions won him answers unsatisfactory and enigmatical, and that even the pompous announcement of his title and state had no more effect than to bring a faint smile to the thin lips of the hermit. So Duke Baldwin rode away in something of a huff, and spoke severely of recluses for some time afterwards.

It was believed that the hermit came from abroad; it was believed that he was exceedingly aged; it was believed, no one quite knew why or wherefore, that in a distant past he had been neither hermit nor holy; and it was whispered by a few beneath their breath on winter evenings, when there was leisure to loll by the fire and talk gossip, that the stranger had practised in his youth the black art and had been an accomplished sorcerer. Whatever the old man had been, and whencesoever he had come, there could at least be no doubt of his present sanctity. He fasted, vigilled, prayed, macerated his nature, lacerated his flesh, read on the Great Book till far into the night, and was at his devotions in the open at the earliest coming of the day, be the weather fair or be the weather foul. The few who ever saw him found in his reverent features no trace of dissatisfaction with his lot, and Sir Jaufre de Brabant, who rode with Duke Baldwin on the occasion when Duke Baldwin spoke with the hermit, declared that the anchorite had the peacefullest face for an old man that he had ever beheld.

On the morning of the day when slaughter reigned in the distant Theban plain, the hermit was sitting in the open air after his first devotions, quietly conscious of the freshness of the air and the color of the hour. He was busy in scattering the larger part of his scanty meal as a pasture for a multitude of birds that fluttered and hopped around him, and chirped and twittered, and sometimes, to his pathetic consternation, battled among themselves as they scrambled for the spoil. "My little brothers," he began, the phrase of St. Francis in his mind, as he observed with sorrow the contest of one large bird with three smaller ones for the solace of a single crumb. But even as he began to speak he became aware that his familiar solitude was invaded. A girl was coming towards him down the slope, a girl tall, stalwart, blue-eyed and yellow-locked, a girl with naked arms and legs, in a kirtle of white stuff. Though the girl came running rapidly towards him over the grass, the birds a-nigh him showed no signs of disturbance at the stranger's coming, but picked and chirruped as unconcernedly as if they were still alone in their timidity with their ancient friend.

It was Argathona who came thus upon the old solitary and his untroubled birds. The moon was still shining when she gained the shelter of her forest on the night of her flight from Athens, and she made at once for the cave where she had so often lain through the ages, her cave in the heart of the wood. There she hid the golden apple, and there she stripped off her male attire and clothed herself in her woman's weeds, according to the old wont. Then she lay down on a couch of fern and slept the dreamless sleep of the immortals that have no need to double their little lives with false seeming. Indeed, she was very weary of the world of men, and wished to forget it and all that belonged to it, save only her lover, who she was very sure must come to her soon in the woodland.

Being of the immortals, she had her will, and awoke refreshed and free of the contamination of the city. But yet her mind was troubled because of her lover and her longing for him, and though she knew that his hurt was nothing, and though she knew that he was fated to escape from danger till he obeyed her call to the woodland, she was conscious for the first time in her young-old life of the length of a long day. She wandered in the forest, visiting all the haunts and hollows, grottos and thickets, that she loved, talking with beast and bird and insect, every creature of the wood. But always in her divine heart she stifled the human desire for her lover, and that day of late spring lagged tardier in his passage than ever yet day of spring had travelled.

Now when she had slept again through the same sweet oblivion, and had wakened to greet a new day, she found her spirit so troubled with unfamiliar regrets and with unwonted fears that there suddenly came upon her a strange sense of loneliness, such as she had never known before, and a wish for the wisdom of another. And even as she wished, there came into her mind the thought of the hermit of whom her lover had spoken to her on the night of their first meeting. She knew, indeed, that such an one dwelt in the confines of the forest, unheeded by her. She did not remember when he came there; he was no more to her than the distant shepherds and yet more distant citizens. But since her lover had urged her to come with him to visit this ancient stranger, her troubled heart inclined towards him, and she resolved to seek him out, she scarce knew why, if it were not that perchance she might speak to him of her lover. Thus it came about that the hermit beheld her descending the slope, what time he was feeding his birds.

As Argathona approached the ancient and saw that he was aware of her coming, she gave him good-morrow in her sweet, clear voice, and the old man, looking steadfastly upon her, thought her indeed the loveliest creature that he had ever seen, even in days when his eyes were daily familiar with loveliness.

"Good-morrow, daughter," he said, gently. "Of what kin are you that are not of my kind?"

Argathona marvelled that the glamour of the woodland could not prevail against the old man.

"Why are you so wise, father," she asked, "that you seem to know what no others have known?"

"Daughter," answered the hermit, "you speak to me with a speech that is not spoken of men, and yet I understand you, and when I speak to you, you understand my tongue though it is unlike yours. Also the birds have no fear of you, the shy birds that fly from a shadow or a sigh."

"Why should the birds fear me," asked Argathona, "that have never hurt living thing? And who has given you the gift to know that I speak the speech of the gods?"

The old man turned, and, going towards the shrine, knelt for a moment before the image of the Redeemer. Then he rose again and faced the girl.

"My Lord and yours," he said, pointing to the crucifix, "has granted me to see and know the things of this world as they truly are. Time was when my eyes were blinded by pride and my heart was big with evil, but the time has been, and I, long dead to the world, wait in patience for the hour of my true translation."

Argathona pointed to the figure on the cross, which she was looking at with a childlike curiosity.

"Is that your Lord?" she questioned, gently. She remembered that she had seen kindred images at Athens, and that Simon had told her hurriedly how they made part of the new faith that had usurped the ancient rule. But she had paid them little heed, being so busy on her own purposes. Now, however, in the silence of the lonely woodside, the image to which its guardian paid so profound a reverence seemed to assume a new significance. So, "Is that your Lord?" she asked.

"Your Lord and mine," the old man answered, "and the Lord of all the souls living in the world."

Argathona looked from the image to the old man, and from the old man again to the image. If that face in its beauty presented the features of a god, why was that god so slaughtered? Why was the brow of divinity crowned with a crown of thorns? For the first time since she passed into the world of men, Argathona felt herself in the presence of something that was higher than herself and her kindred, and for the first time, she knew not why, she felt abashed and astray.

"I know little of the world of men," she faltered. "Few and bitter have been the hours I passed among them, and in those few hours I heard little speech of any lord of the world, though, indeed, I can remember seeing images like unto this to which men paid a kind of reverence, though not with that joy and humility wherewith we of the woodland reverenced our gods. Your Athens seemed only to care for laughter and banquets, and the making of false love, and the waging of false war, and from first to last I heard little speech of this Lord of the world, save when now and then one strengthened an oath with His name. Will you tell me of Him, for of Him I am ignorant?"

The old man saw that he had to deal with a daughter of simplicity that was yet no simpleton. So he addressed her with all gentleness, as a father to a child.

"Yours must have been a strange life," he said, "if the story of our Lord be strange to you. Tell me first your tale, my daughter."

Then Argathona told him her story, even as she had told it to Simon of Rouen in the woodlands such a little while ago. Then she told of all that had happened since, of her encounter with the wounded knight that proved to be the young Prince of Athens, and of their plighted loves, and of the treachery of Esclaramonde, and of her visit to Athens and what came of it, and of her resolve to wait in the greenwood till her true-love came to find her. While she spoke the old man listened in silence, and though there was much in her story to marvel at, yet in his eyes there was no signal of disbelief, and the hope burned hotly in his heart that it might be vouchsafed to him to save this spirit. When Argathona had told her story he turned to her, and his eyes were vessels of pity and his voice was the promise of charity. Gently he bade her sit by him on the grass beneath the image of silver, and tenderly he bade her hearken to the words he had to say. And Argathona obeyed him and sat by him, watching his face and feeding on his words in silence.

Then the old man told her the story of the Redeemer. He told of the prophecy and the fulfilment, the angel and the birth, of the cruelty of Herod the king, and the flight, and the shining of the star, and the coming of the wise, and the worship of the babe in the manger. He told of the going to Jerusalem, and of the child amid the doctors, and the growth in glory; of the meeting with John the Baptist, and the temptation through Satan, and the many miracles, the changing of water into wine, the walking on the water, the feeding of the multitude, the raising of Lazarus from the dead. He told of the danger of the Master, and the treason of Judas, and the last supper, and the passion in Gethsemane, and the trial before Pilatus. He told of the crucifixion. He told of the resurrection.

Argathona sat by the side of the old man in the quiet of the hill-side and hearkened and wondered, and ever as he spoke she seemed to hear far off in the woodlands the voices of the old gods complaining. And the hours waned, and the sacred tale went on, in the solitude of the forest. Far away to the east a great massacre had taken place in the Theban plain, and the levies of Baldwin were flying like sheep on the road to Athens. But no noise of the killing, no echo of the flight came to trouble the ancient and the maid in their business of telling and hearing the mystery of the redemption.

When he had made an end, when the lid of the sepulchre had rolled back and the apparition of the Master had been manifest to the apostles, the ascetic looked at Argathona and saw that her eyes were pools of tears. Then she asked him, sadly, if he had been by when this tragedy came to pass.

"Nay," answered the ancient, "all this happened thirteen hundred years ago"—but he saw that she did not understand him when he said this—"and yet, in a sense, I am one of the Lord's apostles. For there has been a head of the faith ever since from that day to this, and will be to the end, and the opening of the heavens and the yawning of the pit. And in the fulness of time it pleased the Lord to uplift the humble, so that they who had been poor fisherfolk and scriveners, and the like, became rulers of the Christian world. Wherefore, in my turn, Heaven made me the greatest prince in the world. Great kings of great kingdoms, mighty emperors of mighty empires, looked up to me as to their master, and I spoke to them as a school-master speaks to his pupils, as a tyrant speaks to his slaves. For when I lived in the world, who have long left the world, I sat in the seat of St. Peter in Rome, and I held the keys of heaven and hell, and men called me by the name of Boniface the Seventh. But it pleased God to punish me for my arrogance and my pride, and the King of France compassed my destruction, and his partisans made to slay me, and wellnigh did me to death, but my servants saved me when I was left for dead and hid me in a little house. In my sufferings I repented of my sins, and resolved to expiate them in a life of piety. So I caused it to be blown abroad that I was dead that I might escape the vengeance of my enemy, even Philip the Fair, and so live to redeem my soul. Wherefore I journeyed hither, to the country where Paul preached, and here have I lived these many years, daily drawing, as I trust, a little nearer to the desired end, and here when the Lord calls me I look to die. Because I have sinned and suffered in my past days of wickedness I am sick with pity now for all who sin and suffer in the world, and if I could I would help you, my daughter."

Argathona marvelled at his speech and at the strange things he told her, and though she did not fully understand the import of much that he said, she understood that he was good and that he meant her well. Then the old pope asked the pagan maiden what she thought to do when her lover came to her, and she answered him that she and her lover would live forever in the greenwood. Then the old pope raised his hand in warning, and his voice was sad and stern as he told her that this thing could not be. If her tale were true, and she were indeed one of the old people permitted by the providence of God to dwell undying upon earth, such grace was now given to none other in the world, so that within a little while her lover must needs die and she be left alone.

Now the renewal of this assurance stabbed at Argathona's heart, and she knelt at the old man's feet and besought him, asking if there were no way by which her gift of abiding youth and enduring life could be given to a mortal. Boniface answered her that there was no such way, though poets had dreamed of a fountain of youth which blessed those that drank with renewed youth and length of years. But no such fountain existed in the world. Then Argathona began to weep, remembering her mother's sorrow, and seeing its renewal for herself, and for the anguish in her eyes the solitary strove to comfort her.

"I cannot give your lover endless life in this world," he said; "but I can give you the life of a mortal, with its grace beyond the grave." When Argathona stared at him wide-eyed in wonder, he told her that if she would embrace the true faith and be baptized a Christian, in that moment her birthright of immortality would depart from her and her gift of endless youth, and she would become a mortal woman with all a woman's cares and sorrows and a woman's certain death. He told her that if she did this her beauty would fade from her year by year, and ugly age would creep upon her, with many aches and pains in its company, till her time came to pass away. Then he painted the joys of paradise, and the fellowship of the saints and angels, and the endless pleasure of the elect. But only by baptism and acceptation of the burden of death could she hope to be happy with her lover, here for a little while, and hereafter forever.

Argathona mused a little while nursing her chin in the hollow of her hand, and after musing rose and thanked the anchorite gravely and discreetly for what he had told her, and so bade him farewell.

"I will abide for a while in my forest," she said, "and think upon these things that you have told me, and if it prove that my spirit shall see with your eyes, and my heart shall speak with your voice, then I will come to you again."

So she rose and went her way up the mountain path into the forest, and the old pope knelt at the feet of the Crucified and prayed.

27

THE DREAM OF ARGATHONA

When Argathona left the ancient and pursued her homeward path, the fervor of the day was on the wane, and the sky flamed as with the conflagration of a hero's funeral pyre. The west was a medley of reds and yellows, peach color, gold color, rose color, copper color, orange color. All the splendid metals fused in that limbec; all the luxurious fruits and flowers wantoned in that garden. The sun had fallen behind the dark clouds that girdled the horizon; he had vanished as a king might vanish through dark, swiftly falling curtains, but his glittering retinue still lingered in the Occidental antechamber, brilliant in the liveries of their imperious king. High in heaven the moon swam in a space of unnamable, unthinkable sweetness; it was no more than a half moon, and showed like a shield held sideways when a knight rides down the lists. Far away the sea slumbered, steel-blue like a knight's sword, and its large, noiseless waves suggested the easy breathing of some fearful force asleep, and sleeping, lovely in its peace.

Argathona paused on the crest of a ridge and gazed in adoration at the majesty of the dusk. It seemed to her as if she could never weary of looking on such loveliness, and her heart grew cold at the new turn of her thoughts. Must she, indeed, set a term to her delight in life, to the joy of the dawn and the noon and the even and the night, joys renewable to her forever and ever? She could not understand what it meant to say farewell to the sunlight and the moonlight and the stars, to be no longer a child of the bright earth, to fade away as her mother's essence had faded away, to live and love, and then, in a breath, to live and love no more. Faces of fear seemed to gibber at her through the tree-trunks, the hands of anguish seemed to clasp at her throat as if to strangle her; for the first time she felt and trembled at the horror of the forest. With a cry of pain she turned from the sunset and plunged into the wood, and made for her resting-place in the heart of the groves. There she flung herself upon the turf, and above her the sky was gray with stars, and, sobbing, she sought and found sleep.

So Argathona lay asleep in the greenwood, and for a wonder Argathona dreamed a dream. She knew in her sleep that she was in the spot where she lay, in that hollow place in the heart of the old forest where always, since her babyhood, she had loved best to linger. Here in the summer days it was sweet to lie awake and see the sunbeams dapple the grass with shadows, or to be lulled to slumber by the droning of the bees. Here in the summer nights it was sweet to lie awake and peep through the branches at the stars, or to be guided by the silence into the region of sleep. But now, in this unwonted dream of hers, she thought that all the winds of all the world were blowing softly through the lanes and alleys and avenues of the wood, and she believed that she, sleeping, stirred in her sleep to hear, and as she hearkened, it was as if the wailings of the winds grew stronger, till they took the tone of many differing sounds, as the beating of the wings of monstrous birds, and the galloping of huge horses, and the straining of great sails at sea. And as she, in her vision, lay and listened to the cunning of the wind, she was made aware that the place where she rested shone with a marvel of faces that she had not seen since she was a dryad child, and she felt that her wood was peopled once again with the presences of the gods of Greece.

She saw them all about her, between the trees and upon the grass, moving upon her like a circle of flakes of white fire, and at first the phantasms seemed to flicker as flame does, inclining this way and that, waxing and waning, but ever coming closer. Suddenly they stood very still, and it was as if she saw clearer and the flamy shapes took substance, and she knew that she was surrounded by the company of the Olympians, and that they showed as she had seen them long ago in her babyhood ere they rode to the hollow land.

Now while Argathona gazed in awe at the celestials, it appeared to her in her vision that behind these mightiest there congregated a throng of forms filling all the spaces of the wood as far as she could see, and she knew these to be the fellowship of the ancient faith. There clustered the lesser gods, the domestic gods, and the sylvan gods, the divinities of winds and clouds and waters, the beautiful sisters of the dooms and the seasons, and the charities and the arts, and the grim deities of the underworld, and the uncouth creatures that dwelled beyond the realm of night, and the demi-gods, that were men and were uplifted. Argathona beheld them all in a single glance, for all their number, each one individual and familiar, as if no other god-like thing waited there and watched in the moonlight, and yet they blended together even as the moonbeams blended. And now she thought as she lay there, sleeping yet waking, that the eyes of all the Olympians, and the eyes of the myriads beyond, were fixed upon her with a look of entreaty and a look of grief. And the ears of her sleep were quickened, and she heard the eternals speak to her one after one.

The first to speak was Zeus, the all-father, launcher of the levin. His hair was wreathed with a chaplet of oak-leaves, and his right hand grasped a staff upon whose head an eagle perched that fluttered its wings as if about to fly and stared around with fierce, unblinking eyes. And Zeus, the commander of the clouds and the tyrant of the thunder, spoke to Argathona, and said:

"Deathless daughter of a divine mother, do not desert your mother's people and your birthright, the gift of your kin. For though we no longer abide in Greece, you remain, and we may yet return. Wherefore be faithful to the old faith of the fruitful earth and await the coming of your kindred."

So Zeus, the all-father, spoke, and his face was compassionate and sad, and the eagle craned its head towards the sleeping girl and clapped its angry wings. The next to speak was Hera, consort of the monarch of the gods. She wore a queenly crown, and on the ball of her sceptre a cuckoo sat and preened its yellow plumes. And Hera spoke to Argathona, and said:

"Daughter of the consecrated forest, do not abandon its sanctuary at the call of a mortal for a mortal's god. That which has gone may come again, and if the time of our triumph arrive we should weep, indeed, were Argathona not here to welcome us."

And so she made silence, and the restless cuckoo cried its cry while the wife of the high-minded drew her veil about her face. And the next to speak was Poseidon, the sovereign of the sea, and Poseidon leaned upon his trident, and his voice was as the lapping of waves in a sunny bay.

"These plead for the fruitful earth. I plead for the fruitless sea. Fair as a maiden in its grace, fierce as a mænad in its rage. Unchanging, ever-changing, pitiful and pitiless, kind and cruel, ceaselessly beautiful. Surely you will not surrender companionship with the sight and the sound and the savor of the sea."

So Poseidon spoke, arrogant, and was silent, and it seemed to the sleeper that from afar, from the side of the sea, there rose unearthly music as from the breath of the sea-people blown through the curling conch. And the next to speak was the divine one with the crested head, she that carries a lance and bears the face of Medusa on her shield, Pallas Athena, protector of Athens. A wise owl rode on her shoulder and made as if it whispered in her ear. And Pallas Athena spoke to Argathona, and said:

"It is better to be wise in the wisdom of the woodlands than wise in the wisdom of mortals, for mortal man is born to trouble, and mortal woman is born to travail, and the life of each is like the puff of breath that an infant spends in a cry. The child of the wildwood lives idly, divinely, knowing neither cark nor care, and day succeeds day, delicious, and shall succeed till the new order changes and the gods return again."

And so she was silent, and the owl on her shoulder ruffled its neck-feathers and winked its eyes benignly at the sleeping child. And the next to speak was Hermes, the subtle contriver, the crafty, with the living wings upon his heels and the twisting snakes upon his staff, and he spoke to Argathona, and his voice entreated wheedlingly, and it had the persuasion of music rippling from the stringed shell of the tortoise. And Hermes spoke to her, and said:

"My kinswoman, put no faith in the words of man, for the lips that praised us yesterday praise another lord today, and who knows what such fluctuant minds may praise tomorrow. Mortal man is guileful and his speech is a snare, but thou, being warned, be wily and deny him and let him die."

So he spoke and was silent, and the wings on his heels ceased to quiver and the snakes stiffened about his rod. Then the girl-goddess Artemis glided over the grass, short-kirtled, the comely huntress, with her bow and arrows upon her, and some stray locks of her pale hair floating on her neck. And Artemis spoke to Argathona as she slept, and said:

"Sweet sister, living the life I loved to live in the dear woodways with the citizens of the wood, take heed to my speech and be cheered. Shun the love of mortal, for your lover will die as Endymion died, and you will remember him for a while and weep, as I remembered and wept for Endymion. But time can sweeten the grief that wrings for a season the deathless heart, wherefore be wise with time betimes, and abide our coming though it be long delayed; for while you wait you have endless pleasure in the changing days and the shifting seasons and the swelling years, in the sunshine and the moonshine and the shining of the stars."

So she spoke and was silent, and the night wind fluttered the fair curls upon her nape and the silver gray folds about her knees. Then the effulgent, the sun-god, moved from his fellows, Phœbus Apollo, with his lyre cradled in his left arm, and his right hand touched the strings, and what he spoke he seemed to sing, and his song was as the song of the wandering stars in heaven. And he spoke to Argathona, and said:

"Daughter of the gods, the gods forbid your unfaith. To be of us once is to be of us forever, and, though we linger in the hollow land, we are still the celestials, and still we desire the remembrance and the fidelity of our kin. It is nobler to hold to our memory than to surrender us for a mortal and a mortal's melancholy god. Wait in the greenwood, watch with the ancient faith, patient in the knowledge of endless youth."

So he was silent, and the sunlight of his words seemed to race all over her body and thread her veins with fire. And thereafter it seemed to Argathona, in her slumber, that god spoke after god innumerable, beautiful gods and grotesque gods in their attributes of benignant or terrible divinity, each appealing to her, or commanding her to stay with the ancient faith, and to shut her heart against the sons of men and the Son of Man. Their voices were eloquent as the rustling of leaves in the forest or the crisping of waves on the shore, so that she could have been content to rest there and to listen to them in gladness through the revolving years.

When it seemed to her that all had spoken, came from that fair company the fairest of them all, Aphrodite, the incomparable, lovelier than all women, loveliest of all goddesses, with her gray doves fluttering about her naked body, and as she moved across the grass red roses burgeoned at her feet. Aphrodite came very nigh to the sleeping dryad, and her eyes were shining with the passion and compassion of love, and her voice was wooing and winning with a music unheard out of dreams. Aphrodite spoke, and said:

"Argathona, I pity you, and I know not what to say, for I, like you, have known what it is to love a mortal, and in very truth I think it were better to love a mortal than never to know the meaning of love. Love, then, this mortal and let him die divinely, having kissed immortal lips and clasped immortal beauty. And when he is but as the dust of yesterday, there will still be comely mortals to love, and you can quench your passing hours of sorrow with golden years of joy. But do not forsake the old faith for the new god, for he that is by my side is still the greatest god in the world, and ever the master of mortal men."

As she spoke, Aphrodite moved a little ways and gave place, and Argathona saw the form and face of a beautiful, silent youth, and his countenance was grave and glorious, and Argathona beheld undazzled the splendor of the godhead of Eros. Eros spoke no word, but he lifted up his hands as if at once in blessing and command, and at that look and sign Argathona's heart seemed to melt within her and to need no other entreaties. But even then there loomed a mighty figure from the forest, making his way through the shining ranks of the divine, a shaggy, puck-nosed giant, with little horns sprouting from his forehead through his tangle of savage curls, and though he was made like a man-god he ran on goat shanks, and he held in his hand a strange pipe, framed of many pieces of reed of different measure bound together by withies. In his presence the other gods appeared to fade and show faint, and the power of the new-comer seemed to inform all the forest and to overshadow all the world.

Pan spoke no word as he fixed his fierce, friendly eyes upon Argathona, but he set his thick lips to the rims of his reeds and blew down them, and his breath made such melody in their channels as Argathona ached with fear and longing to hear, and all the other gods stood spellbound. The piper piped of the red earth and the green grass and the blue sky and the yellow corn, of the straight passions and the simple pleasures of men, of love and pursuit and triumph, of hunger with meat a-nigh, of thirst with the wine-skin between the fingers, of sleep and waking, of jollity and horror, the mirth and the fear of things. He piped of the lowing of cattle and the bleating of sheep, the humming of bees and the buzzing of flies, the flowing of streams and the growing of flowers, the singing of shepherds and the dancing of the nymphs upon the green. He piped till his piping came to a burden, and the burden of his piping seemed to be, "Keep the Faith."

Then all the Olympians cried out in chorus: "Wait, watch, keep the faith." And behind the circle of the greater gods all that populous multitude of the lesser gods took up the call and voiced it, ringing through the forest and filling the sky, and stretching to the ends of the world: "Watch, wait, keep the faith."

And with that cry there arose again the sound of the beating of wings and the trampling of horses and the straining of sails and the wailing of great winds, and then in a breath the Olympians vanished, the vision faded, and Argathona awoke in the strong morning sunshine to find her lover looking down upon her.

28

LOVER AND LASS

When Simon carried Rainouart senseless out of the slough where his comrades perished, he made as hard as his horse could fare on the way to the Eleusinian wood. While the flying forces of the dead duke kept on the main way to Athens, he sought to strike a trail that would lead him more directly to his goal, and, ignorant though he was of the country in which he found himself, the native sense of a war-worn campaigner, acting like a kind of instinct, guided him aright. But the business was slow, first from the unfamiliarity of the region and next from the fact that the good horse could go at no continuance of a steady pace with two heavy men upon his back. Indeed, when they came to the mountainous places, there was much picking of the way and no little stumbling and sliding in the act. So that it happened that the May daylight was fairly spent before Simon felt confident that he was well within the precincts of the Eleusinian wood, and that the purpose of his journey was so far accomplished.

He had been too much occupied for thought of other matter than escape from danger up to this moment, but now, when so many leagues lay behind him and the bloody swamp, now, when what pursuit must have been was afoot in quite another direction on the heels of the Athenian army, Simon decided that the time had come to rest awhile and to consider the case of the young prince, who still lay inanimate before him. Reining his steed, he dismounted. Then, still holding the bridle of the horse, he lifted Rainouart from the saddle and carried him with little difficulty to a shady place a little way removed from the narrow track they had for some time been following. Here Simon laid the unconscious youth on his back beneath a tree, and tethered the horse to another at a little distance.

Now Simon felt very keenly the wisdom of that provision of wine and victual which he had made before riding from Athens, and which he had the presence of mind to preserve in the midst of all the agony of the murderous slough. Unstopping his flagon, he parted Rainouart's lips with the gentle firmness of a strong, sure hand, and tilted some of the red liquor down his companion's throat. After a little while Rainouart began to show signs of returning consciousness. The color rekindled in his cheeks, his lips began to move to a more easy breathing, and presently he opened his eyes with a sigh, and looked around him with the dazed regard of those that wake from sleep in unfamiliar surroundings. Soon his wandering regard fixed itself on the face of Simon, who was looking steadily at him, and, recognizing a known countenance, Rainouart struggled to a sitting posture and clapped his hands to his humming head.

"What are you staring at me for?" he asked first, fretfully. Then, as he glanced about him and saw the carpet of grass that he lay on and the thicket of trees that encompassed him, he continued in amazement, "Where, in Heaven's name, are we?"

To this question Simon answered, solemnly, "In safety, thanks be to Heaven."

Rainouart, with his wits still wool-gathering, wondered. "Safety from what?" Then, suddenly, memory swooped back into her temple, and the young man sprang to his feet swiftly and advanced upon Simon.

"Where are the rest of us? Where is the duke? Where are my comrades?"

To the which hot questions Simon could do no more than render cold answer.

"I hope their souls are in paradise by now, for, indeed, their bodies are no longer quick, and we are the leave of that fellowship."

Then at first the prince began to storm and ejaculate, being shaken out of his native gravity by his strange case and his imperfect understanding of the matter, but Simon presently told him a plain tale that quenched his heat with tears. Simon showed him how the cause of Athens was lost, how Duke Baldwin and his pride of knights had perished, how Simon had saved his prince and himself from the peril, and how his prince's immediate duty was to the girl he loved, the girl who loved him.

Rainouart was silent a little space as the memory of the morning's business came back to him, and he mused on Simon's words and found them honest. Then he held out his hand to Simon, who clasped it.

"Friend," he said, "I had little cause to love Athens or those that dwelt therein, always excepting Guy de Hainault and Jaufre de Brabant, good knights. As for my sire, I will not speak of him, for he made my mother's life bitter, and it may be that I sinned in thinking thereof bitterly. But God knows I would have died with my fellowship. Yet since it has pleased God to save me, by your strength and your fidelity, from the swamp of slaughter, I am clean of any treason and free to seek for my sweetheart."

"Now this is well," crowed Simon, yet he gulped a groan, too, as he spoke, thinking how he had rescued a youth for whom he cared nothing to pleasure a maid for whom he cared much.

By now it was dark, and though the moon filled the forest with white fire, it seemed vain to search the woodland for Argathona that even. So Simon fished some bread and meat out of his wallet, and with that and the flagon the pair made a journeyman's meal of it, and changed many thoughts. There was little in common between the pair, save that they were both strong men and brave soldiers, but at the end of their parley they knew each other better, and liked each other better, though it may be that there would never be any great love lost between them. But at least the friendship was fond enough to prompt Simon to pluck from his bosom a little book and give it to his companion, who, looking upon it, recognized that very volume of the *Romance of the Rose* which he had carried with him on the day, so short a while ago, that brought him acquainted with Argathona. Simon told him cheerfully how dishonestly he came by it, and Rainouart did not quarrel with him for that, for though, indeed, he was pleased to get his book of verses again, he had learned since last he looked upon it that there were better things in the world than the reading of verses or the writing of verses.

After a little more discourse, Rainouart and Simon, the night being now upon them, laid them their lengths upon the turf and slept peacefully through the summer night. Simon dreamed that he was back in that place of pleasure at Byzantium, and would have nothing to do with the women-folk there just because he had fallen in love with an old-time image of stone that stood in the garden and that would have nothing to say to his wooing. Rainouart dreamed that he was in the demesnes of my lord Mirth, and that he walked between Love and Venus to the thicket where the noble rose was throned. So they slept, and woke late when the sun was high in heaven, for the aches and pains of the dead day had been of a kind to compel heavy slumber. They broke their fast with a bite of bread apiece and a few drops from the flagon, which Simon husbanded scrupulously till supply came his way. Then, leaving their steed tethered in ease and safety, they proceeded to explore the forest, and when they had made their way to the very core of the woodland they came to the place where Argathona lay asleep in the shade.

Rainouart gave a little cry of joy and Simon choked a moan of despair, for the girl seemed fairer in her sleep than ever to his eyes. He whispered in his companion's ear that he would leave him with his lass and would wander awhile in the woods for his diversion, but he made a tryst with him that he would come back to that same spot in a little time. So Simon left Rainouart to stand by his sleeping love and drifted into the depths of the wood. Rainouart looked down upon Argathona and loved her with all his soul, and by-and-by her eyelids trembled and then opened, and the girl awoke and gazed into her lover's face.

In an instant Argathona sprang to her feet and caught at her lover's extended hands and looked into her lover's adoring eyes.

"My dear," she cried, "you are welcome to the greenwood," and then she fell to laughing and to crying at the same time like a silly girl that is glad and sad in a companionable moment, and to stay her tears Rainouart was quick to kiss her on the lips, though the sound of her laughter was sweeter in his ears than the chime of blessed bells.

For a while of delicious silence they clung together in the sunlight, murmuring each other's names in little broken spells of speech, and fondling each other after the manner of happily met lovers since the dawn of time. But at last, when the sweetness of their first delicate embraces was sufficiently tasted, and the restraint of two pure hearts glided ghostlike between desire and desire, Argathona drew a little way from her lover, and, holding him at arm's-length with her hands upon his shoulders, asked him what sadness he carried. For her clear eyes saw that there was sorrow behind the joy he had in finding her and fondling her, and she would not be denied to know the care that ate upon his heart.

So Rainouart and she sat side by side upon the grass, each with arms about the other, while Rainouart in a hushed voice told her what had come to pass. How the Duchess of Thebes, strengthened by the secession of the Catalan Grand Company, had defied the pride and power of Athens, and how the pride and power of Athens had ridden forth to beat Thebes to reason, and how the pride and power of Athens were swallowed up in the bloody slough. And he told her how he himself was escaped from that slaughter, dwelling little upon his own stubbornness to turn from the shambles planned by the Catalan Grand Company—for it becomes no man to elaborate his devotion to duty—but lauding to the full the courage of Simon that by his courage and purpose had plucked him from destruction and carried him from present death to the depths of the greenwood, which same Simon he told her was now taking his ease somewhere in the skirts of the forest, having quitted his companion as soon as the pair came upon the sleeping girl.

While he told his tale the immortal maiden clung to him close, and trembled at her lover's peril, and revelled in his strength of spirit that would rather have died than come to her dishonored, but she had little grief in her heart for the tragedy of the Athenian gallants. Beautiful evil creatures they had seemed to her in her short sojourn among them, fair as a snake may be named fair, and dangerous as a snake is dangerous.

And "Oh, my love," she whispered, "I was blithe to spy you"; and "Oh, my love," he whispered, "I was blithe to find you." So they prattled and babbled together, strong man and strong maid, and the world seemed very young to Rainouart, for he remembered nothing but the discovery of his love, and the world seemed very old to Argathona, for she knew, and joyed with a fierce, sorrowful joy in the knowledge, that there was little usage of the world left for her.

After a while Rainouart told her of his plans: how a messenger had gone to Avignon to the pope, there to break him free from his marriage, and how, in the meanwhile, he was now minded to make his way swiftly into Peloponnesus, where he hoped to win help at best from the Duke of Corinth, or at worst to take ship for France and the court of Philip the Fair, bearing Argathona with him to be his bride and wife in France.

Argathona listened as he whispered his will, and when he had made an end of his aims she turned to him suddenly and stretched out her arms and cried out to him, "Take me in your embrace, beloved, and kiss me once with all your heart and with all your soul, for never again shall you kiss me as I am now at this hour."

Rainouart, amazed, entreated her meaning, and she answered him sad and simple: "All my life I have lived in a faith strange to you, the faith of us who have lived in the woodlands since the days beyond the dawn, but now I intend to take your faith and to share your worship and to praise your God. So let us rise and go to the home of the holy man, and he will bless me and make me as you are, and all shall be well between us till the time comes when nothing can be well for either of us."

Now Rainouart did not very clearly understand what his sweetheart meant when she said these words, but rather took her to mean that she had been bred in that form of the Christian faith which was practised by the Grecians, and he rejoiced that she was so ready to come from the tents of error and dwell in the serenity of what he held to be the truth. So he kissed his mistress long and lovingly upon the lips with his arms bound about her body, kissing her with all that strength of his clean heart and his clean soul, and she gave him back both kiss and clasp, and as she did so she gave also the good-bye to her deathless life.

Then they rose to leave that place and go towards the hermitage when their purpose was stayed by the sound of running feet through the brushwood, and Simon came upon them, hurrying through the trees. Now Rainouart had forgotten Simon, being all absorbed in his joy at finding Argathona, but Argathona was glad to see him, just because he had saved her lover. They saw that Simon's face was grave, yet not with the gravity of sadness, and when he beheld them he quickened his pace till he came up with them, and when he was up with them he gasped, being breathed from his hurry, "Be happy, lass and lad, you can be married this morning."

29

WHAT SIMON FOUND IN THE FOREST

Simon made his way through the forest idly and at all adventure. He was trying to think what the world would have been like if a girl of the kind of Argathona had chosen to take him for mate. But by-and-by he found this manner of musing too melancholy, and did his best to banish it by pricking a lively interest in his surroundings, looking hither and thither at woodland sights that pleased him, reminding him of Normandy. So by degrees he made some way across the wood, steering, as he guessed, in the direction of the highway, when suddenly he became aware of something bright and golden glancing through the tree-trunks. Curious to see what that could be which glittered and twinkled so brilliantly through those sombre aisles, Simon pushed his way rapidly till he came to a little open space where the trees were thinner, and there he saw a strange sight.

From the boughs of one of the trees a man was hanging that was clad in coat of gold and had a cloth bound about the lower part of his face, but the man was not hanging free, for his feet were firmly planted on the saddle of a dappled horse that seemed to wait very contentedly beneath him. As Simon came into the clearing he saw the eyes of the poor wretch that was pinioned and gibbeted thus fixed upon him in the very eloquence of entreaty, and Simon's purpose was very instant to answer the appeal. He trod at a brisk trot across the interval of grass that divided him from the piteous fellow in that perilous pillory, and when he had come near him he coaxed and wooed the horse cunningly for a moment or so lest he should start and put his surmounter's neck in danger. But the horse stood still and allowed him to come close, and when he was hard by Simon caught at the bridle with a gentle firmness to stay the animal from stirring. Slipping the bridle over the hook of his left elbow, he clasped that arm around the legs of the pendulous fellow, while with his right hand he plucked his sword from its sheath and sheared at the rope that was about the pinioned man's neck. In another moment the captive was safe in his arms, and the next Simon had set him on his legs on the grass. Simon cut the bonds that bound his wrists, and then, pulling the gagging-cloth from the victim's face, recognized to his astonishment the page Bohemond, that was wont to wait so dapper and alert upon the Duchess of Thebes.

At first the poor lad could scarcely speak, but when he had wit and skill to articulate he cried in an awful voice: "The duchess, the duchess, where is the duchess?" Then it seemed as if he could say no more, but after Simon had plied him with a little of the scanty liquor that yet remained in his flagon the boy grew voluble, and told in scraps and tags of passion and anguish a most monstrous story.

It seemed that overnight the Duchess of Thebes had asked Ximenes to lend her men of the Catalan Grand Company for a certain purpose, and when he had refused her she bade Bohemond find for her the men she needed. What the duchess's purpose was Bohemond did not know, further than that he believed she wished to make sure of some enemy of hers that she held to be lurking in the secrecy of the Eleusinian wood. Chance had made Bohemond acquainted with a kind of freebooter whom, from the lad's description, Simon had little difficulty in recognizing as his one-time waylayer Captain Fox. This footpad promised to pick up a fellowship, and he kept his word. Early in the present morning Esclaramonde, with Bohemond for companion, slipped away from Athens, joined a band of six spadassins outside the walls, and rode for the forest, the duchess ahead in a rigid spirit of silence. At first all went well enough, though it showed strange to Bohemond to see his duchess travelling in the company of half a dozen ruffians. But it seemed that when the party had got within the confines of the wood the bearing of the men suddenly changed towards the lady that led them. The fellow that no doubt was Captain Fox had fallen somewhat behind as they rode with one of his pillagers. The pair kept whispering apart, and between them it is probable that they changed their plans from one crime to another crime. The first that Bohemond knew of their intent was when he suddenly found himself stricken from his horse by a brace of the knaves, while the rest of the malefactors set upon the duchess and snatched her from her saddle though she raged at them like a fury. Two of the miscreants dragged the screaming, struggling woman—whose clamor was now the more horrid in contrast with her former silence—into the wood, while Captain Fox gave the horses in charge of another, and bade the two that had hold of Bohemond to treat him in the fashion in which Simon had found him. "For," quoth the rogue, "I would not have the lad's blood on my hands, since he helped us to this booty, but if it pleases Heaven to hang him by spurring his horse to stir, why then let him swing for me." So Bohemond had remained there, for how long he knew not, standing on his steed that by the bounty of Providence was content to keep still until Simon came through the trees to save his rider.

All this amazing tale was blurted and stuttered out in gasps and spasms of speech, its hearer grasping at half words and interpreting much from little. Now when Simon had heard it, and it took but a few hot seconds in the telling, he saw one thing plain for him to do, which was to try to rescue the duchess, much as he hated her. Simon would willingly have left Bohemond behind, thinking him too pretty a stripling to be of grave use in a scuffle. But Bohemond would by no means be persuaded to stay, seeing which Simon liked his mettle and clapped him on the back. Then noting that the rogues had stolen the lad's sword, he lent him his great dagger. "For," said Simon, "if we find the fly-by-nights, you may busy yourself in putting out of their pain any that I chance to leave unfinished."

Now as they started on their search, which did not prove a long one, as you shall hear, Bohemond, babbling at his companion very incoherently, for he was weeping himself sick for his wicked mistress, told all that had chanced in Athens after the slaughter in the marsh. How of Duke Baldwin's knights only two came off with their lives that were made prisoners by special charge of Fernand Ximenes, and these twain were Count Ernault of Toulouse and Sir Jaufre de Brabant. How the Catalan Grand Company, marching on the track of the scattered army, entered the city of Athens unopposed and unimpeded. How the estates of the slain knights were divided among the followers of Ximenes and their women distributed among the victors, so that many a sturdy Catalan mercenary received for wife some noble lady for whom the day before the battle he would have counted it an honor to carry a basin for her washing of the hands. How Ximenes compelled the archbishop of Athens to wed him in state to Esclaramonde, insisting that she was a widow, which was, indeed, the common belief. Simon already knew how, on the morning after her latest marriage, Esclaramonde had left the city to seek for Argathona in the forest with the intent to slay her.

While Bohemond was moaning out his story Simon was using his eyes as well as his feet. Indeed, there was little difficulty for a keen campaigner in getting on the track of the duchess and her abductors. A scrap of silk clinging to a twig, and recognized by the page as being of the color of his lady's gown, first set them on a trail that thereafter proved easy to follow. Simon's keen glances could read the record of the journey in snapped branches and trampled grasses, even if his guesses had not been confirmed again and again by bits of silk and bits of lace and once a fallen pearl. So, going warily, Simon and Bohemond came by-and-by to the edge of a little hollow place in the thick of the trees, and there, looking down, saw that which would have made the boy cry aloud in rage but that Simon clapped his great hand over his loyal mouth and silenced him.

There was a single tree in the little hollow, and to that tree Esclaramonde was bound, quite naked, with her hair about her face. The six bandits were huddled together a little way from her, kneeling on their leader's mantle which was spread upon the grass, and all were intently absorbed in playing at dice. Simon was an old battle-hand, and such ugly sights were familiar enough, yet he could not help raging to think of that beautiful evil being as the prey of those filthy fingers. The boy's fury was not to be restrained, and, drawing his dagger, he began to spring down the slope regardless of odds. In a moment Simon was after him, and the astonished robbers, looking up from their sport, beheld a giant and a lad come thundering towards them. As they scrambled to their feet and snatched at their weapons their foes were close at hand. Simon was first in the field, his long legs outstripping Bohemond, and he was upon the desperadoes with his great sword sweeping and swinging like the sails of a windmill.

The caitiffs were six to one, or, at best, six to one and a quarter. For a lad with no more than a dagger was no match for the meanest of that gang, but for all their advantage they could make no head against the whirlwind assault of Simon. Two of the felons were headless before the band could rally, and now they were but four to two, for Bohemond had caught up a sword that had fallen from one of the dead scoundrels and showed that he knew how to handle it. Simon's mighty weapon rose and fell, and another of the rapscallions was despatched, while Bohemond wounded a fourth. Then, while the woman tied to the tree lifted her head and stared through her black hair at the battle, the three recreants turned and fled in different directions.

Captain Fox as he ran made for where the prisoner was pinioned, and before Simon could reach him he passed his sword through her body. Then, with his weapon red with the woman's blood, he turned on Simon, his face all warped and white, hideous with lust and hate and fear, and he began to scream out something to the effect that Simon should not have her; but he never finished the sentence, for Simon sliced him like a pear, and the sword bit to the breastbone. Wrenching his weapon free, Simon turned to where Bohemond was being pressed by the two remaining rogues, who, finding only a lad at their heels, had turned to tackle him. Again they fled, but Simon was swifter than they and slew them as they ran. Thus in a little pinch of time there were six dead men and one dying woman in that dismal hollow, where still the white dice shone ironically, scattered over the black mantle on the grass.

Simon unbound the duchess, for Bohemond, now that the fight was over, could do nothing but bite at his hands to keep himself from crying, and indeed she was a tragic sight with the blood dabbling her whiteness. Simon wrapped her decently and tenderly in a mantle, for, after all, she was a woman, and a dying woman, and he laid her gently on the grass. The simplest knowledge of wounds was sufficent to assure him that her hurt was mortal, and, indeed, in a few seconds she expired without having spoken a word. To the end of his days Simon, when he remembered that time, wondered what were the thoughts of the duchess as she peered through her hair at the battle.

30

RENUNCIATION

This was what Simon had to tell to Argathona and to Rainouart when he came upon them side by side in the forest. This and the order he had taken thereafter. For he had found the horses of the robbers with the horse of the duchess tethered in a glen, and he had bound the body of the dead woman decorously upon her horse's back and intrusted the corpse to Bohemond's care, charging him to ride at a walking pace to Athens and tell the tale to Ximenes. With the aid of the other horses, Argathona and Rainouart and he could make their way quickly to Peloponnesus and safety before any pursuit could reach them if pursuit were attempted.

When the maid and the man heard Simon's story they were silent for a while, troubled alike with sad thoughts and glad thoughts. To Rainouart the news meant that he was free to marry his true-love, but to his true-love it brought fiercely the knowledge of mortality, and her spirit shivered in its house, and suddenly she snatched at her lover's hand, and in the clasp caught back strength and comfort that had threatened for a moment to abandon her. And so in silence they turned and went their way with Simon after them till they came in sight of the hermit's hut, and they halted before the shrine with its glory of the silver image of the Redeemer pierced upon the tree.

Then Argathona turned to her lover and begged him to let her approach the holy man alone, and Rainouart, who would not have said her nay in anything, granted her prayer. Then she bade him wait where he stood, and he and Simon knelt before the shrine and prayed, while Argathona quitted him, and coursed fleetly over the grass and came to the hermit's door and knocked at it for admittance. The anchorite was within, and he opened his door, and he welcomed the maiden as if he had been awaiting her, and he took her by the hand and drew her within the hut and saluted her with, "Peace be with you, daughter." Argathona surveyed the palace of the anchorite with its mean walls and its naked floor, and its wooden table laden with a great book and a vessel of water and a crucifix of ivory.

Argathona said to the ancient, "Father, I have slept and dreamed and wakened, and I return to you to pray you to take me into your faith and to change me, immortal, into a mortal maid."

The hermit bade her kneel before the table, and he knelt by her side and prayed awhile in a great agony of beseeching, after which he said certain sacred words to the girl for her to repeat to him; he then arose and blessed her and sprinkled holy-water upon her, and baptized her into the rites of Christ. When he had done Argathona was still Argathona in all her outward seeming, but from her mind all memory of her gift of immortality had vanished, and she thought of herself and of her life as a shepherd girl might think of herself, and of the eighteen years that she had laughed and danced through since her mother, that died in her childhood, had borne her to the sire that she had never seen. As for the old gods, there was no more memory of them in her mind than if no man had ever paid them praise in Greece, and the old speech of the gods was no longer upon her lips, but, instead, the speech of her mortal lover. All things else she remembered clearly: the finding of Simon and the coming of Rainouart to the wood, and the treason that took him from her and her journey to Athens to save him, with all that followed thereupon. All these things she remembered just as a girl of eighteen to whom they had happened would remember them, just in that way and no other way. For Argathona was now no more than a girl of eighteen years that had lived unwittingly without religion till she had met the holy man who had welcomed her into the faith of her fellow-mortals. But the thing that she remembered clearest and best of all things was that the lover she loved so dearly was waiting for her outside in the sunlight.

Outside in the sunlight she found him, she walking with the hermit hand-in-hand. And outside in the sunlight the old pope blessed Rainouart and Argathona in wedlock, man and maid kneeling before the shrine. Then Simon brought horses and the three made their escape into Peloponnesus.

www.ingramcontent.com/pod-product-compliance
Lightning Source LLC
Chambersburg PA
CBHW011718240626
47153CB00009B/2908